Changeling's Return

a novel approach to the music

Book Cover Design: Changeling's Return interwoven threads of myth, folklore, and magic are also present in Linda Snyder's mosaic, representing the triumph of light over darkness at dawn, that liminal moment when the borders between the worlds are ill-defined, if not non-existent. Difficult to see in the photo, the owl is actually projecting from its background in the mosaic, an element of sympathetic magic in a modern work, done in an ancient medium, representing the folklore belief in an owl's ability to navigate between the natural and supernatural realms.

Changeling's
Return

a novel approach to the music

by Travis Edward Pike

Otherworld Cottage Industries
Los Angeles

Pike, Travis Edward
Changeling's Return

  1. Sci-Fi Fantasy 2. Musicals 3. Song Lyrics
  4. Music, Popular (Songs, etc.) 5. Western Mythology
  6. Western Folklore 7. Supernatural
  I. Travis Edward Pike II. Title
  III. Title: A novel approach to the music

813.54

ISBN-13: 978-1-892900-07-4

Printed in the United States of America

BOOK DESIGN BY TRAVIS E. PIKE

I dedicate this story, its music, and its mysteries, to my wife, Judy; my daughter, Lisa; my brother, Adam; and to all the family members, friends, and fans who never stopped believing that some dreams may come true.

Travis Edward Pike
Otherworld Cottage
November, 2019

ACKNOWLEDGMENTS

Thanks to the 1975 Changeling Troupe: Melodie Bryant, Ann Sanders, Marian Petrocelli, Steve Pugliesi, Greg Bischoff, Phil Cataldo, Ken Park, and David Pinto, for their outstanding performances for the first *Changeling* demo recording, to Woody James, who introduced me to musical modes at CalPoly, Pomona, and again to David Pinto, who in 1987 recorded nearly all the parts of my evolved *Morningstone* version, using synthesizers and emulators advanced for their time, and the vocalists still heard in parts of the current compilation, Lois Young, Cheryl Lewyn, Tyana Parr, Elissa Valentino, Joann Paratore, and Katherine Garret, and to my daughter, Lisa, who co-produced those sessions.

A special thank you to my brother, Adam, who sweetened, mixed, and mastered the *Morningstone* recordings in his studio in 1988, and beginning in 2013, co-produced, played, recorded, mixed, and mastered nearly my entire back catalog, along with my newer material, including some now added to *Changeling's Return,* and to Colleen Stratton, Karen Callahan, Lauran Doverspike, Barbara Jordan, Kris Snyder, Terry Hagerty, Saba Mwine, Alana Shannon, Bridget Shannon, Phyllis Elliott, Ariel Pisturino, and Elaine Alaoglu, for their vocal contributions.

Thanks, too, to my early nineties motion picture department heads, who scouted locations with me: Peter Anderson, Britt Lomond, George Costello, and George Johnsen, and my colleagues in the British Film Commission, for their assistance in my U.K. recce, Andrew Patrick, Dorothy Hobson, Hugh Edwin Jones, and Sue Lathan.

And thanks to Gary Schneider, Lenny Helsing, Lee Zimmerman, Andy Pearson, Mike Stax, Pat Prince, Kent Kotal, David Kessel, Rob Bailey, Mole Lambert, Larry Battson, Mark Nardone, Jim Kaplan, Tim Perlich, and especially Harvey Kubernik, for keeping the legend alive, and finally the New Playwrights Foundation; Jeff Bergquist, Randy Ball, Alice Lunsford, Michele Hart, Phyllis Elliott, Syrie James and Terry Hagerty, and to my wife, Judy, who has supported my creative endeavors for more than fifty years.

CONTENTS

It gives me great pleasure to announce *Changeling's Return*, and introduce Travis Edward Pike, the man who made it possible for readers and/or listeners, to escape into a supernatural world of magic, myth, and music unlike any hitherto known. Born and reared, like the hero in his novel, in Boston, Massachusetts, Pike provides two approaches for listeners, readers, or both to experience the wonder of his 1976 musical screenplay *Changeling*, optioned, but never produced, and now released in a music album he calls *Changeling's Return: a novel musical concept*, and this book, *Changeling's Return: a novel approach to the music*, both happy results of his more than half-century career in music, film and literature.

Listen to the mysterious music and song composed for the unrealized movie; read the occult fantasy exploring Western mythology, folklore, and the supernatural, woven together by the music of the spheres; both, individually and jointly, providing a window on a supernatural world where the survival of humankind is being weighed in the balance, and the outcome is still uncertain.

In a pre-Beatles world, Pike, a twelve-year-old student at Boston Latin School, was censured for writing poetry and short stories in study halls. Two years later, while waiting to speak to Travis' father, filmmaker James A. Pike, American journalist and author John Gunther, renowned for his sociopolitical books about various parts of the world, read some of 14-year-old Travis' short stories and poetry he found on a coffee table in the Pike's parlor, asked to meet Travis, told him his writing showed promise and encouraged him to consider a writing career.

But Travis was also interested in music, and at fourteen, he became lead singer for a teenage rock band. He had just turned eighteen when he composed his first movie title song for *Demo Derby* in 1963, later penned ten tunes and starred in the pop musical *Feelin' Good,* shot on location in Boston, Massachusetts, and in 2017, "Watch Out Woman," one of his songs from that film was finally released on a vinyl 45 in the U.K., and made it to #3 single on *Shindig!* magazine's *Best of 2017* list.

It is no coincidence that Pike's fictional main character in *Changeling's Return*, Morgen, was reared in Boston, became the lead singer, songwriter, and front man for Beantown Home Cookin', a fictional band, drawn from the author's own musical adventures in that city where Travis Pike's Tea Party was formed and performed in the sixties, making Pike both witness and participant in this musical sci-fi fantasy.

In his portrayal of heathen ritual, Pike explores the light and dark spaces between the equinoxes and solstices, and introduces us to the colorful shadow people spotlighted in his ambitious, nutritious, peripatetic out-of-body adventure, not preaching, but teaching and reaching listeners and readers with his expressive musical and literary style. In *Changeling's Return,* "songs are spells, going 'round and 'round in your head, even when there's no music to hear."

I embarked on Pike's fantasy-adventure, secure in the knowledge that the composer, lyricist, novelist, and tour guide, would not abandon me inside the Tomb of Every Hope, but wherever we might roam, would bring me home through his non-fear-based approach to the characters and situations encountered in his supernatural realm of otherworldly music and megalithic shrines.

Changeling's Return is Pike's invitation to explore a world where mystery and destiny are forever intertwined. Having sipped from *Changeling's Return's* Cauldron of Inspiration, I emerged from its Stream of Consciousness with renewed hope and a firm belief that humanity can and will learn to understand our planetary environment as it is today, and resolve to live in harmony with Nature's Laws.

Harvey Kubernik is an award winning author of 15 books. His literary music anthology *Inside Cave Hollywood: The Harvey Kubernik Music InnerViews and InterViews Collection Vol. 1*, was published in December 2017, by *Cave Hollywood.* Kubernik's *The Doors Summer's Gone* was published by Otherworld Cottage Industries in February 2018, and has been nominated for the 2019 Association for Recorded Sound Collections Awards for Excellence in Historical Recorded Sound Research.

Changeling's Return

a novel approach to the music

by Travis Edward Pike

Otherworld Cottage Industries
Los Angeles

CHAPTER ONE

The BBC interview started well enough, especially since April 29th had been a busy day for Morgen, and he'd been awake for the entire Virgin Atlantic night flight from Boston's Logan Airport to Heathrow, researching British May Day festivities and traditions, including May Eve, aka Walpurgis Night, April 30th, the same night for which his first live TV concert broadcast was scheduled. He'd planned to catch some z's before the concert, but he'd barely had time for brunch when he was picked up by a BBC limousine and taken to the radio station. Morgen, a veteran interviewee, was fully prepared for the typical ice-breaking questions interviewers ask: when and how Beantown Home Cookin' came together, did he really write all their songs, and so forth, but the first question this BBC interviewer asked was why his name was spelled with an "e," instead of an "a." He'd thought Morgen with an "e" was a variant used for a girl's name. As off-the-wall as that was to start an interview, Morgen was prepared for it, because he'd been hearing variations of it ever since he'd started elementary school.

"That's generally true," Morgen replied. "Morgen with an 'e' or an 'a' are both names given to children of either sex, but as far back as first grade, my teacher tried to correct my spelling from Morgen with an 'e' to Morgan with an 'a.' I began spelling it the way the teacher told me to, until my mother saw it on a paper I brought home from school, and told me it was incorrect, and my name was spelled with an 'e.' As you might imagine, that led to my first visit to the principal's office and a follow-up visit with my mother, resulting in it being officially changed back to Morgen with an 'e,' because that was the name, in fact the only word, scrawled on the note attached to my blanket, when I was found outside the entrance to the hospital."

"Really? You were a foundling?"

"I am a foundling. It's not something you outgrow."

"No, of course not," the interviewer said. "When did you first learn that's how you came by your name?"

"I was there when the counselor explained it to the couple adopting me. It was particularly important to keep the spelling, because it was a bit unusual, and might be my birth mother's name, or my father's name, or even a family name that might help to identify me if anyone ever came looking for me."

"And has anyone come looking for you?"

"Not yet. At least, not to my knowledge."

"How old were you, then?"

"I was five."

"That must have been tough for a five-year-old to hear."

"Not when the five-year-old is about to go home with a father and mother of his own."

"I must say, you seem pretty well-adjusted to me, for being abandoned at birth. Does a thing like that haunt you?"

"Not really," Morgen replied. "I don't remember much from before I was adopted, but once I was taken in by my adoptive parents, I enjoyed a wonderful, loving, childhood that got me started in music."

Morgen thought that setup would lead to a discussion of his career, but the host either missed his cue, or wasn't ready to move on.

"Amazing," he said. You've named your band 'Beantown Home Cookin', a reference to your home town, Boston, Massachusetts. Are all the members from Boston?"

"I didn't name the band. They were already Beantown Home Cookin', when I came aboard, and wherever the band members came from, we all lived in Boston, and most of the guys had gone to the Berklee College of Music in Boston, and that should certainly qualify them as a Beantown band."

"Are the Trashbabies all Bostonians, too?"

"They all make their home in Greater Boston," Morgen answered, "but they're not only cosmopolitan, they're international. Their families, like almost all American families, emigrated to America, some when we were still British Colonies, but several more recently, displaced by wars, famine, poverty or persecution in other parts of the world, to enjoy the freedom and opportunity that has made the United States famous around the world as a melting pot of cultures, making the Trashbabies a sterling example of the unique diversity and opportunity that makes America great."

"Spoken like a true patriot. I guess that's to be expected from a Bostonian, but isn't it true that to avoid harassment, all the ladies have to go by stage names?" the host asked.

"I know them by their stage names, and I understood stage names afford celebrities some protection from harassment, but are sometimes also part of the act. What about your Spice Girls: Scary, Sporty, Baby, Ginger, and Posh, if I remember correctly."

The host laughed, then said, "That sounds about right, but everyone knew their real names, too. Today, Posh Spice is better known as Victoria Beckham, wife of Manchester United's outstanding former football player, David Beckham. But the Trashbabies all have secret names, like something out of *Old Possum's Book of Practical Cats*."

The Trashbabies were the nine gorgeous singer-dancers featured in Beantown Home Cookin's traveling stage show, but if there was a question in the host's prattle, Morgen had missed it. Broadcast radio doesn't tolerate dead airspace well, so when Morgen failed to answer, the host prodded, "T. S. Elliot?"

"What about him?" Morgen asked.

"I believe he came from a distinguished line of Bostonians, didn't he?" the host ventured, starting to feel as lost as Morgen, but blessed with a prompter's voice in his headset suggesting he stay with sports, and ask Morgen what he thought of the New England Patriots' stunning, final two-minute, come-from-behind, overtime win over the Atlanta Falcons in Superbowl 51.

"What am I thinking?" the host blurted. "You're from Boston. How did it feel to see the Patriots' spectacular comeback Superbowl victory over the Atlantic Falcons!"

"Atlanta Falcons," Morgen corrected.

"And a fifth Superbowl ring for your quarterback! What's his name?"

By then, Morgen felt like he was witnessing the interview from the other side of Alice's looking glass. As for the name of the quarterback, he drew a blank, but tried to fill the empty airspace with what he knew of the quarterback's family history, gleaned from local newspaper and radio interviews.

"I can tell you this much," Morgen stalled, hoping his mental review would reveal the quarterback's name, "and he wasn't born in Boston, and only became a New Englander when he came to the Patriots, but his family originally emigrated to Boston during the famous nineteenth century potato famine, and his name isn't Sullivan."

Prompted by the voice in his headset, the host exclaimed, "Tom Brady!"

"Right!" Morgen concurred, "I knew that."

The host laughed and said, "Jet lag will do that to you."

Later, sitting in the back seat of the limousine taking him to the ruined abbey where his live U.K. premiere concert broadcast was to originate, he shuddered. How could he possibly have forgotten Tom Brady's name, with five Superbowl rings, easily the most famous name in New England since JFK.

"And his name isn't Sullivan," Morgen groaned aloud.

Morgen saw the limousine driver glance back at him in his rear-view mirror.

"Just thought of something funny," Morgen explained. The driver grinned and turned his attention back to the road.

"How long before we get there?" Morgen asked.

"An hour, possibly a bit more if we run into traffic. Do we need to stop?"

"No," Morgen answered. "I'm fine."

He settled back into his seat, and stared out the window, but everything whizzed by so quickly, it made his eyes tired, so he closed them, and thought about how he'd come to this day, lead singer and front man for Beantown Home Cookin', an American pop star from Boston, Massachusetts, riding in the back seat of a limousine, on his way to his first live concert telecast, the first stop on a six-week European tour that would end on the same day he'd been fired from his dishwasher job in a Cape Cod rock and roll joint three years ago.

In addition to being hot and muggy, Boston was relatively dead in summer and would stay that way until the student bodies returned to fill the Greater Boston colleges and universities in September. The well-heeled locals' destination of choice was anywhere on Cape Cod, but Morgen, on the G.I. Bill, and just having finished his first year at Boston University, didn't belong to the well-heeled crowd. With no G.I. Bill benefits coming in until the start of the fall semester, the only way he could escape to the Cape was to land a summer job there. And escape he must, because the roommate whose name was on the lease was graduating, one of the other two students who shared the apartment was going home to Connecticut, and the other, going home to New Hampshire for the summer. Morgen had been working part-time, driving a delivery truck, but his pay barely covered groceries, much less rent.

In a matter of days, he'd be out on the street, so he was perusing the bulletin board in the long corridor, where most of the listings were for ride-shares to distant destinations, when he noticed one on a 3 x 5 card, that stuck out like a sore thumb: a help-wanted ad,which must have been thumbtacked to the bulletin board quite recently, since unauthorized ads were quickly taken down. Given that policy, Morgen felt no guilt as he took it down and slipped it into his pocket. The job on the Cape paid less than driving the truck, but other than that, read like a paid vacation in paradise. It was a dishwasher job at a Falmouth nightclub with live entertainment, close to the water, included free meals, and a private cottage.

Morgen had never worked as a dishwasher, but a summer job with room and board at the beach was exactly what he needed to carry him over until school recommenced in the fall. When he called the number, the gruff voice on the phone said the job was his, and he could start as soon as he got there. Morgen trotted back to the bulletin board, called a few numbers offering ride-shares to the Cape, and found one passing through Falmouth on the way to Woods Hole.

The driver's name was Terry. Morgen arranged to be picked up on Commonwealth Avenue the next morning. Terry would be driving a bright yellow 2014 Chevy Camaro Super Sport.

That night, except for underwear, socks, a T-shirt, and the blue jeans he planned to wear, Morgen packed all his clothes, shaving kit, and travel alarm into his sea-bag. His pea coat was too bulky to fit, but worst case, he'd wear it.

The following morning, he was at the curb early, sitting on his sea-bag, waiting for his ride, when the fully-loaded, yellow, 2014 Chevy Camaro SS stopped to pick him up. Terry was no more than 19-years-old, and Morgen was his only passenger, but even so, there was no room in the trunk or on the back seats, so Morgen stowed his sea-bag on top of the gear Terry had piled up, where it partially blocked the rear window, but it stayed put, one advantage of sea-bags over suitcases. It was already warm, so Morgen took off his pea coat, climbed into the car and sat with his neatly-folded pea coat in his lap.

As soon as Morgen buckled up, with a roar and squeal of tires, Terry sent the car screaming out into the early morning Commonwealth Avenue traffic. That might have been meant to impress Morgen, but it only suggested that Terry was not to be entirely trusted behind the wheel, and unless he settled down, the trip to the Cape might be a white-knuckler.

Starting out, the traffic was terrible and the lane changes as they looped around from the Mass Pike onto the South East Expressway were intense, but on route 25, the east-bound traffic thinned and by the time it swung south, it was reasonably easy sailing. Once they crossed the Bourne Bridge, Terry relaxed and began calling out the names of places he'd visited along General MacArthur Boulevard. Morgen relaxed too. The road signs showed they were getting close to Falmouth.

The English limousine suddenly swerved, throwing Morgen sideways across the back seat, and returning him to the present.

"Sorry, Gov. Something in the roadway."

"What was it?" Morgen asked.

"Don't know, but whatever it was, we missed it," the driver answered. "But you might want to buckle up."

Morgen put on the seat belt. "Do you anticipate running into more obstacles on the roadway?"

"We missed that one, but you never know."

Morgen remembered that Terry had swerved to miss something on the roadway on General MacArthur Boulevard, then remembered it wasn't something. It was someone. Two someones, both male, staggering across the road, drunk, or stoned out of their gourds. Welcome to the Cape.

Terry dropped him at the front door of the club around 10:30 a.m. and watched until the door opened, and Morgen waved goodbye, before waving back and quietly driving away.

7

The waitress who'd come to the door glanced at his sea-bag, said he was expected, and led him into the dark interior, where she introduced him to Salvatore, a balding, heavy-set, middle-aged man sitting on a bar stool, who made Morgen think of a large-scale Danny DeVito.

Sal eyed the sea-bag, looked Morgen in the face, and rasped, "So, you're Morgen, are you?"

Morgen smiled and answered, "That's me," as he set down his sea-bag and reached out to shake hands with Sal.

Sal muttered "Whatever," and ignoring Morgen's outstretched hand, turned his back, slid off his bar stool and started walking toward the back of the room.

"The kitchen's back here."

Morgen snatched up his sea-bag and followed, peering through the dimly-lit interior and fixing the room's layout in his mind. The long bar was on his right. In the middle of the room, there were a number of small tables, each with chairs stacked on top of them, and beyond, against the far side wall, a row of booths. As they neared the rear wall, Morgen noticed that where the tables ended, a dance floor began.

Up against the rear wall was a platform for the house band, with microphones, amplifiers, and a drum set already in place, and as they approached the double, swinging doors to the kitchen, Morgen noticed on the right, between the bar and the back wall, were doors to the restrooms.

Sal burst through both swinging doors, into the kitchen, with Morgen close behind, managing to get through without losing his sea-bag by leaning into the door on the right.

"Yo, Lonzo," Sal shouted over the noisy kitchen exhaust fans, "Here's your new dishwasher!"

The tall, black cook glanced up just long enough to acknowledge Morgen's presence, then nodded curtly to Sal and turned his attention back to whatever he was doing in the prep area beyond the huge stove and range hood that stood in the middle of the kitchen. Sal pointed toward a small space on the floor to Morgen's right and shouted, "Put your stuff over there. Lonzo will show you what to do."

Sal turned on his heel, threw open both doors and headed back to his seat at the far end of the bar.

"What's your name?" Lonzo shouted.

"Morgen, with an 'e,' " Morgen shouted back.

"Well, I'm Alonzo," the cook shouted back, "with a big capital 'A' right at the front. Stow your gear over there," he continued, jerking his head toward the spot Sal had indicated.

"I'd like to get settled in, first," Morgen shouted back.

"You're working for me now, Morgen, with an 'e.' What time you start?"

"Eleven o'clock," Morgen replied.

"And what you gonna do when you start working?"

"I expect you'll tell me," Morgen replied pleasantly.

"You ever been a dishwasher before?"

"I've washed a dish or two in my time."

"Here you're gonna wash thirty, maybe forty at a time. You see that washer machine?"

Morgen saw a lot of stainless steel, but nothing he recognized as a dishwasher.

The tall, sinewy cook moved quickly around the stove and started toward him. Morgen smiled and stood his ground, as the intimidating 6' 3" black man went to a large stainless steel box, slid up one side door and then the other, and pulled out a rubber-coated basket that looked a lot like the ones that came with dishwashers Morgen had seen in TV commercials. Brushing past Morgen, he opened a cabinet door under the table, took out what looked like a white, hockey puck, and dropped it on top of the machine.

"That's the soap," he said. He took a dish off a stack of clean dishes on a shelf above the steam table on Morgen's side of the stove, gave the dish a couple of sharp raps on the big rubber collar protruding from the top of the table, and said, "When the dishes come in, they're stacked on this side. You make sure the garbage can is under the table, then bang the dishes on the collar like I showed you to get the scraps off, then stack them on edge in the basket, shove the basket into the machine and shut the door. Make sure you've got both doors completely closed, and pull down this red lever."

Listening to the rush of water inside the dishwasher, Morgen nodded that he understood. Alonzo pushed the lever back up and the rush of water stopped. He then lifted the left side door, and pulled out a hot, steamy, tray still gleaming with soap bubbles, pushed it back inside the dishwasher, and pulled down a blue lever. Again, Morgen heard a sudden rush of water inside the box.

Alonzo slid up the door on the other side of the dishwasher and pulled out the fresh-rinsed tray. "You check the soap from time to time to be sure there's enough soap on top to clean the dishes, and always check to see the garbage can is there, unless you want to spend a day scrubbing the floor on your hands and knees. You got that?"

"I think so," Morgen replied. "Soap goes on top, garbage can underneath, thump the dishes on the rubber collar to knock the scraps off, place them on edge in the tray, open the right side door to push the dirty dishes in, pull the red lever to start the hot water spray, and push up when the dishes are done."

Alonzo interrupted. "You don't have to push it up. It knows enough to shut itself off when the dishes are done."

"Aye, aye, Chief," Morgen affirmed.

"I ain't no Chief," Alonzo snapped, "and I was never in any branch of the armed forces. You got that?"

"Got it," Morgen replied, wondering how Alonzo came by

his military posture and commanding presence.

"I pushed it up because I don't have time to stand around here listening to it, when there's no dishes inside," Alonzo said. "Then what do you do?"

The way he said it, made Morgen think there might be something more to the process that he hadn't been told. "Does the rinse lever shut itself off?" he asked.

Alonzo nodded.

"Then I open the door on this side . . ." Morgen began.

"Not if you've just done a load of dishes, you don't," Alonzo said. "I failed to tell you that the blue rinse lever, just because it's blue, don't mean it's not hot. This machine has a hot water rinse. If you don't wait at least ten to fifteen seconds before you open that door, you're liable to get scalded by the steam. And don't try to re-stack dishes for another ten to fifteen seconds, after you pull them out, or you'll burn your hands.

"The hot water helps the dishes dry fast, but that means they're hot when they first come out."

By the time they'd finished the cook's tour, it was eleven o'clock, and orders started coming in. Morgen discovered he also manned the steam table and deep fat fryer on his side of the stove–fried clams and fried shrimp in one, French fries in the other, because "nobody wants no fishy-tasting French fries." Manning the deep fat fryers was hot work, and since the fries and fish were frozen, the fat would sizzle and pop if you dropped them in too quickly, which Morgen learned the very first time he put a basket of shrimp into the fryer.

Morgen also ladled out the soup de jour and chili from the steam table on his side of the stove, providing him with an opportunity to enjoy a spoonful or two (always on a clean spoon and never from the ladle), just to make sure it was all right and warn the waitress if it was very hot (another condition he learned on his first day), but it was his soup-tasting that introduced Morgen to Alonzo's New England clam chowder, that quickly became one of his favorites.

CHAPTER TWO

Morgen and Alonzo took a lunch break between three and four o'clock, and Alonzo showed him the cottages across the alley in back, used by delivery trucks and the garbage truck when it came to empty the dumpsters.

"The one on the left is yours," Alonzo said, handing Morgen the key.

"They look the same," Morgen remarked.

"Mirror images," Alonzo said, and smiled as he continued, "but mine is further from the dumpsters."

"So, we're neighbors," Morgen said, waving flies away.

"Not really. I only use mine to wash up and change before I go home. My woman won't let me in smelling like garbage."

"One last thing," Morgen asked, "Where's the water?"

"You mean the beach? That's about a forty-minute walk, there and back, more if you stop to stick your toes in."

"Oh."

Brushing away the buzzing flies, Alonzo fled back into the kitchen. Morgen unlocked the door to his cottage, and was hit with a blast of heat from inside. With all the flies buzzing around outside, he couldn't leave the door open, nor could he open the single, alley-facing window. There was no screen.

Morgen decided to unpack after work, but noted the room had a narrow single bed covered with a thin, thermal blanket, topped with a hard, flat pillow, a small bureau, with a small mirror attached to the wall above it, a chair and small writing table, and a shallow closet with double sliding doors, that lurched and dragged more than slid when he tried them.

It also had a tiny bathroom with a door that opened outward, into the room, a necessity because just inside the three-quarter bath, on the left, was a three-by-three shower stall, and directly in front of it, on the opposite wall, was a three foot wide, six foot tall, built-in cabinet base with shelves above, on which there were towels and washcloths. Beyond them was a pedestal sink with a mirrored medicine cabinet above, and, although it couldn't be seen from the doorway, Morgen guessed that the toilet was on the far side of the shower stall.

He quickly washed the sweat from his face, and saw it, a rather nice dual-flush job that looked quite new, all cleverly laid out in a six foot-by-six-foot room. He guessed the cottage next door shared the wall between the two toilets and shower stalls. That would be the most cost-effective use of the tiny space as far as plumbing was concerned.

He was already starting to sweat, again. Deciding he'd had enough, Morgen fled back through the flies to the relative cool of the sweltering kitchen and roaring exhaust fans.

Alonzo was cleaning pots and pans when Morgen came in. "That was fast," he said.

"You said I still had a lot to learn."

"This is your job, too," he said, scrubbing a deep pot.

Alonzo continued, "You gotta keep these pots and pans clean and ready, so whenever there's some slack, you get to work on them. Here, you try it."

Alonzo handed Morgen the steel pad and Morgen took up where Alonzo left off.

"I've been trying to work it out. Where's the 'e' go?"

"I must have left it in Boston when I took this job."

Alonzo looked puzzled, then let out a hearty laugh when he realized Morgen thought he'd said "ego."

When Alonzo laughed, Morgen realized why, but didn't let on, enjoying the notion that he sounded clever, and added, "It's a little 'e' between the 'g' and the 'n'."

Alonzo nodded. "That's about what I figured."

At eight o'clock that night, when the band started playing, they couldn't converse at the top of their lungs, so they didn't.

Morgen worked steadily, staying ahead of the dirty dishes as they came in, cleaning the pots and pans, but when the band started playing "Lucille," Morgen began singing along at the top of his lungs, letting his voice rise to a shriek the way Little Richard made famous in his 1957 version.

Alonzo stared at Morgen, amazed by what he saw and heard, as Morgen shifted from foot to foot in time to the music and shrieked out the song.

When it ended, Alonzo grabbed Morgen and propelled him out the back door into the alley. At first, Morgen thought he was in trouble, but Alonzo only brought him outside so they could talk, and hear what they said to each other.

"Where'd you learn to sing that song like that?" he asked.

"That's how Little Richard did it," Morgen answered.

"I know how Little Richard did it. How do you know?"

"My parents were middle-aged when they adopted me," Morgen explained. "They met at a Bill Haley and the Comets rock and roll show when they were kids, and loved to dance. At five years old, watching them jump, twirl and toss each other around made me laugh and laugh. I used to think they did it for my benefit."

"They probably did," Alonzo said.

"They loved to see me happy. They had boxes and boxes of 45s, and I began singing along with the records. My mother used to say rock and roll made us a family.

"After my Dad's first stroke, when all they could do was sit, snuggle, and hold hands, they let me go through the records, stack them on the spindle, and sing the songs to them.

"After Dad died, I stopped playing the records until, one day, my mother asked me to put on some records and sing to her.

"I did, but when she began to cry, I thought my heart would break. I was almost sixteen, and promised never to play them again, but she hugged me like I was a little kid, and told me her tears were happy tears. Those records just didn't sound right if I wasn't singing along with them, so she could remember all we'd shared together. And whenever I sang 'Lucille,' she thought of Dad telling her to put on 'Little Morgen'."

"Is your Mama gone, too?" Alonzo asked gently.

"Oh, yeah," Morgen answered dispassionately. "She's been gone more than five years now. I was nineteen and joined the navy when she passed away."

"Well, just so you know," Alonzo said, "when you start singing and carrying on, you make me happy, too."

The dinner hours were as busy as Alonzo said they would be, and when the kitchen closed, Alonzo started prepping ingredients for the next day's specials, while Morgen split his time between cleaning pots and pans, running dinner dishes through the machine, and mulling over all the dangers of his new job.

As Alonzo put it, "Working in a kitchen is hazardous. You gotta be aware when you come near this griddle, that it's more likely hot, than not."

Morgen had seen the open flames under the steam tables, and he'd already learned why he should be careful putting baskets of frozen shrimp and clams into a bubbling deep fat fryer. And he'd had the lecture about concentrating on whatever he was doing, as long as he was doing it, and told a man can get just as maimed chopping salad as filleting a fish, and to never forget, when scrubbing pots, pans, and oven racks, there's sharp things lurking in that soapy water. In less than an hour, they shut down the kitchen, and locked up.

Morgen was sitting on his bed, remembering his youth when Alonzo tapped on his door. "You still awake in there?"

Morgen opened the door and standing on the single step below him, Alonzo was still a bit taller, but what really struck Morgen was how fresh and clean he looked with his jacket over his shoulder, and wearing a white shirt and tie.

"I been thinking, I should call you Little E," Alonzo said.

"Little E?" Morgen mused. "Okay, I'll call you Big A."

"Big A and Little E," said the tall cook with a smile so wide, it completely erased his normal scowl, and shaking Morgen's hand, said, "Deal! Get some sleep. See you in the morning."

Big A, without looking back, strode off down the alley to the parking lot, but the next morning, when he arrived, he brought Little E an old, sliding window screen, warning him not to use it except on days the garbage men left a fresh dumpster, or the room would stink.

Then, Little E found the nearest laundromat, but it took nearly three hours between walking there, sitting while his load washed and dried, and walking back, barely making it in time for work. The laundromat was open 24 hours, so he'd have to come up with an alternate schedule to do his laundry. The next morning was cool and breezy, so he walked to the nearest beach. It was deserted at that hour, and had no refreshment stands in sight, so it might always be deserted.

His job as a dishwasher continued as it began, including his singing along in the kitchen when the band out front played its first set. During the band's first break, Big A and Little E would shut down the kitchen, lock up, go to their cottages to scrub off the sweat, then Big A would go home to his family, and Little E was left on his own.

That first week, tired as he was after each day's work, Little E took his chair outside in the cool of evening, went around to the parking lot and sat against the wall of the club to listen to the band, but too exhausted to stay awake for long, he'd fall asleep during a break, and wake up stiff all over. He was sleeping in his chair the night Salvatore rousted him.

"Whaddaya think you're doin'?" Sal yelled, pulling the chair out from under him. Standing over him, wielding a baseball bat, back-lit by the overhead lights, Sal was a nightmare.

"Customers been complainin' there's a bum hanging around out here. It's lucky I recognized you before I let you have it!" and shoving the chair into Little E's hands, continued, "Now get outta here, and don't let me catch you out here again!"

On the Friday night of Little E's sixth week, a fight broke out in front of the club during the band's first break. Little E and Big A were just closing up when they heard screaming. They rushed around to the front in time to see a car race away in a cloud of black exhaust. The band's singer was sitting on the ground, blood squirting from a wound in his arm. Big A pulled off his belt and applied a tourniquet to slow the flow, but a police car that must have been cruising nearby, howled into the parking lot, and the two cops inside took over. Calling for backup, they loaded the wounded singer into the patrol car's back seat.

A second police car arrived. One of the first officers on the scene stayed, while an officer from the second squad car climbed into the back seat with the singer, and the first car sped off to the hospital.

The two officers remaining began taking statements, one questioning the band members, the other questioning potential witnesses. Sal blocked the doorway to keep customers inside from leaving, but when they settled down, he turned and spoke to the officer questioning the band.

"Officer," Sal said, managing to sound obsequious, "some of the customers inside wanna go. They didn't see nuthin' and they're pretty shook up. Whadda you say? Can I let 'em go?"

"You're sure they were inside the whole time?"

"I'm sure, officer. Five of 'em. The band won't be goin' anywheres, and if they go in and start playin' that should quiet the crowd, and maybe you could question them later, okay?"

17

The officer replied, "I'm through with these guys for now, but nobody leaves the club until I get names and numbers."

"Thank you, officer," Sal called back, "Could you start with them five over by the door?"

Both officers went to question the five customers who wanted so desperately to leave, and Sal went over to the band.

"You heard him," he snarled. "Get in there and get to work. You ain't exactly ornamental."

One musician whined, "We're a group. Our singer may be dying! We should be on our way to the hospital!"

"You ain't goin' nowheres, except back on that stage."

Big A intervened, telling Sal, he'd handle it.

"Whadda you know?" Sal challenged. "You're the cook!"

Again, Morgen was impressed by Big A's military bearing. If he hadn't been a chief petty officer, or high-ranking sergeant, he must have had some training. He spoke with unmistakable authority to Sal and the band when he said, "I know we've got one hell of a singer standing by, and if you put him on, you'll have this place jumping in no time." To the rattled band members, he said, "And don't worry. He knows every song in your repertoire, and how to deliver them."

"I don't know . . ." one of the band members began.

"But I do," Big A said, "Salvatore will check with the hospital and keep you informed, so let's get these frightened people back inside and start rocking the house down! I suggest, you start with 'Lucille.'"

Morgen suddenly realized Big A was talking about him! He couldn't run without attracting the attention of the police, so he drifted toward the ally, and didn't start his mad dash to his cottage until he was out of sight.

Meanwhile, Salvatore protested, "I don't even know which hospital where they took him."

Big A suggested, "There aren't that many options down here. If you can't figure it out, call the police. They'll know."

As they went back inside the club, the whiny player called back to Sal, "His name is Charlie Taylor."

"You're supposed to be on stage," Big A said, and the guy scampered inside. Turning to Sal, Big A said softly, "Don't you have phone calls to make?"

"I've got phone calls to make, all right," Sal growled, "And you can be sure one of them will be to Mr. Rico!"

"Good thinking," Big A replied.

Sal turned and hurried inside the club.

Big A walked to the alleyway, and then broke into a run, arriving outside his cottage just as Morgen came out of his, wearing jeans and a clean T-shirt.

"What do you think?" Morgen asked. "I washed up and put on deodorant."

"I've got a shirt for you," Big A replied. "It'll be long, but if you roll up the sleeves and tuck it in, it should look great."

In less than 30 seconds, Big A reappeared with a shiny, multi-colored shirt with streaks of shiny gold in it.

"Put it on. We'll enter through the kitchen. When you hear the opening bars of 'Lucille,' you get on stage, grab a mike, and knock 'em dead!"

Mr. Rico arrived shortly thereafter, with his lawyer in tow, but when he heard Little E rocking down the house, he smiled and nodded at Big A, who was standing by the kitchen doors. Big A smiled back, slipped into the kitchen, locked up, cleaned up, changed his clothes, and went home to his family.

Morgen finished up the weekend, and to give him time to change and clean up in time for the two eight o'clock show starts, Big A finished the dishes, pots and pans, and heard two full sets before he left on Saturday and Sunday night.

Monday was payday, and Morgen, with three successful nights of singing to a full house, was excited when he went into Mr. Rico's office to pick up his pay check, but taken aback when the check was the same as the previous week.

"Excuse me, Mr. Rico. Is this all? You know I sang with the band all weekend. Don't I get something extra for that?"

"Not from me, you don't," Mr. Rico replied, "but thank you for filling in. Under the circumstances, you did very well."

"I worked three night in a row."

"I pay you to wash dishes," Mr. Rico explained. "The band got paid Sunday night, packed up, and moved on. If they owe you money for singing, you'll have to take it up with them."

"That's bullshit!" Morgen fumed.

Mr. Rico said, "I'm sorry you feel that way," and he pushed the button hidden under his desktop.

"I don't work for the band. I work for you!"

"Not any more, you don't," Mr. Rico said.

Salvatore burst into the office.

"Get this bum out of here," Mr. Rico said, "get his shit out of my cottage, and get me a new dishwasher."

"Consider it done, boss!"

"I save your ass, and you fire me?" Morgen shouted, whereupon Sal, while never the sharpest knife in the drawer, but a formidable brute when let off his leash, grabbed Morgen and threw him bodily out of the office into the main room. Before Morgen could get up on his own, Sal was on top of him, jerking him to his feet, then dragging him toward the kitchen. When Morgen tried to twist free, Sal threw him across the dance floor for good measure.

Big A stuck his head out the kitchen door. "What's going on?" he yelled.

"This little shit's been fired," Sal snarled. "And I'm going to help him pack."

"I'll take care of that!" Big A volunteered. "He's got some of my things in his room, and I want them back."

Sal glared at Big A for a second or two, then snarled, "Okay, Lonzo. He's all yours, but Mr. Rico wants him gone, and if he ain't gone in fifteen minutes, it's on you . . ."

20

"It won't take that long," Big A promised.

Morgen couldn't believe it was really happening. Big A spoke softly as he helped Morgen to his feet.

"Listen up, Little E. You've no idea what these animals are capable of. You've gotta get out of here, now."

"I worked three nights, and Mr. Rico refused to pay me. It's not fair."

"It's not fair," Big A agreed, as they walked out to Morgen's cottage, "but you don't belong here. You're not a dishwasher. You're a singer, a hell of a singer, and your three-night stand proved that to me, you, and everybody who heard you."

"Did you used to be a cop?"

"No. Start packing."

"Well, where'd you get your military bearing and the voice of command I hear whenever you decide to take charge?"

"Keep packing." Big A said, and Morgen did.

"I'm six foot three," Big A continued, "I was born six foot three. I was so much taller than all the other kids, I used to go around stooped over, to try to fit in. If I stand tall now, it's because my mother drilled it into me. When she saw me stooping over, she'd yell at me to stand up straight."

"Well, it looks good on you now."

"As for the commanding voice, I was in ROTC when I was in high school. You done?"

"I guess so. And you never went into the service?"

"I graduated in '73. I know that's before your time, but they had this thing going on in Vietnam. President Nixon promised to end it, and late in January of my senior year, the Paris Peace Accords were signed, marking the official end of that war. Personally, I was thrilled and relieved to hear it. I was finally able to start planning a future that didn't start and end with me getting myself killed."

Then Big A took Little E in his long arms, and hugged him goodbye.

"That's it," Big A said. "You've got to git, and I mean right now."

"Take care, Big A!" Morgen called and he took off down the alley, "Be seein' you!"

"Not here, you won't," Big A shouted after him, and sadly, that was the last they ever saw of each other.

It wasn't quite noon, when Morgen, walking north on General MacArthur Boulevard, thumbed down a bright red Mustang convertible driven by a pretty young lady wearing a white halter top, white shorts and white sandals that fastened above her calves.

"How far you going, sailor?" she said with a smile like sunshine breaking through the clouds on a stormy day.

"Boston," he answered.

"Me too," she said, happy for the company.

Morgen dropped his sea-bag on the floor by the back seat.

"I'm Bonnie," she said as he climbed into the convertible.

"You're all that, Lassie," Morgen said in what he hoped was a Scottish accent, "and I've been out and about for more than a year, now."

Bonnie's eyes widened. "Were you in prison?" she asked, looking less confident than before.

"I was in the navy," he replied, dropping his affected accent. "You probably thought I was a sailor because of the sea-bag."

"Actually, it was the pea coat. Kind of hot for today, isn't it? So, what do you do now? Are you an actor?"

Morgen, not wanting to admit he was an unemployed dishwasher replied, "Would it surprise you to know I'm a rock and roll singer, looking for a band?"

"You're kidding?" she squealed happily. "My friends have a band, a really good band, and they're looking for a singer!"

CHAPTER THREE

That afternoon, Bonnie introduced Morgen to her boyfriend, George, who lived in a big, old, wooden house he rented on the cheap in a part of town desperately in need of urban renewal. His band, Beantown Home Cookin', regularly practiced in his heavily-draped, boarded up living room. Roger, the drummer, was a Canadian percussionist who met George at the Berklee College of Music, and Frank (Franklin, not Francis), the electric bass player, was another Berklee grad, all living in the same neighborhood. Tony and Mike, the lead and rhythm guitarists, who also sang backup, shared a rental on the other side of the Mystic River.

Morgen's audition was simple. George setup a floor mike, plugged Morgen into his P.A., gave Morgen a playlist and asked Morgen how many of the songs he knew. Morgen was familiar with most of the songs, and Morgen's singing impressed them all. As for the songs he didn't know well, he promised to learn them, and even added a few Jerry Lee Lewis and Little Richard tunes, all songs the band recognized, and George was thrilled to add them to his playlist, not least because they gave him a chance to showcase his skill on the piano parts.

By four o'clock that afternoon, Morgen had become the sixth member of Beantown Home Cookin', and would go on with them on Friday night, when they were scheduled to begin a three night stand at a popular local dance bar, and that meant they'd have to practice every day for the rest of the week, to nail down the new playlist.

Morgen had been having a wonderful time, but when George announced the rehearsals, for the first time, he saw doubt on Morgen's face.

"Do you have a day job?" he asked.

"That's not it," Morgen replied.

"Where are you staying?" Roger asked. "Do you need a ride?"

"That's it," Morgen said. "I don't have a place to stay, I'm short of cash, and it's too late to cash my last paycheck."

"How much do you need?" George asked.

Morgen handed his check to George. "It's not much," Morgen said, embarrassed by the amount, and explained, "The cottage was covered by the club, and I ran a tab for my meals, so after they deducted it all, that's all I cleared."

"No wonder you quit," George remarked.

"It's summer," Frank volunteered, "The Cape is wicked expensive this time of year."

"Well, you can crash here tonight," George said, "and if that works for you, I'll take you to the bank, and we'll see what we can do about getting you settled in tomorrow morning."

Morgen said, "I don't want to put anybody out . . ."

"No problem. We'll start rehearsal at two, tomorrow afternoon," George said, making sure everyone in the band was aware that they'd be starting an hour later than usual.

Bonnie had sat contentedly through the audition, feeling good about introducing Morgen to Beantown Home Cookin', but wasn't happy with the sudden turn of events.

"Do I need to cancel our dinner reservations?" Bonnie asked, sweetly.

They had no reservations. Bonnie had spent the weekend with her family in their place on Cape Cod, and it was George's promise to take her out to dinner that had her driving back to Boston when she picked up Morgen. It was Bonnie's subtle way of reminding him of his promise.

"I was going to ask Morgen to join us," George said.

"Thanks," Morgen said, "but I don't have anything to wear. Everything I have is wadded up in my sea-bag."

"That's all right," George said. "I know a great Chinese restaurant. We'll order take out and dine in!"

"Are we using the fine china, or the paper plates," Bonnie asked, pointedly.

Aghast, George replied, "Paper plates, of course. I didn't invite you up to do dishes!"

That settled, the band made their farewells and Morgen, still feeling like an intruder, asked George, "Is there a spare room, or will I be staying in here?"

"There is a spare room," George said, "but it's on the third floor and unfurnished. If you can stand it, you can sleep here on the couch."

"The couch will be fine," Morgen said.

They dined at the kitchen table, sitting on the three matching, chrome-legged kitchen chairs with faded vinyl seats. The chrome-legged Formica table had seen better days, but looked presentable with a clean, white tablecloth and two Indian brass candlesticks with tall, red candles. Whether they were intended to suggest passion or danger ahead, wasn't clear. But the whole business about the paper plates had been an in-joke shared by Bonnie and George. In fact, the Melmac plates all matched, as did the stainless-steel utensils preferred over the plastic ones that came with the take out order.

Bonnie brewed a pot of Oolong tea, and the Chinese food was incredible and abundant. Spread on the table, it looked like Bonnie had ordered one of everything on the menu, and included a bag of soft sesame seed candies for dessert.

As Bonnie and George began clearing the table, Morgen excused himself, to allow them some privacy.

"If you don't mind," Morgen said, "I'm ready to turn in."

"No," Bonnie answered quickly, "go right ahead. We'll see you in the morning."

"Thanks for a really wonderful dinner."

"Thank you," George said. "With you here, I got to enjoy a number of my favorite dishes that we generally don't order."

"See you in the morning," Bonnie added, clearly a signal that it was time for him to make his exit.

"Sure thing," Morgen said, and left the relatively clean kitchen, with a screen door that allowed fresh air in to mingle with the aroma of the Chinese food. In contrast, the odor captured in the couch in the rehearsal room was enough to gag a maggot. Morgen had trouble finding a way to turn his face to reduce its impact on his nose.

With all his tossing and turning and trying to get to sleep, with his head on one side or the other of the saggy-cushioned sofa, he saw something that had escaped his notice earlier. A large part of the living room was taken up by a grand piano, a huge thing that George hadn't played once during the audition, but what now caught Morgen's eye was that the three legged piano had two firm legs, and the third, nearest him, was broken, and the piano was made level by the addition of three thick books, stacked under the broken leg.

Morgen couldn't help but wonder how the leg had become broken, and why George hadn't had it repaired, and the riddle of the piano was still unsolved when he finally drifted off to sleep.

Bonnie slept in, and when George came down and found Morgen, awake, he offered to take Morgen out to breakfast at a place near George's bank, where he was sure they'd cash Morgen's check.

The restaurant was a railroad-car inspired diner, where breakfast could be ordered, cooked, served and eaten, all within twenty minutes. They both ordered one egg over easy two sausage links, and were allowed to substitute a short stack of buttermilk pancakes, with real Vermont maple syrup. instead of home fries, The only problem was that they still had twenty-five minutes to go before the bank opened, so they ordered a second cup of coffee and bear claws, heated in the microwave, which made them way too hot to even try to

26

eat for another ten minutes, and they allowed Jim to freshen their coffee while they waited. The diner was busy, but the turnover was generally quick, so they didn't feel rushed.

Making small talk, George asked Morgen if he'd slept well, and Morgen's reply was that regretfully, he hadn't.

"I've got to say, George, that room stinks, literally," Morgen said. "It was like trying to take a nap in a football stadium locker room after halftime."

"I guess I'm just used to it," George admitted, "but that gives me another idea. I told you I had a spare room up on the third floor. I could pick up some furniture at Ace's Place, a great used furniture store I know, with lots of very reasonably priced old furniture. I'll furnish the room, and later, when you can afford digs of your own, if you want it, I'll sell it to you for what I paid for it."

"That's generous George, but what if things don't work out."

"Then I'll have a furnished guest room for the next guy."

"When I get my check cashed, I'll want to buy a new mattress, and if things don't work out, I'll let you keep it for whatever I pay for it."

"This is starting to sound like a plan," George said with a smile. "You don't have to worry about bedding. I've got plenty of sheets, blankets, and pillow cases. I suppose you'll want a new pillow."

"That, too," Morgen agreed

"There is a drawback," George warned. "The third-floor bathroom is out of commission, so you'll have to use the bathroom on the second floor, but you'll have it all to yourself."

"That sounds doable," Morgen agreed.

Jim, the short-order cook and counterman, added some fresh coffee to their cups, and they finally enjoyed their bear claws, cooled off enough to eat.

With cash in his pocket, Morgen and George went back to the house so Morgen could see the spare room. Bonnie, still in her bathrobe, was sitting at the kitchen table having coffee and toast when they arrived.

"Did you bring me something?" she asked.

"No, sorry," George said, sounding like he really meant it. "We just stopped at Jim's for a quick bite and went to the bank."

"Oh." Bonnie said

"Yes," George continued. "Morgen's going to stay in the spare room on the third floor for a while, and we've just come back to see what we need to do to get it ready for occupancy."

"I see," Bonnie said, sounding like whatever she saw was not entirely pleasant.

Thinking quickly, George added, "and once Morgen's settled in, you and I will go out for that dinner."

"Uh-huh," she replied, making it sound affirmative and doubtful at the same time.

"C'mon," George said to Morgen. "Let's go see that room."

Two flights of stairs later, George put his shoulder to it, and managed to push the swollen door to the spare room open. They shooed all the pigeons out the broken window, taped a large piece of cardboard over the broken window pane, and then managed, with the aid of a crowbar, to open the swollen closet door that they removed and placed in the hallway.

The room didn't smell like a men's locker room, but was thick with an eau de neglected aviary that Morgen hoped he could eliminate with a good scrubbing. Once it was cleaned up, all it needed was furniture, and it would be ready for occupancy.

George wanted to get the furniture, but Morgen insisted on cleaning up the room, first.

"There's a reason they call sailors 'swabbies'," Morgen said.

George was able to produce a wastebasket, broom, dustpan and brush. Morgen said he'd need a sponge, a large bottle of liquid bleach, and a box of detergent, so George promised Bonnie they'd be right back, and drove Morgen to the store. They were back in less than thirty minutes, and Bonnie was fully dressed when they returned, waiting for George in the kitchen.

"I'm back," he called cheerily.

"Good," Bonnie replied. "I've got shopping to do, too."

"I'll go with you," George volunteered, "as long as we can get back by two."

"Rehearsal," Bonnie said.

"Thanks to you," George added happily, "we've finally got a lead singer and a lot of tunes to get down before Friday night."

"Lucky I ran into him," Bonnie said.

"That wasn't luck," George said, smiling appreciatively. "It was fate. You done good, girl."

"If you can tear yourself away . . ." Bonnie said.

"You've got everything you need, right Morgen?"

"Everything I think I need," Morgen replied, "and finished or not, I'll be down in time for rehearsal."

"Great," George said, and he and Bonnie left.

Cleaning that room was more trouble than Morgen had anticipated, and having to refill and empty the bucket on the second floor got old in a hurry, but true to his word, he came down on time for rehearsal, actually a continuation of the audition of the day before, mostly made up of selecting songs they all knew well enough to play, rather than actually rehearsing any new material. At four o'clock, George said they had more than enough songs to cover the gig, and told everyone to come back tomorrow at the usual time, and they'd start nailing down the playlist. Then, it was off to the used furniture store. Morgen and George arrived about an hour before closing, giving them plenty of time to pick and choose and negotiate fair prices for a headboard and steel bed frame, a chest of drawers, an end table and a table lamp. George paid for everything, insisting it had to be delivered that same day, which proved to be problematic.

The delivery truck had already left, but Ace reached the driver on his cellphone, already caught up in rush hour traffic.

Ace and the driver negotiated until the driver finally agreed, that for another $25.00 dollars cash, he'd come back, pick up the furniture and deliver it that same night, but couldn't promise what time he'd arrive, so George had to be sure there was someone home to take delivery, curbside.

That settled, George and Morgen hurried over to a mattress store, bought a new mattress on sale, arranged for immediate delivery, and hurried back to the house.

Bonnie looked beautiful, all dressed up for their dinner date, and was obviously not happy to learn their dinner date had to be postponed a second time. As she stomped upstairs to change into something more comfortable, George shouted after her that he'd order the pizza.

Morgen waited until he heard her go into George's room and slam the door, before he went up to finish cleaning before the furniture arrived, leaving George to order the pizza and deal with Bonnie when she came down. He'd nearly finished when the pizza arrived, and shouted he'd be down shortly, and for them to start without him.

Ten minutes later, most of a large Pepperoni, and a large Canadian Bacon and Pineapple pizza were still left over, when Morgen came down. They looked great, and might have tasted great, had his hands not smelled so strongly of bleach.

The mattress arrived before the furniture, and the driver and his helper carried it all the way up the stairs to the third floor. Bonnie gave George a look, and he quickly gave the driver a ten-dollar tip.

It was almost an hour later that the furniture was delivered to the sidewalk in front of the house. The chest of drawers was awkward to carry up the flight of stairs to the front porch, and then up the two flights of stairs inside, because they had to carry it tilted back to keep the drawers from sliding open.

It began to rain, gently, at first, but then harder, so Bonnie pitched in. She carried the small side table and the table lamp up the front stairs and set them inside the front door, while Morgen carried the headboard, and George carried the awkward steel bed frame upstairs. Morgen came back down for the lamp and end table, while George began assembling the bed frame, a simple matter of unfolding and thumb-screwing its two sections together. They then realized they'd failed to buy a box spring or planks to lay across the metal bed frame to support the mattress, which meant that Morgen spent that night smelling like bleach, sleeping on a new mattress in a room that smelled of bleach, with no way to open the window, probably a good thing, because if he had, the flock of pigeons lurking on the phone lines outside, might have taken it as an invitation to move back in. Happily, when they plugged in the lamp, it worked, so at least the wiring was adequate.

Friday afternoon, the band moved their equipment into the dance club. It had a good-sized podium with a raised plywood platform in the center rear, for Roger and his drums. George set up his L-shaped four keyboard array downstage to Roger's left, with Frank and his bass amp set up in between.

Tony and Mike, the guitarists, were accustomed to being downstage on Roger's right, opposite George, and regularly reeled and rocked with the music they played and sang, drawing the lion's share of audience attention, but on Morgen's first night, when Morgen sang Bob Seger's "Old Time Rock 'n' Roll," all that changed, and by the end of the song, the crowd belonged to Morgen, who not only grabbed their attention, but held it as he introduced the band members and himself, and he kept their attention right up to last call, singing, prancing and dancing back and forth across most of the front of the stage, incidentally forcing the guitarists to retreat to make room for his energetic, charismatic performance.

Bonnie was there. She saw it all, and screamed right along with the crowd, thrilled by their performance, excited by the knowledge that she had been instrumental in bringing them together. She went with them to the Saturday night performances, too, arriving with Beantown Home Cookin' twenty-minutes before they were to start.

They ran a sound check. Everything sounded fine, but after the sound check, Tony warned Morgen not to get between him and the audience, and to stick to his spot, center stage, in front of the drums. Morgen said he couldn't. If he did, the crowd wouldn't hear anything but the drums. George settled it. Without any announcement, he and Frank moved his keyboards back so Morgen could easily get past them to address the crowd on George's side of the stage, and then told both guitarists to back up, too, so Morgen could work that side of the stage just as easily. Tony and Mike protested that the crowd always cheered their reelin' and rockin' routines. George said he didn't mean they should stop reelin' and rockin,' just that they should back up enough for Morgen to be able to work the entire room. The crowd's reaction to the previous night's performance, was the loudest and most sustained they'd ever had.

George then made it clear that the crowd loved Morgen's strutting, howling performance, and if that's what they wanted, that's what Beantown Home Cookin' was going to be serving from then on.

Bonnie witnessed the exchange, and saw Tony and Mike grudgingly accept George's decision. Morgen also knew they were not happy with the new deployment, and did everything he could to involve them in the show, joining them, sharing his microphone with them on some songs, adjusting his own performance to include and call attention to some of their routines, reelin' and rockin' along with them in others, even inviting Frank front and center to join them in some. He also managed to sometimes share his microphone and the spotlight with George, too, the chef responsible for Beantown Home Cookin', mostly pretty much hidden behind his four-keyboard array.

Word of the band's new lead singer had reached the *Boston Herald* and the *Boston Globe*, and both newspapers had columnists in attendance, and the reviews were better than good, guaranteeing a standing room only crowd for the following weekend. Morgen had never before performed with such talented musicians, and that next week, he composed his first original song for them, calling it simply, "Rock and Roll," a deliberately derivative number that set the crowd jumping and made good copy for the press. Summer was coming to an end, and George was already lining up college gigs, armed with the recent Beantown Home Cookin' reviews, when Bonnie suddenly broke up with George to go back to Wellesley College to continue her education.

Morgen was distraught, feeling responsible for the breakup, He told George he had enough money to get a place of his own, if that would help, but George said the breakup was bound to happen, sooner or later.

When Morgen argued that Bonnie was a prize, and he'd be a fool not to go after her, George studied Morgen for a moment, then asked, "How old are you Morgen?"

"Almost twenty-four," Morgen replied.

"I'm almost thirty-two," George said. "Bonnie's young, beautiful, smart, and just about everything a guy could want."

"So, go after her!" Morgen advised.

"I have nothing to say to her that she'd want to hear," George said mournfully.

"She loves you!" Morgen insisted.

"And I love her. But she loves the me she'd like me to be, not the me I am. She doesn't understand that I'm a musician because I love to play music. She doesn't want to hang around in bars and get hit on by guys all night long, and she doesn't want to be left home alone every night, or every weekend. She's been after me to 'grow up,' and accept a day job teaching at Berklee, so we could settle down, make a home and have a family. When she first brought you to me, I thought she might have begun to come around.

"In fact, I had less time for her than before, because we had so much material we had to get down to be ready to perform. I'm a musician. I live, love, work, and play music. It's not just something I do to make money. It's who I am. You had nothing to do with our breaking up. It was just time."

"I'm really sorry," Morgen said.

"You and I are a lot alike," George continued. "Your music is you, too. It's why you were born with the gifts you have, what you were put on earth to do, and I see it in you every time we do a show."

"I hope you're right," Morgen replied.

"You know I am," George said.

Morgen was depressed when he began to compose "Oh Mama," but by the time he was finished he was eager to introduce it at the next rehearsal, a genuine rehearsal in which they worked up Morgen's new song, with a drumbeat that grabbed the crowd by the heart and never let go, an integrated melody line for lead guitar, and with George's help, got it all together in time for their next performance.

Tony and Mike both liked the new song, but Tony wanted to improvise a long, howling lead guitar part. He and Mike both fancied themselves guitar heroes, ready for the big time, and had hoped to move Beantown Home Cookin' into heavy metal, but George seemed to be all in on what they considered retro rubbish. They knew George enjoyed the spotlight provided by the honky-tonk piano parts, but there was plenty of room for some really wild psychedelic synthesizer in the heavy metal genre, if George would only give it a chance. In two rehearsals, they'd nailed Morgen's "Oh Mama," and at the next rehearsal, like it or not, Tony was going to do his improvisation.

They went to George's house, an hour early, to propose the idea to George, but he wasn't home, so they let themselves in and waited in the rehearsal room.

Roger had made time to drive Morgen around to look for an apartment. The most affordable were all taken when they called, and they still hadn't found anything suitable when they realized they only had time for one or two more before they'd have to break off the search and get over to George's for rehearsal.

George, having replenished the snacks and beverages he ordinarily laid out for rehearsals, drove to the back of the house and brought his purchases in the kitchen door. He put the bags down on the kitchen counter, and heard voices coming from the living room. He glanced at the wall clock, and saw that it was almost an hour before the band was due.

George's neighborhood was not only run down, but stripped-down, stolen cars were regularly found on its streets, burglaries were common, and gang activity was on the rise.

Fearing vandals or thieves might have gotten into his house while he was at the store, George armed himself with a cast iron frying pan, and stealthily moved toward the voices. Heart pounding, he stopped outside the door to listen to what the intruders were saying.

He heard the first voice say, "Hey, altered states, man. It might open him up to it."

"It'll blow his mind!" the second exclaimed, and laughed.

"We'll know soon enough when I drop this tab in his Moxie."

George recognized Mike's voice, and heard Tony's reply.

"A little tab'll do ya!"

Furious, George burst into the room.

"Early, aren't you!" George snarled.

"We came to talk," Tony said, forcefully.

"Really?" George snarled, "Before or after you dropped acid in Morgen's Moxie?"

"It's time to open his mind to new possibilities," Tony said, with an evil grin.

"You've opened my mind to new possibilities," George said. "I'm wondering what Beantown Home Cookin' will sound like without you."

"Oh, don't be like that, man," Mike whined.

"And you're opening my mind to a world of new possibilities," Tony snapped back.

"I didn't even do it, yet," Mike protested.

"Both of you, pack up your shit and get out of here!" George snarled.

There were more words, mostly expletives, each one more vulgar than the one before, as George supervised them packing up their guitars, stands and amplifiers, and taking them out to Mike's car.

It wasn't easy, but they managed to fit everything in, no one dropped acid, and George didn't brain anybody with his cast iron frying pan. The only serious casualty in the aftermath of George's outrage was that the ice cream, sitting on the kitchen counter for nearly half an hour, had melted into a cool soup. George was trembling, his mind racing, having just fired a third of the band, needing to replace them and rebuild a playlist in less than a week before their next gig, and wondering how he'd explain it all to everyone.

Ultimately, George's official explanation was true enough.

They did break up over creative differences. He later told both Frank and Roger what really happened, but swore them to secrecy about the plot to send Morgen on an acid trip without him knowing it, and both agreed it was an evil thing to even contemplate, and they deserved immediate dismissal.

That evening, George went over to Berklee and recruited replacements, Emery, an excellent guitarist who managed to double on lead and rhythm guitar, and Jeff, a second keyboard player, with an excellent collection of orchestral samples as well as all the most popular synthesizer apps.

Both had no trouble mastering the playlist, and with Morgen's energetic and charismatic performance, the Beantown Home Cookin' show didn't suffer at all. It was visually better balanced, too, with Jeff's keyboards and Emery's guitar arrayed on Roger's right, George's keyboards and Frank's bass on Roger's left, and Morgen free to roam the stage at will.

CHAPTER FOUR

"We're here, sir."

Morgen opened his eyes to see the English chauffeur holding the door open for him.

"I must have dozed off," Morgen said.

"You did, sir," the chauffeur answered, "Jet lag will do that! Your dinner's waiting for you over there, in the marquee."

Morgen saw they were stopped outside the ruined, roofless abbey, where a dining hall tent had been pitched and dinner was being served. Morgen was greeted with "Tom Brady," shouted in unison by the band and the Trashbabies alike. Morgen wagged his head, but then laughed with them as the ribbing continued.

Roger, the drummer, wailed, "We'll never be booked in Boston again," followed by Frank, the bass player, wailing, "I can never go home!" Morgen, particularly liked the double-barreled Q and A started by Emery, the excellent guitarist George had recruited from Berklee, shouting, "Who's that?" followed by the guitarist, Grant, Rodney had added to the group when he became their manager, answering, "I don't know, but it's not Sullivan." Everyone was having a great deal of fun at his expense, not that he didn't deserve it. Rhoda, a Trashbaby, sounded horrified when she shouted, "Do you even remember why we're here?"

Morgen put his hands up in surrender, but Jasmine, the sole East Indian dancer fretted, "If jet lag can erase Tom Brady, how will he possibly remember his lyrics?"

"That's harsh, Elsie," Morgen answered, looking directly at Jasmine.

"Elsie?" Jasmine cried.

Alice, sitting close by, with a sense of humor as wicked as Morgen's, sprang up from the table, threw her arms around him and said, "You haven't forgotten your Sally, have you?" Morgen hugged her back and said, "I could never forget my Sally," getting laughs from all.

Finally, they settled down and made room for Morgen at the table, where a cute waitress, glowing with excitement, presented Morgen with a menu card, and pointing to her name tag announced with undisguised glee, "I'm Sally!"

Alice, saw the name tag and yelled, "She really is!" She offered Sally her hand, and said, "Pleased to meet you, Sally. I'm Alice," she said loudly, as if to remind Morgen.

Hit with laughter and greetings from all, Sally smiled broadly and told Morgen, "I'll take your order when you're ready. Just give me a wave."

Sally then demonstrated her little wave, and concluded "Don't worry if you don't see me. I'll see you."

On their U.S. tour, they'd endured everything from fast food, to backstage takeout, to room service, and generally agreed that the best they'd had to date was luncheon at the Hermitage House Smorgasbord in Nashville, Tennessee, but this early dinner, provided by the BBC, served on picnic tables in a tent at a ruined abbey, eclipsed even that.

The menu card offered a choice of entrées including Roast Turkey, Roast Beef, Baked Ham, or Meatless Baked Lasagna with all the fixings. So much for the oft-repeated warnings about English food. They all settled down to hearty, scrumptious meals.

They still had a few hours before the concert, so they watched the lighting crews erect light towers on either side of the stage in front of a particularly picturesque ruined abbey wall, and when they finished, Beantown Home Cookin', the Trashbabies, and the sound crew ran a sound check.

Sunset would be at eight-thirty, and the concert was scheduled to start at nine. The production van, camera crews and security were all in place by eight o'clock, when the remote location was opened to the concert-going public, many of whom brought picnic baskets and blankets, or cushions to sit on before the show began, all useless when the show started, because as soon as the music began, everyone leaped to their feet, and the area before the stage became standing room only.

It was just past ten minutes to ten, in the ballroom of the Great Country House, hired for the occasion, in clear weather and medium traffic, little more than an hour's drive from the ruined abbey where the live broadcast was originating, that Rodney Hazelton, Beantown Home Cookin's manager, was in the hallway outside the ballroom, on his cell phone, talking to Maggie, his administrative assistant, who had called him from the office at his Massachusetts estate.

"I have no idea whose it is, or was, but I can tell you this," Rodney said softly. "It makes my place look like a gatehouse."

"So, what do you want me to say to *Variety*?" Maggie asked.

"As soon as you get pictures, you'll send them some."

"Will I have them by tomorrow?"

"I don't know, but as soon as I do, I'll email them to you. It's not our fault they didn't send someone to cover this."

"You want me to tell them that?" Maggie asked innocently.

"Hell, no! Look, they're coming to the end of 'Witchy Stew.' I've got to get back in there."

"Knock 'em dead, boss!"

Rodney turned off his phone and went back into the ballroom. The show, already considered an international sensation by the assembled movers and shakers of the U.K. and foreign press who'd been watching the show on the big screen TV, and some had already been glancing furtively at the open bar and snack buffets provided for the press conference after the show, knowing they would have to wait another 90 minutes or so before the stars appeared for photos and interviews. But at that instant, they were all going just as wild as the concert-goers on the big screen TV.

At the ruined abbey, follow spots scanned the crowd, all screaming for more, and all caught on camera. It didn't seem possible, but suddenly, the screams grew louder, as the stage lights came up on Morgen, the Trashbabies, and Beantown Home Cookin', playing the introduction to "The Stranger."

On screen, Morgen strutted to the front edge of the stage, addressing his song to the crowd, but especially to the most desperately excited young ladies in the front rows, pressed against the security barriers, hoping against hope he'd notice them and make eye contact.

"Baby, won't you tell me all your dreams?
And, Baby, if things aren't all you dreamed they'd be,
Listen. I'll help you if I can."

Morgen crouched down and reached out toward a young lovely in the front row.

They could not touch, but the gesture was enough, as the girl stretched and struggled frantically against the security barrier.

"Closer. Let me take you by the hand."

He looked genuinely disappointed as he rose, master of all he surveyed. Live, the crowd reaction was deafening, but the music captured by the television crew was clear enough for the home television audience.

"I'm the one they call *The Stranger*."

Continuing his song, Morgen pranced along the front edge of the stage to favor a new group of frantic young female fans.

"I can help make your dreams come true.

I'm the one they call *The Stranger*."

And again, he reached out and sang his next line to a particularly attractive young lady in the second row.

"Listen and I'll tell you what to do . . ."

The frustrated young lady kept shouting his name, but could not be heard over the music and the roar of the crowd.

Managing to look forlorn, Morgen rose and made his way slowly back across the front of the stage, further than before, seeking a new target.

"Poor child. Close and rest your eyes.

Lie back. Soon you'll realize, you can trust in me.

Listen, and the world will go away.

Closer. Listen only to what I say . . ."

The Trashbabies abandoned the band as they sang their chorus, moving slowly downstage toward Morgen, all the while scanning the young ladies in the front rows, selecting his next conquest.

"So pret-ty, pret-ty, per-dee-per, dee-per, dee- per . . ."

Morgen watched as the Trashbabies scanned the front rows, making and breaking eye contact with a number of young women, seeking an appropriate target for their master.

The Trashbabies huddled briefly, and Theresa broke away from the others, went to Morgen and whispered in his ear. The other Trashbabies all looked directly at the selected young lady, and as the song continued, making way for Morgen, who moved closer, singing his song, his focus on that girl alone.

"Poor thing. You're really feeling sleepy.

Lie back. All those eerie feelings will go away.

Softly. Surrender is no sin.

Easy. Open up and let me in."

The Trashbabies repeated their hypnotic chorus.

"So pret-ty, per-dee-per, dee-per, dee-per . . ."

Morgen went as close as he dared to the edge of the stage nearest his prize, crouched, and reached out to her. For her part, the girl tried frantically to climb over the security barrier, screaming with frustration as the security guards stopped her. Morgen abandoned the girl, rose for his last verse, celebrating his ability to manipulate and control his audience.

"I'm The One, *The Stranger*.

I'm The One. I make your dreams come true.

I'm The One. *The Stranger*.

Listen, and I'll put my spell on you."

It was great theater, and elicited meter-bending roars from the live audience, stunned the millions who watched the broadcast in their living rooms, and at the exclusive recording industry soirée intended to showcase Morgen's talent to the media, brought the British and select foreign mavens to their feet, their enthusiastic ovation punctuated by shrill whistles, and delighted screams from the ladies present.

Content to bask in the success of the turnout, the underwriting recording industry moguls graciously allowed Morgen's manager, Rodney, to play master of ceremonies. The lights came up, the screen went dark, and the cheering continued.

Standing before the dark screen, Rodney shouted, "Milords, ladies and gentlemen! Beantown Home Cookin' and the tantalizing Trashbabies will be here, in person, before midnight, to pose for your cameras and answer your questions. Meanwhile," Rodney continued, "please enjoy the offerings set out on both sides of the room, or refresh yourselves at the complimentary open bar!"

The guests were quick to take advantage of Rodney's invitation, and flocked to the long tables on both sides of the great room, displaying a scrumptious assortment of hors d'oeuvres, fruits, cakes, candies, and other assorted treats, and bartenders and hostesses at the bar began taking orders.

"Take your time, folks. There's plenty for all. It's early, and we've got the room until dawn, and you'll have plenty of time for photos and interviews when the talent arrives!"

By the time Rodney finished his speech, almost everyone had made their ways to the bar or the food tables. Rodney saw the grinning recording industry moguls applauding him from the back of the ballroom, took it as permission to make his own survey of the offerings, but was cut off by Alan Fuller, the record label's happy A&R man.

"Great show, Rod," Alan said, "and the Chairman of the Board just gave me the okay for the new album, so when you finish the tour, you'll be coming back here to record."

"Excellent," Rodney replied. "Where?"

"I haven't scheduled it, yet" Alan replied, "but you can be sure it will be the best available."

An attractive lady appeared at Alan's shoulder, and addressing Rodney, said, "Excuse me. You're Morgen's manager, aren't you?"

"Angela!" Alan exclaimed. "I don't believe you've met Rodney Hazelton."

"Mr. Hazelton," Angela said, taking Rodney's hand and in the act, pulling him closer to herself.

Alan enthused "Angela Knight, hostess of *Knight on the Town*, the most-watched entertainment talk show in the U.K."

"And widely syndicated," Angela added with a smile, as she and Rodney shook hands.

"Angela," Rodney said with a matching smile. "How nice to meet you! Of course, I've heard of *Knight on the Town*, but I have to admit, I've never seen it."

Alan quickly added, "Rodney only arrived today. I haven't had a chance to tell him how fortunate we are to have you here."

"Thank you, Alan," Angela said.

"What did you think of the show?" Rodney asked.

"It was incredible," Angela answered, "Look! That finale gave me goose pimples!"

"Excuse me," Alan interjected. "You two need to talk, and I'm starving!"

"We'll talk later," Rodney called after him, but Angela moved in, turning Rodney so her still photographer could take photos of them together, and as they both smiled for the camera, said in a voice not-to-be-denied, "I want him."

"Everybody wants him," Rodney replied.

"An entire show," she said, "Interview, video clips . . ."

Rodney replied. "Just say when and I'll make it happen!"

"Do you prefer Rodney," she asked, feigning innocence, "Or should I call you . . . Rod?"

It was raining outside. Rodney sat in a corner near the double doors, exhausted by a day that started yesterday in Boston, became today in London, and as midnight approached, would soon be tomorrow. Since yesterday, apart from a snooze on the plane, he'd been on the go for almost thirty hours. The record industry moguls had departed, and the international media crowd had broken up into a number of cliques, apparently interviewing each other. Beantown Home Cookin' and the Trashbabies hadn't arrived yet, and Rodney's tank was running on fumes, when his cell phone buzzed.

He snapped it up and said, "Where are you?"

The chauffeur answered, "Just driving in the gate."

"I'll meet you in front!"

Rodney slipped out the door into the long gallery, grabbed someone's umbrella from an umbrella stand, and hurried downstairs to the ground floor. He switched on the outside light as he hurried through the service entrance door, slithered by the exotic red sports car parked inside the barrel vault under the main stairs, and as the limousine arrived, opened the umbrella, and dashed to the passenger door. He climbed inside leaving the door slightly ajar, with his left hand holding the wet umbrella outside.

"Wakey, wakey, Morgen," he said, shaking Morgen's arm.

Morgen groaned as he opened his eyes.

"You look like hell warmed over, but the show was great!

Morgen, still bleary-eyed, managed an insincere "Great."

"The sound was everything they said it would be, the girls were never better, and you were sensational," Rodney continued, "C'mon. I'll sneak you up the back . . ."

Dismayed, remembering a media crowd was waiting for him, Morgen groaned "Oh, no! How many?"

"A hundred or more select members of the media. Angela Knight is here, and she can't wait to meet you."

Angela's name meant nothing to Morgen. Daunted by the thought of the ordeal ahead, he confessed, "I'm really not up for this."

Rodney sympathized. A few moments before, he'd been feeling the same way, sitting in a corner of the great room, but with Morgen's arrival, he'd found his second wind.

"C'mon," he chided, dragging Morgen toward the car door, "You can be tired tomorrow."

Rodney pulled Morgen out of the car, bringing the umbrella up to shield them, and was unpleasantly surprised when water from the upturned umbrella poured down over him.

"C'mon," he urged, as they hurried into the barrel vault.

Out of the rain, Morgen reacted to the gleaming, wine red sports car.

"Wow! Whose car is this?"

"It's yours, rented for the duration of our U.K. tour."

"Mine?" Morgen gasped, caressing the sports car's hood.

Rodney let Morgen enjoy the moment, thinking it would reawaken him to his obligation to the record company, and the media powers that awaited his arrival upstairs.

When Morgen opened the driver's side door, the interior light came on, inviting him inside. He slid behind the wheel, one foot still outside on the ground. The keys were in the ignition. He turned the key, not enough to start the car, but enough to illuminate the dashboard.

"It's got a full tank," he exclaimed.

"I expect that comes with the rental," Rodney said. "They'll charge you to refill it when it's returned."

Morgen pulled his right leg inside, shut the door, and turned on the ignition.

"Morgen!" Rodney shouted.

Morgen pressed down the accelerator pedal, and grinned when he heard the hearty purr of the engine. He lowered his side window a crack and asked Rodney, "Care to take a spin?"

"Are you crazy? It's late, raining, your guests are waiting, and here, everyone drives on the wrong side of the road!"

Morgen put the car in gear and drove slowly out from under the barrel vault.

"You can't go anywhere!" Rodney shouted.

"I'm just taking it for a test drive."

"Everyone's waiting. The band and the girls will be along any minute!" Rodney shouted as Morgen revved the engine.

Exiting the barrel vault into the rain, the car's automatic windshield wipers came on. Rodney pulled at the driver's side door, but it had locked automatically when the car started.

"I'll be right back," Morgen shouted. "It'll wake me up!"

Rodney was stunned when Morgen sped off. To him, ducking a carefully arranged and catered meet and greet with top media movers and shakers, especially after that sensational televised performance, was tantamount to refusing to talk to the press after winning a Grammy.

A flash of lightning, followed by an immediate thunder clap heralded a sudden downpour. Although less windy inside the barrel vault, the temperature dropped precipitously.

Beantown Home Cookin's bus was the first to arrive, stopping directly in front of the barrel vault. Rodney hurried toward it with the umbrella, but a voice from inside shouted at him to "Get out of the way."

Rodney jumped to one side as one by one, the band members leaped from the bus, through the curtain of rain, and into the barrel vault, where they stood, shivering, as the band's bus moved on, and the Trashbabies' bus pulled up, revealing Linda, the lead dancer, standing in the open doorway, dressed to kill, her hair beautifully done up, and wearing high heels.

"Jump," Rodney shouted.

"Not on your life," Linda shouted back. "Get some umbrellas or something. We can't be soaked through when we meet the press!"

In a voice not audible outside the barrel vault, Owen, the other Rodney addition that brought the band up to nine, including Morgen, observed, "Might make page three."

Rodney cracked a smile. Until very recently, the British tabloid *The Sun*, had featured a photo of a topless model on page three, and the idea of any one of the Trashbabies, cold and soaked to the skin, appearing on page three, was titillating.

"Well?" Linda shouted.

Rodney shouted back as he hurried past the cold and soaked band members, "Wait here! I'll get some towels and umbrellas and be right back."

Rodney twisted the handle on the service door, but it didn't budge.

"Shit!" he snapped, then pulled out his cell phone and quickly punched in some numbers.

"What's the holdup?" Roger shouted.

"The door's locked!" Rodney shouted back.

Grant, one of the two guitarists said, "Ring the doorbell!"

Rodney shouted, "There is no doorbell. I'm on it, okay?"

CHAPTER FIVE

The din on the convertible roof was deafening, more like a waterfall than a rainstorm, and the car's windshield wipers hadn't been able to penetrate it, forcing Morgen to pull over to the side of the road, where he turned on the car's flashing emergency lights and hoped, if anyone else was on the road, they'd manage to stop before they plowed into him. Then, as suddenly as it started, the deluge stopped.

It was still raining steadily, but the squall had passed, and through the windshield wipers, Morgen could see the road ahead. Deciding he'd had enough adventure for one night, and it was time to turn around and go back to the great house, he left the emergency light flashing, and drove cautiously out onto the roadway, the soft purr of the motor underscoring the steady, gentler rhythm of the windshield wipers.

Peering through the rain, exhaustion finally began taking its toll, and hypnotized by the drone of the motor, the rhythmic swish of the windshield wipers, and the Trashbabies' chorus from "The Stranger" playing in his head, urging him to an ever-deeper sleep, Morgen began to blink and nod. He thought he heard a woman's voice gently call his name, opened his eyes briefly, and as they began to close again, heard her call more urgently. He raised his head, but his eyes remained closed.

The third time she called, louder than before. He opened his eyes and saw, standing in the middle of the road ahead, a doe, frozen in the glare of his headlights!

Morgen hit his horn, stood on the brakes, and swerved to avoid the doe, crashing through a patch of Rhododendrons and landing, miraculously, right side up on a narrow country lane. Now, wide awake, he looked into his rear-view mirror, but the doe was nowhere to be seen.

The final verse of the song that had nearly killed him, played on in his mind, and his confidence soared.

"I'm The One, *The Stranger.*

I'm The One. I make your dreams come true.

I'm The One. *The Stranger.*

Listen, and I'll put my spell on you."

The windshield wipers stopped with the rain.

Morgen climbed out of the car, and inspected it, but apart from bits torn from the Rhododendrons he pulled from the front bumper and grill, and a bit of mud he was able to brush away, was relieved to see the car was undamaged.

Morgen walked back to the rural road, but finding no trace of the doe, began to wonder if there ever was a doe in the road. For all he knew, he might have dreamed it.

The air was especially fresh and cool, bracing, as the natives might say. Unsure where he'd picked up the expression, he guessed he'd probably heard it on some British TV show he'd seen on WGBH. Above, the moon shone brightly, and the sky was clear enough to see millions of stars, until they were suddenly blocked from view by a ghostly barn owl that silently flew over him and disappeared into the woods, making it, in all, a wonderful night to be alive.

He put the top down. Fresh, cool air would help keep him awake, and by now, Rodney, the media guests, the band and the Trashbabies would be wondering where he'd gone.

When he put the car in gear, he realized the wind-chill in the moving car, was too cold for comfort, but rather than put the roof back up, he turned on the heater, laughing at himself for driving with the top down, and the heater going full blast.

The rain had stopped, but the roads were still slippery, so he drove slowly. Trees formed a canopy over much of the country lane, and he was hit by rain falling from the branches overhead. He thought that would help keep him awake, and where the trees parted, he saw a beautiful star-filled sky.

Suddenly, he thought he saw something moving in the woods, and through a break in the trees, saw a magnificent white stag, looking back at him. He stopped to get a better look, but it turned and majestically walked away, disappearing into the denser woods as if, having shown itself, it had fulfilled its duty and could now move on. It was a magical moment, and the thought struck Morgen, that perhaps it came to thank him for avoiding the doe.

Not much further on, Morgen came to a narrow, arched stone bridge, but as he approached it, three statuesque beauties in fantastically wrought body armor, designed more to provoke than to protect, rose into view over the top of the bridge, any one of them, if they had the voices and the moves, physically qualified to join the Trashbabies.

Morgen stopped the car, and as they came down his side of the bridge, rose to sit on the back of his seat to show himself, and ask for directions.

They eyed his car as if they'd never seen one before (and that may well have been so, at least not one as fine as this), and he greeted them with a big smile.

"Good evening, ladies," he said. "Late night?"

In that instant, a huge, brindled mastiff emerged from the Rhododendrons on the far side of the car and barked a warning. Morgen quickly slid back down into his seat and said, softly as the first beauty drew near, "Big dog."

"What brings you here?" the first one snarled.

Obviously, she didn't know who he was, but he had done nothing to offend her. Whatever was eating her, had nothing to do with him, and he needed directions, so he smiled and answered, "You want the truth?"

The brindled mastiff came right up to the far side door and still standing on all fours, stuck his enormous head inside the open car, sniffing Morgen, studying his face, effortlessly invading Morgen's comfort zone.

"That is slyly spoken," the second one answered.

"Like a deceiver spoken," the third volunteered in a nasty, accusative tone.

"Intended, perhaps, to mislead?" concluded the first as she passed by.

Still in need of directions, and intimidated by the enormous dog in his face, Morgen hoped they were practicing for a U.K. Comic-Com, putting on their attitudes the way they put on their costumes, and with one eye on the dog, Morgen answered, gently and reasonably, "Perhaps the truth will serve me?"

"Truth serves not," the second stated empirically.

"It is its own unbending master," said the third with finality.

"The Tomb of Every Hope," said the first, dismissing him, and killing any hope of help these three might ever offer.

The ladies having passed without incident, the brindled mastiff released Morgen from its baleful gaze, and trotted off after the three women.

"Then I shall serve Truth," Morgen said, loud enough to be heard, but eliciting no response. Vexed, and dumbfounded by his idiotic final remark, Morgen watched them in his rear-view mirror as he began driving slowly up and over the hump-backed bridge, tilting the mirror to keep them in sight as he crested the bridge and started down the other side. Then, firmly gripping the steering wheel with his right hand, he braced himself and rose in his seat for a last look at the trio, but in that instant, the steering wheel spun to the right, and trying to regain his balance, Morgen's right foot came down hard on the accelerator. The motor roared. The car lurched forward. Morgen spun, dropped back into his seat, cut the wheels enough to clear the stone wall on the bridge, and stood on the brake. The wheels locked, but on the wet, slippery road, the car skidded to the edge of a watery ditch on the right, only coming to a stop when the front right side dropped to the ground, leaving the car suspended over the ditch, its right front wheel hanging uselessly, its elevated left rear wheel, not touching the road.

For a moment, time seemed to stand still. Morgen sighed with relief, a half-second before the rain-soaked side of the ditch upon which the right side of the car had come to rest, gave way, and the car suddenly lurched sideways and thudded into the ditch, with just enough of a jolt to cause the driver's airbag to explode in his face.

Stunned by the blow of the airbag, it took Morgen a moment to realize what had happened, but when the chilly water seeping into the car from around the driver's side door, rose above his shoe, the shock of the cold water spurred him into action. He scampered over the center console onto the passenger side seat, then out over the door, but unable to get a footing in the rain-soaked dirt wall of the ditch, leaned out over the shoulder of the country lane, pushed himself up, rolled over onto the muddy road, and soaked, and shivering, rose to his feet.

Morgen would need help to get the car out of the ditch, and the only immediate source of help was the trio of women on the other side of the bridge. He sprinted to the top of the bridge, but the women were nowhere to be seen. The night was still, and even if they'd entered the woods, they should still be able to hear him, so he shouted, "Hello! Ladies?"

He paused and listened, but no answer came. He tried again, shouting, at the top of his lungs, "Hello! Can anyone hear me?" Again, he listened, but all he heard was the gurgle of rushing water. As he trotted back to the car, the gurgling grew louder. The storm runoff, backed up by the dam caused by the car, was forcing the water to carve new passages on both sides of the ditch. Morgen climbed down into the car, felt it settle deeper into the mud, and standing above the console, reached down to retrieve the ignition key and switch on the flashing emergency lights. He then climbed back up onto the road, where the flashing taillights were clearly visible to anyone who might use the narrow country lane, but in that gray twilight, his taillights, flashing and ticking their warning, seemed unlikely to attract any help.

The adrenalin rush caused by his mishap having worn off, Morgen sat at the end of the stone wall on the side of the bridge where he'd gone into the ditch, and dozed fitfully. Each time he awakened, cold and shivering, he got up and did jumping jacks for minutes at a time, to try to warm up, until as dawn approached, he was startled by a nerve-jangling shriek.

Suddenly, from the rain-soaked tree opposite the car on the left side of the road, a barn owl flew out, circled over his head and flew away into the woods. Whether it was the same owl or a cousin, Morgen didn't know, but he saw something white, partially hidden by the tree's low hanging branches. He went toward it, lifted the branch, was showered with rain water for his trouble, but what he found was well-worth the soaking.

It was a white, arrow-shaped directional sign, with faded black letters spelling out "Morningstone 1 km." revealing a previously unseen, overgrown, unpaved lane that no doubt led to Morningstone. Farm, inn, village, or scenic wonder, whatever it was, it was only one kilometer away, a destination where he might find help.

He set out along the muddy, overgrown dirt road, thinking of the last birthday gift he'd received from his adoptive mother, *The Poetry of Robert Frost.* What lay before him was definitely a road less traveled, possibly no more than an overgrown driveway, but whatever he'd find at the end, it offered hope, and hope was enough to start him on his way.

As he trudged on, his colorful, romantic notions were replaced by the harsh reality of his current situation. By now, the media after-party in his honor would be over, and he'd failed to make an appearance, and Rodney would be furious.

Depending on how the evening went, the band and the Trashbabies might have enjoyed some well-deserved attention, but sooner or later, he'd have to explain himself, and the wrecked car. What would he tell them? What could he tell them? He got lost in the rain? True enough, but how would he explain going off the road into the ditch? He could say the car skidded on the wet road when it went over the bridge. He'd managed to stop it before it went into the ditch, but before he could back away, the wall of the ditch collapsed, the car slid down into its muddy bottom, and triggered the airbag that blew up in his face.

All true, as far as it went, but how would he answer why he, the guest of honor, decided to go joyriding, instead of going in to meet his media guests?

As he walked that lonely kilometer, he thought long and hard about how he might explain his actions. He'd been exhausted, was feeling bad about how lame and dimwitted he sounded in the morning interview, and wanted to clear his head before going into what promised to be the biggest, most important, and intense session ever, with the cream of the crop of the U.K. and foreign media reporters, photographers, reviewers, and critics, all in attendance. His test drive had seemed like a good idea at the time, but hadn't gone according to plan.

Profuse apologies were in order for the terrible inconvenience and worry he'd caused.

By the time he'd reached the hillside above the quaint little hamlet of Morningstone, he'd worked out a number of answers he hoped might suffice.

There was no activity to be seen in the hamlet below, and Morgen didn't wear a watch, but judging by the warmth of the sun bathing that open hillside, it was probably no later than eight, or eight-thirty when he started down the hill toward the bright red phone booth in the center of the village green.

The mouth-watering aroma of fresh baked bread drew Morgen's attention to the bakery on the left side of the green, but the glare of the sun on its window prevented him from seeing the attractive, middle-aged lady with the gleaming, silver-white, mid-length hair, cut to frame her face, and accent her dark, lovely eyes, who watched him from inside.

With more than enough British coins in his pocket, he went directly to the red phone box on the village green, and although he didn't know any local phone numbers, was confident information would give him the number of the record company and he would soon be on his way back to civilization. Alas, it was not to be. He deposited the coins, heard them drop, but never received so much as a dial tone. He tried three times in all, each time substituting different coins, each time, getting them all back, and was forced to conclude that the fault was not in the coins, but the phone. Between attempts, he'd been staring blankly through the phone box window at an antique, hand-primed Texaco gasoline pump, but as he hung up the phone, he noticed the sign across the front of the building by the pump, declaring it to be "Smythe's Forge & Auto Repair." Better yet, one of the big double doors in front of the barn-like building was ajar, suggesting the repair shop was open.

When he entered the garage, the ruddy, dark, muscular Smythe greeted him, and Morgen quickly explained that he needed a tow truck to get his car out of the ditch out by the bridge, and asked if Mr. Smythe could arrange that.

"I'd be glad to, sir. Honored to be of service, sir," Mr. Smythe replied, "soon as I get this back together."

"This" was Smythe's tractor, its disassembled motor in boxes or spread out all over Smythe's cluttered work bench.

"When will that be?" Morgen asked.

"Should have it up and running by tomorrow morning, sir."

"Terrific," Morgen said. "Is there another garage nearby?"

"Oh, I'm afraid I'm it, sir."

"Great," said Morgen. "Do you have a phone I can use?"

"Yes, sir," Smythe replied, and started toward the double doors, Morgen following close behind.

"There, sir!" Smythe exclaimed, glad to be useful and pointing toward the red phone box in the center of the green.

"I tried that. It's out of order."

"Aye," Smythe commiserated. "It rained last night. Rain can knock out phones."

"Is there a car rental nearby?"

"I'm afraid not, sir, and no way to call," Smythe answered.

Morgen was crestfallen, but Smythe, although looking doubtful, suggested, "You might try The Owl."

Flabbergasted, attempting to process Smythe's remark, Morgen asked, "You mean like in *Harry Potter*?"

"The pub," Smythe answered, pointing the way, "Right around the bend, sir."

"Oh, the pub. Will it be open at this hour?"

"The bar won't be, but the door will."

"Thank you. I'll give it a shot!" said Morgen, and started on his way.

"I'll stay on this, just in case," Smythe called after him, but Morgen didn't look back, and never saw Smythe's grin, or his subtle nod toward the bakery.

CHAPTER SIX

What Morgen did see, as he rounded the bend, was, a large, well-maintained, two-story, Tudor-style building with a hanging sign reading "The Owl" and a sign across the front of the larger, attached structure declaring it to be the "Morningstone Inn." The building itself had settled, suggesting it might be authentic 16th century, but if so, it had clearly been recently restored.

As Morgen approached the door to the pub, he heard strange music coming from within. It was unlocked, so he went inside, where the gentle music was louder, but the interior was dark, except for an irregular colorful glow flickering in a large room to his right. A mechanical whirring sound mingled with the music.

Morgen went toward the sound, entering a large, low ceiling room where a movie was being shown on a pull-down screen. A half dozen figures, seated at a long table, stared up at the screen, as the camera panned from a pretty young lady playing a harp, dressed in what appeared to be classical Greek costume, to another pretty young lady, similarly dressed, swaying gently and playing tambourine, and then to a third pretty, who stirred a cauldron supported by a tripod of iron owls, finally coming to rest on yet another, even more beautiful young lady, wearing a floral tiara with multi-colored ribbons streaming through her long hair, standing in front of a man-sized monolith, framed by a Stonehenge-inspired trilithon. When she started to sing, Morgen sat quietly on a bench at one of the booths at the back of the room, not wishing to interrupt her song.

"Come share this with me. Make my dream your own. It will ever be . . . *Morningstone*."

The scene changed back to the women by the cauldron, but Morgen's thoughts were stuck on the singer.

Her voice made the hair on his nape rise, her song was an invitation, and something about it, the exotic melody, or the way she sang it, made it seem she was singing it to him. As enchanting as her voice was, he wondered if the half-dozen figures up front were as stricken as he was? Whoever she was, the lady was a talent to be reckoned with.

Suddenly, she was back on screen, and her song seemed to cause the sun to rise, bathing her, and her world in its light.

"Mystery and destiny, forever intertwined
Revealed for all the world to see,
That all who seek may find.
I provide the key. Through me, the path is shown.
Behold your legacy, *Morningstone*."

A long shot revealed the Stonehenge-like set as the sun rose, and for the first time, Morgen made the connection between the song and the place, the inn and the hamlet called Morningstone. But the show wasn't over, and to his shock, the three mean-tempered women he'd met on the road appeared, marching angrily toward three other women, sitting on the hillside above the stone circle, weaving an enormous tapestry.

The weavers appeared to be young, beautiful, and serene, except that their eyes were startling miniature moons.

They wore cowls on their intricately embroidered robes that at first glance, seemed to blend into the enormous tapestry they wove.

The weavers spoke first, not all at once, but finishing sentences for each other, all of one mind suggesting they might be more than a match for the belligerent trio approaching.

The first, spinning fibers for the tapestry, turned her blind gaze toward the angry ones and said, "The thread is short."

"And thin," said the second, who actually wove the thread into the tapestry, and the third said, "It calls for skill."

Whereupon, the first ill-tempered, armored belligerent complained, "All-knowing Fates, how can you sit and weave?"

The three ladies who'd been playing music and stirring the cauldron arrived in time to hear the second armor-clad complain, "The goddess lies defiled!"

"All Nature weeps," accused the third.

The spinner, the first Fate so named by the first armor-clad woman, warned, "Gently!"

The second Fate, who wove the tapestry, warned, "Lest, by your own violent moods," and the third Fate finished the second's statement, "this slender thread be broken."

"Let it break!" shrieked the first ill-tempered iron-clad.

"Man thinks himself divorced from Nature's law," the second one raged,

"And, in contempt, upon Greed's altar spends his craven lust!" spat the third.

"Shall Furies now guide Fate?" the lovely who'd previously tended the cauldron asked, directing her question to the Fates.

"Do Muses still guide Man?" the first Fury snapped back.

"Enough! Enough!" the first Fate intervened, and the second said, "Even as the Furies gird for vengeance . . ."

"So, the Muses seek with sacred Truth to wean Man from his folly," the third Fate concluded.

"Fates, hear us!" the second Fury roared.

"No single champion comes to sip their brew," complained the third. "No single hero does their song inspire," said the first Fury contemptuously.

And the second Fury closed, by saying, "Our loving sisters are, themselves, bemused, if they seek good in Man."

"Enough! Enough!" said the third Fate.

The spinning Fate said, "The thread is short and thin."

"It calls for skill," said the weaving Fate.

"The Laws of Nature are beyond appeal," acknowledged the first Fury. The second Fury, needing no permission, said, "So now, sisters, by your leave?"

"Farewell!" said the Fates in unison.

The Furies, glaring at the Muses, turned and marched away.

"We too, must bid farewell," said the Muse carrying the harp, and gave the third Muse, who had danced and played tambourine, a nudge with her elbow. The surprised third Muse saw that the second was rolling a single hair between her finger and thumb, and realizing her meaning, kissed each Fate farewell, starting with the cutter, then the weaver, and finally, the spinner, where, plucking a single long hair from her own head, the Muse added it to the spinner's skein, then hurried off to join her sisters. As the Muses exited, the Fates turned their sightless gazes upon each other and smiled, for being Fates, they'd known all along what the third Muse would do.

The Furies had also seen the Muses' ploy and were outraged.

The third Fury hissed, "Have they no shame?"

"The Fates are with the Muses!" accused the first Fury.

The second Fury snarled, "They conspire to frustrate justice."

"Nature lies betrayed!" the third shrieked at the Fates, but from the hillside the Fates turned toward the Furies, and their unspoken answer rang loudly in the Furies minds.

"See you not the wheels within the wheels?" the first Fate's voice asked.

"Would you deny their final, loving gift?" the second Fate's voice asked.

"A single hair upon which all depends?" said the third.

"The thread is short," added the first Fate.

"And thin," said the second.

"It calls for skill," the third reminded the Furies, but the Furies remained angry and defiant.

"We are not moved!" shouted the third Fury at the Fates.

"Things shall be as they will," came the Fates unspoken reply.

Scribbles appeared, marking the end of the reel. The projector was turned off and the house lights came on.

Morgen recognized the iambic pentameter, but not the source. He'd read *The Complete Works of William Shakespeare* during the summer break between seventh and eighth grade, what he saw on the screen hadn't been in it, but he'd never read any of Marlowe's plays of the same period, and knew he also wrote in iambic pentameter. At least, the mystery of the ill-tempered iron-clad women was finally solved. They were obviously method actresses, playing Furies, determined to stay in character, even between takes.

The lights came up. The figures at the table were teenagers. A lady dressed in sensible country tweed, her long hair exquisitely braided and pinned up to give the appearance of a business-like cut, emerged from behind the projector, walked to the front of the room, and raised the screen to reveal a blackboard, upon which was a circle with a horizontal line running through it labeled "threshold."

The lady wrote something inside the circle above the line and something below, and speaking with her back to the room, began, "What do the characters . . ."

Morgen was about to stand up and make his presence known, when she turned, saw him, and finished her question with just the slightest hesitation, ". . . represent?"

It was her, the singer, the woman who sang "Morningstone." He quietly sat back. She'd seen him, might have asked who he was, or why he was there, but didn't, and as long as she allowed it, he was content to sit and listen quietly.

"Nature deities," a boy called out.

"The Ninefold Muse," a second boy answered.

"The denigration of the goddess," a girl called out.

"Oh," the singer ventured, "Why do you say that?"

"Well, ever since society became patriarchal, men have been putting women down. The embodiment of the female principle, the mother goddess, is reduced to a bevy of ineffectual, bickering, departmental nymphs."

One girl must have made a face. The singer asked, "Comment, Calypso?"

Calypso said, "What Barbara says may be so, but in this instance, I think it is safe to say that the fragmentation of the goddess is a device of exposition, used to reveal the crisis dramatically through a confrontation between various aspects of her character."

"Who are the Furies?" the singer asked.

Barbara quickly volunteered, "Goddesses of vengeance."

"Force of Nature opposed to humanity," the third boy suggested.

"The obstacles to be overcome," the second boy said.

"The guardians of the threshold," offered the third girl.

The singer turned and doubled the horizontal line on the blackboard. Then, obviously into her topic, she spun back to her class and asked, "And the Muses?"

The second boy was on top of this one. "Goddesses who seek to inspire Man," he said.

Calypso followed with "The keepers of the cauldron."

"The Cauldron of Inspiration," the singer said, obviously pleased at how engaged her pupils were. "What about it?"

The first boy jumped on this one. "It's the reward," he said.

Calypso had a completely different take on it. "The womb through which the enlightened one becomes the twice born."

Morgen thought he'd been keeping up pretty well, but Calypso threw him a curve. Fortunately, the third boy brought him back on track when he said, simply, "Enlightenment."

"Enlightenment," the singer repeated as she turned and added it to the half-circle below the threshold. She turned back to her class. "What about the Fates?" she asked.

The first boy's answer was "The Past, Present, and Future," but the third girl saw it differently. "Impartial Nature," she said. "What shall be, will be."

"What are they doing?" the singer asked.

The first boy answered, "Weaving the thread."

The excited singer snatched that one up. "The thread! All right. What about the thread?"

The third girl spoke up again. "It's short," she said.

"And thin," the first boy added, and then they all joined in to say, "It calls for skill!"

The singer had them, then, and she knew it. "It calls for skill," she repeated thoughtfully. "What does it symbolize?"

"Time," the first boy answered.

"More than time," the third girl said. "There's an implied threat in the delicacy of the thread. It could snap."

But the second boy nailed it. "Doesn't the thread," he asked, "the strand of the Muse's hair, doesn't it represent the hero?"

"The hero!" the singer exclaimed. She was glowing as she turned to the blackboard, scribbling "hero" above the line.

"The key! The Chosen One!" she continued, then turned back to her class.

Morgen suddenly felt dizzy. He'd slept fitfully, only minutes at a time, during the long, cold night, and had nothing to eat for hours. The room started spinning. The last thing he heard, just before the lights went out, was the singer saying "The single hair upon which all depends."

Suddenly, Morgen was back inside the sports car, driving through the gentle rain, the throaty drone of the motor, the rhythmic swish of the windshield wipers, and the Trashbabies' vocals urging him to go ever-deeper. And through it all, he heard the singer gently call his name. And he heard the teenagers' voices, and knew each by his or her voice.

It was the second boy who first recognized him. "It's Morgen," he said.

The duly-impressed third boy asked, "The rock star?"

"What's he doing here?" Barbara asked. Morgen knew her voice. It was she who'd complained the mother goddess was reduced to ineffectual, departmental nymphs.

Morgen was thinking he'd have to be wary of Barbara, when the first boy said, "The Stranger."

The second boy spoke up right away, as if to prove he'd followed the broadcast every bit as closely as the first. "Bit of the old 'Witchy Stew,' eh?" he asked, and the first boy answered in an eerie, spooky tone of voice, "The cycle begins anew," and the singer spoke his name again. The third boy asked, "Just passing through?"

For a moment, Morgen thought the boy was asking him, and realized that he was staring at the raindrops on his windshield, and had to force his eyes to refocus to view the wet road ahead. And then, it was the singer's voice again, slightly more urgently calling, "Morgen?"

He heard Barbara say, threateningly, "Perhaps he's come to stay." The Trashbabies' voices sent him blissfully deeper, but Morgen was still distressed that he didn't know the singer's name.

"Wouldn't be a hero, then," said the first boy, and continued, "nothing but an adventurer."

The third teenage girl said, "The cycle would be incomplete."

The singer raised her voice, demanding his attention, urgently calling, "Morgen!"

Morgen saw the doe frozen in his headlights, hit the brakes, pulled the wheel hard over, and jerked awake, on the floor of the pub, looking up into the eyes of the beautiful singer, who held his hand, smiled down at him and said, "Welcome back."

"What happened?" Morgen asked.

"You seem to have fainted. Are you all right, now?"

"I think so."

A girl crawled across the bench on the other side of the booth and drew open the curtain, letting sunlight flood the room, and a boy opened the curtains over the next booth.

"Lend a hand," the singer said, and another boy stepped in, took Morgen's other hand and between them, they helped

Morgen up enough to sit him on the end of the bench from which he'd fallen. Still holding Morgen's arm to steady him, the boy gushed, "You're Morgen, lead singer of Beantown Home Cookin' aren't you?"

"Yeah," Morgen answered.

"Have you come for our Spring Festival?" a girl asked.

Morgen looked at the teenager, who, by the sound of her voice, could only be Calypso, the girl who'd suggested the fragmentation of the goddess was a device of exposition, but before he could answer, the boy who'd helped him up asked, "Will you be performing?"

The singer said, "Class, please!" and the teenagers came to order.

"Sorry, gang," Morgen answered. "I just came in to use the phone."

"I'll get it!" volunteered the third boy, and hurried to fetch it from the bar.

"I can get up," Morgen said, but he was trembling.

The singer gently held Morgen where he was. "You stay still," she said. "The cord will reach."

Morgen didn't protest. The third boy hurried back to the booth with the phone. The singer took it from him, thanked him, set it on the table and then addressed her class. "Manners, please. Introductions are in order."

"Which one of you is Calypso?" Morgen asked. Calypso lit up, smiling happily, thrilled to hear Morgen say her name and said, "That's me!" delighted to be the first named. Morgen looked directly at Barbara, and said, "And if I'm not mistaken, you're Barbara."

"Here," Barbara replied, as if answering a roll call.

"And I'm sorry to say, I don't know your name," Morgen said, looking at girl number three.

"I'm Amy," she said. "Pleased to make your acquaintance."

65

"I'm sorry, guys," Morgen continued, "but I never heard any of you called by name," whereupon the first boy, hitherto known only by his voice, said his name was Kevin; the second boy, who had helped him off the floor, was Billy; and the third, who'd fetched the phone, introduced himself as Nigel.

"I was impressed with all your answers," Morgen said. "I had a year of college before I went into music, and never have I enjoyed a class as much as I enjoyed monitoring this one."

As the teens began expressing their gratitude for his kind words, the singer interrupted, dismissing her class, saying in that tone that teachers sometimes use, "All right. That's all for now. Final fittings this afternoon!"

The groaning, grumbling teens obediently left the pub.

"Sorry, if I messed things up," Morgen said.

"Not at all. We managed to cover all the important bits."

"I'm glad," Morgen said. "They're bright kids."

"They are that," she replied, pleased that he'd noticed.

Morgen took the handset out of the cradle and lifted it to his ear, explaining, "My car ran into a ditch and the local garage can't get to it before tomorrow."

"So, you'll be staying over?"

"No. I'll be missed. By now they'll be scouring the countryside."

Morgen depressed the cradle several times, but failed to get a dial tone.

"It's dead," he said, his hand beginning to shake involuntarily as he handed the receiver to her.

The singer held the receiver to her ear, pressed the cradle a few times, then thoughtfully returned it to its cradle.

"Do you have a cell?" he asked.

"A cell?"

"A cellphone? Wireless?"

She shook her head no as she answered, "I'm afraid our links with the outside world are tenuous, at best."

Morgen shuddered.

"You're trembling," she observed. "You're sure you're not hurt?"

"I'm all right. Delayed reaction, I guess."

"You've had a shock."

"No," he protested. "I'm fine, now, really. Just tired."

"You need a lie down."

"You're probably right," he agreed. "I haven't really slept in two days. The sign outside said this is an inn."

"It is, but it's fully booked now. Spring Festival, you know."

"If they could spare a room for a couple of hours . . ."

"I can do better than that. There's a cottage, a bit off the beaten track, but you could rest there. No one would dare to bother you."

"Why? Is it haunted?"

"Nothing as exciting as that, I'm afraid. Protected by tradition is more like it. It's ages old, built to house pilgrims to our ancient shrine."

"Sounds fascinating."

"I can drive you there."

Morgen brightened. "You have a car?" he asked.

She smiled as she answered, "No. Not exactly." She helped him to his feet, and took his arm. "Shall we?"

"By all means," he replied.

CHAPTER SEVEN

Morgen wondered what she drove. She definitely wasn't a soccer mom, so a minivan was unlikely, but in this rural area, she might drive a pickup truck, or a motor scooter. He knew that motor scooter rallies were fairly common in England's beach cities. But if England had helmet laws, he couldn't imagine her trying to fit her exquisite hairdo under a helmet.

Nothing had prepared him for her pony cart. At first glance, it appeared to be made of flowers growing out of a sturdy wooden frame, supported on a fixed axle yoke that extended a full foot beyond the floral enclosure above, fitted with relatively enormous wooden-spoked wheels, held round by flat iron tires. Her beautifully-groomed, white pony was harnessed between two wooden shafts, bolted to the frame, so the two-wheeled cart was drawn and steered by the pony, which meant that the driver had to be skilled to direct it, either through its reins, verbal commands, or the touch of the woven buggy whip on the pony's flanks.

As they approached, the pony tossed its head, but whether in greeting or as a warning, was not immediately clear.

"I don't believe it," Morgen said.

"Beautiful, isn't it?" she said. "Traditional this time of year. A dozen people worked through the night to decorate it for our festival."

"You're big on tradition around here, aren't you?"

"Definitely."

"Sounds like our Rose Parade," Morgen remarked.

"Rose parade?"

"Flowers and entries from all over the world, volunteers working for days to glue all the flower petals onto the floats."

"Glue?"

"Well, how do you do it?" he asked.

"The stems are woven into the wicker-work."

As they approached the cart, Morgen saw the green stems of the flowers, woven through what looked like the backs of wicker patio chairs, cut to fit and lashed to rigid, arched, bent-wood frames that supported the floral display.

"Impressive," Morgen said.

"You like it?"

"That's what I call going green," he answered.

The singer grasped a half-round side rail, stepped on an iron pedal suspended under the back of the cart, and effortlessly stepped up into it, turned, smiled and said, "All aboard."

Morgen tried to do as she had, but the iron pedal swung up and away under the cart, and he nearly fell.

"Did I break it?" he asked.

"No," she said. "It has to be able to swing like that, should we run over anything hard enough and high enough to hit it. I should have warned you. You must get a firm grip on the side rail, then, with your left foot over the pedal, tip your toe down to keep it from slipping away, shift your weight forward, and step up into the cart, all in one move."

She reached down, took his right hand and placed it on the solid curved wooden side rail. "Hold tight to this," she said.

Morgen tightened his grip.

"That's the idea," she said. "Now, toes down, step onto the pedal with your left foot, and step up into the cart."

He tried to do as he was told, but didn't get his right foot high enough to clear the floor, tripped and stumbled headlong into the cart.

Smiling, she admitted, "Well, it does take practice."

Morgen, on his hands and knees, tried to stand up, but one hand sank into the floor, that lurched, independent of the cart, and he quickly rolled over to sit with his back to the side rail.

"I think your floor needs repair," he said, and pointed. "It's gone soft, there."

The singer shifted her weight from side to side, causing the floor to sway.

"It's not rotted out," she explained. "The leather strap floor is suspended above the hard frame to save the driver's knees and spine."

"Takes a while to get used to all this new technology."

"New technology?" she laughed. "Hereabouts, we've been making them this way for more than 2,000 years."

The pony nodded its head up and down, whether agreeing with her history lesson, or eager to be on its way, Morgen couldn't say. Watching the pony, he asked, "Can that little guy handle the both of us?"

"He thinks he can," she replied. "Shall I help you up?"

"I'm comfortable on the floor."

"Suit yourself," she said, then clucked at the pony, but instead of lurching forward, the cart spun in place, which made it look to Morgen like the inn was moving, so he shut his eyes.

"You're sure you know how to drive this thing?" he asked.

"The little guy's clever enough to keep us out of a ditch."

Morgen fell silent, listening to the clopping of the pony's hooves, watching the road recede behind them.

"I don't usually go in for this sort of thing," he said.

"What sort of thing is that?" she asked.

"Riding around in pony carts with strange ladies."

She smiled, for a moment enjoying her strange lady status, then reached down to shake his hand and said, as if making it up, "I'm Laura. Laura Webster."

"Laura Webster," Morgen repeated, wondering for a moment if that was her real name or her stage name, but considering he'd told her his real name, decided the name she gave him was probably her real name, too, and smiled.

After a moment of silence, Laura reminded him, "And you're Morgen."

"I am."

"Are you ready to stand up?" Laura asked.

"Must I?"

"You're missing all the sights," she said, turning her attention back to her driving. "Our flowers are famous, but our greatest attraction is Morningstone, itself."

"I'm not so sure about that."

Laura smiled at his subtle compliment, and turned her attention back to being his tour guide, but whatever she said, her voice became music in Morgen's ears, and her description of the countryside, an obbligato line to the new love song he silently sang to her.

"I've never seen *The Likes of You.*

Are you a dream, or a dream come true?

You're more than my imagination can conceive.

Please let me touch you, that I may believe."

Before another verse could be born, he saw her staring at him. "You haven't heard a word I've said, have you?"

"I've been listening," he replied.

She touched the pony's flank with her buggy whip. The pony wheeled off the country lane and onto a winding dirt trail on a gently sloping hillside.

As the pony cart wended its way up the hill, Morgen again heard Laura singing, if only inside his head, but falling silent as the megalithic shrine came into view.

"Well, here it is," Laura said, "Morningstone."

"Incredible!" Morgen exclaimed. impressed by the megalithic shine site. "I thought it was a movie set."

It was a thing of wonder, a large circle of rough-hewn stones, extending from the hillside like it was offering a hug, with a massive trilithon entrance to its sacred precinct within the circle, in the center of which stood a man-sized monolith, and behind it, the dark entrance into what appeared to be the entrance to a mine.

The view of the valley below, all the way to the distant hills, was a breathtaking patchwork of fields of grain, garden vegetables, rich green pasture land, blossoming orchards, and fields of flowers planted as much to attract the bees that fertilized the crops, as for their inherent beauty, and the slightly diluted scents that wafted all the way up to the shrine.

71

The combination of the shrine and the valley view was a testament to the centuries they had both flourished, venerated by countless generations, proof of Nature's eternal provenance, and the persistence of the human spirit.

"Come along, if you wish," Laura said, springing from the cart, and moving toward the entrance to the stone circle. "It's safe enough in broad daylight."

Morgen climbed down, clinging to the pony cart side rail, and said, amused by his infirmity, "My legs feel wobbly."

Laura grinned and said, "That's to be expected. You're on sacred ground."

"I've seen ancient Greco-Roman theaters in Turkey," Morgen said, "but I've never seen anything quite like this."

"It's not a theater," Laura explained. "It's a shrine, and the dark opening you see in the hillside is an entrance to the Tomb of Every Hope."

Morgen moved to enter the circle, to get a better look at the man-made hillside. "A beehive tomb?" he asked.

She blocked his way and warned, "According to legend, one of three fates will befall a mortal brave enough or foolish enough, to tread upon this sacred ground by night. The hoped for one is rarely granted."

"And that is?" Morgen asked.

"That communion with the Ninefold Muse that makes bards of minstrels," she replied.

"And the more common fates?" he asked.

"Madness or death," she answered.

"That would tend to keep the lines down," Morgen muttered, and then said, "I'd really like to see inside, and as you pointed out, it's broad daylight."

"You're tired, and not ready, yet," she said, taking his arm and leading him back toward the pony cart, disappointed, but clinging to the vestige of the romance he sensed in the air.

Morgen took a long look back at the stone circle set into the rocky, forested hillside that embraced the retaining wall of massive stones, rising at its center to a height of approximately fifteen feet, with the hillside rising steeply another thirty feet or more to its rounded peak, bearing silent witness to its creators.

Laura allowed the long, last look, then asked, "All set?"

Morgen sat on the floor, clinging to the side rail.

"All set," he answered.

"It's not much further to the cottage," she promised, clucked to her pony and once more, they were on their way.

Morgen noticed the dolmen, near which the Muses had played "Morningstone," the song Laura sang in the film, inviting him to share it with her, and regretted that moment, at the stone circle, when he believed the magic slipped away.

"I don't get it," Morgen said.

"What don't you get?" Laura asked.

"You. Here."

Amused, Laura looked back at him and smiled. "Where else would I be?" she asked, playfully.

"I saw you in the film. You know you've got talent."

"A local effort for the heritage class."

"And I suppose the other ladies are all locals, too?"

Laura's smile broadened. "Yes. Why do you ask? Did one of our ladies catch your fancy?"

"Could be."

"How intriguing! One of the Furies? Their charms are obvious enough, and if you enjoy a challenge . . ."

"They're too method for me."

"What's 'method'?"

"Don't get me wrong," Morgen explained. "They obviously really get into their roles, but between scenes, a little civility couldn't hurt."

"Ahh. A Muse then. Be a help in your career . . ."

73

"My career's doing fine," Morgen said.

Laura, feigning surprise, "A Fate?"

Morgen's expression indicated she wasn't even close. All that was left was Laura herself. They both smiled as their eyes met, but the pony cart hit a bump, and Laura quickly turned her attention back to the narrow-wooded trail.

His confidence restored by their banter, Morgen heard Laura's song again, inspiring new lyrics and renewing his hopes.

"When you come near, I feel dazed and weak.

I dare not move, I dare not speak,

I don't know why, this feeling's new.

I've never seen *The Likes of You*."

And then, their separate melodies entwined, each a promise to the other.

"Will you, like a lover's moon, flee the morning sun,

Or will you constant be? Are you the one?"

Suddenly, Laura frowned, snapped the reins, and the beautiful moment vanished with a splash as she drove the pony cart into and across the stream that flowed past the cottage. Sitting on the floor, Morgen never saw it coming, and the rattling cart and chilly water dampened his ardor as quickly as it did the hide that covered the woven leather floor.

As the cart started up the bank on the other side of the stream, Morgen had to cling to the side rail to keep from sliding out the back.

"Regular all-terrain vehicle," he muttered.

Reining in the pony, Laura proclaimed, "We're here. Our Guest Cottage," but frowning, pointing to the smoke from the cottage chimney added, "Apparently, you've got company."

Morgen's heart sank. If someone was occupying the cottage, would he be allowed to stay? Would he still want to?

"Shall we go in?" Laura asked.

"What do you think?"

Laura jumped down from the pony cart and started toward the door, saying, "I, for one, would like to know who's here."

Morgen quickly slid to the ground, and followed.

Laura knocked thrice, then, without waiting for an answer, opened the door and entered, Morgen right behind her. The cottage was all on one floor, and the entire front section was a single great room, with a massive fireplace protruding from the left side wall, and what looked like a back door, directly across from the front, on the far wall. But their attention was drawn to the kitchen on the right, where a lovely, mature woman stirred a bubbling pot on the stove top.

The woman shouted gleefully, "Laura! I thought I heard you," and wiped her hands on a kitchen towel.

"Fiona?" Laura replied, "Aren't you supposed to be in the village?"

Fiona smiled warmly and said, as she hurried toward them, "Without a bite to eat or a drop to drink in the cottage? A fine how-do-you-do that'd be, for a famous guest who's come all the way from America."

She stopped in front of Morgen, held out her hand to him and introduced herself. "I'm Fiona," she said.

The way she held out her hand, horizontally rather than vertically, Morgen bowed slightly, and raised it to his lips.

"Fiona," he said, and introduced himself. "I'm Morgen."

Laura rolled her eyes. "I thought you were seeing to the costumes."

"First things first, dear," Fiona replied, and turned her attention, and warmest smile, to Morgen. "Welcome to the Guest Cottage."

"Thank you," Morgen replied. "I'm glad to be here."

Fiona turned to the nearby kitchen table, took one of several wine bottles out of a large wicker basket, pulled its cork, and poured the golden beverage into three goblets standing ready on the table top.

"This calls for a toast," she said, handing out the goblets. I brought along some of my nectar for a welcome, made entirely from our local fruits and herbs."

"Careful Morgen," Laura warned. "It's potent!"

The beaming hostess offered her toast. "To you, Morgen. May your needs be provided, your desires fulfilled, and your memories commend us!"

"I'll drink to that," Morgen answered, taking a sip that caused his eyes to water, and continued, when he caught his breath, "Is this what you drink when you're out of tea?"

"Oh! If you wish, I could put on the kettle," Fiona offered.

"No, this is fine!" Morgen said, wiping tears from his eyes.

"So, you'll be joining us for our festival," Fiona continued.

"Morgen's only staying until his car is back on the road."

"Long enough," Fiona replied, with a twinkle in her eye, and then to Laura, "but I haven't made up his room . . ."

"I'll do that," Laura said, going to the other door that opened onto a hallway and bedrooms at the rear of the cottage. "You finish up, and I'll drive you to the village."

"So much to do and so little time," Fiona muttered and returned to stirring the stew pot bubbling on the stove.

"Something smells delicious," Morgen observed.

"Ambrosia," Fiona volunteered happily. "It's traditional at the cottage, and removing her apron, turned back to Morgen and said, "Morgen with an 'e.' "

Smiling, Morgen said, "I'm surprised you'd know that."

"Something as important as that, I make it my business to know," Fiona said. "All those people, trying to correct your spelling, and you, fighting to keep it as originally written. You were right, you know. It singles you out from all the Morgans. It identifies you, should anyone come looking for you."

"So, I've been told," Morgen said. "Whoever signed me in changed the 'e' to an 'a,' but the head nurse insisted she copy it exactly as it was on the note."

"Good for her! There's a lot in a name," Fiona said.

"Well, so far, no one's come looking."

"Sure of that, are you?"

"Well, not that I've heard of."

"It's like having a festival name," Fiona suggested.

"A festival name?" Morgen asked.

"Names like Fairchild, Merriweather, and Greenwood, all surnames given to children conceived at festivals."

"Really?"

"Well, under the circumstances, a girl couldn't be expected to know just who the father might be, could she?"

As Morgen tried to process Fiona's explanation, Laura came back into the main room.

"Are you ready, Fiona?" Laura asked.

"Done so soon?" Fiona said, and then, looking around, began listing the cottage's amenities for Morgen.

"You've wood for a fire, plenty to drink and a pot full of ambrosia, but it still needs to simmer for a few hours," Fiona said, "and if you feel peckish before then, there's bread in the basket, all baked fresh for the festival."

Laura took up the inventory, eager to get on with it. "And there's matches on the mantle, and pen and paper, on the writing desk, should you feel inspired. You know how to light the lamp?"

Morgen saw the kerosene lantern on the writing desk, and answered, "Yes, thank you."

"Sorry to have to rush off like this, but the festival . . ." Laura began.

Fiona interrupted, "So much to do and so little time."

"I'll be fine," said Morgen, following Laura and Fiona as they moved quickly out the front door to the pony cart.

"Oh dear!" Fiona exclaimed. "Look at those flowers!"

In fact, some of the flowers woven onto the cart had taken a beating when the pony dashed across the stream.

"I'll deal with that," Laura said, and called back to Morgen, "Bye for now. Get some rest!"

Morgen couldn't help noticing they seemed in an awful rush to get away, but called back cheerily, "I will, thank you!"

And it happened again. As his and Laura's eyes met, she smiled at him, wheeled the pony cart in place, and sent it back across the stream.

Once more, their song welled up inside him, and he silently sang to her and her alone, as the pony cart slowly, carefully crossed the stream, without any of the splash of its arrival.

"Don't go away. Stay near me now.
I'd keep you close, if I knew how."

The pony cart rose onto the far bank and began ascending the narrow dirt trail, but Laura didn't look back.

Morgen continued sharing their song, and heard the orchestral accompaniment return.

"If I sound strange, please trust me do.
I've never seen *The Likes of You*."

Despite the orchestra, it seemed the magic was gone, until Laura suddenly turned to look back at him, as if to prove his song had reached her heart, and again, her obbligato merged with his verse for the finale.

"*The Likes of You. The Likes of You!*"

The pony cart went out of view, swallowed up by the thick woods, but Morgen dared hope an unbreakable bond between them had been forged.

Inside the cottage, the delicious aroma of Fiona's ambrosia drew Morgen over to the large, cast iron stove to see what was brewing in the pot. He saw cut up carrots, potatoes, and onions through the thick broth boiling on the top, but not much else.

He resisted the temptation to taste it, and looked for a control to turn down the heat. Finding none, he realized the temperature was controlled by what fuel and how much was burning under the stove top, and the position of the pot on top of it, decided not to meddle with it, and instead, looked into the wicker baskets on the table, one containing five more bottles of Fiona's nectar, the covered one, fresh-baked bread.

Pulling back the covering, he was surprised to discover the loaf of bread on top was baked in the form of a nude woman, sunny-side up! Morgen smiled, thinking of how Fiona must have anticipated his reaction. She couldn't be much over forty, and maybe younger, but she was a naughty one, and probably got a kick out of shocking the younger generation.

He turned the loaf this way and that, wondering where one should bite into it, and what that would tell an observer. No doubt, Fiona would attach significance to where one bit in: head, feet, or ripped in half and eaten from the middle. He scanned the room, trying to imagine where a camera might be hidden, but saw none, then laughed at himself for being so paranoid, especially in a location that didn't even have phone service, so he poured himself a goblet of nectar, which finished off the first bottle, tucked the loaf of lady bread under his arm and, goblet in hand, checked out his accommodations.

The kindling and wood in the fireplace was all set to go, needing only a match to set it ablaze, and there were some large, stick matches on the mantlepiece, next to a big, old-fashioned hour glass and without any idea how long it took for the sand to run out, Morgen couldn't resist turning it over to put the sands of time in motion. In front of the fireplace was a coffee table and a saggy old sofa that served as a room divider, setting the living area apart from the kitchen area.

The writing desk stood below the single, multi-paned window in the front wall on that side of the cottage, overlooking the stream and narrow wooded trail beyond, and in front of the table was a curved-back, wooden captain's chair with a cushion, tied to the spokes in the back, to keep the cushion in place. The table's single drawers on both sides held stationery, and on top of the writing desk was a blotter, inkwell and quill.

Morgen went to the saggy sofa, placed the lady bread on top of the coffee table, and sat down to sip Fiona's nectar.

CHAPTER EIGHT

He awoke to a tiny explosion in the fireplace that heated and provided light to the living area. He didn't know who lit the fire or covered him with the quilt, but saw the hourglass had run out, and the sunlight was gone from the front window. He was stretched out on the lumpy sofa, covered by a quilt, and when he sat up, discovered he'd been clutching the loaf of bread to his chest. The kerosene lamp atop the writing desk was lit, and on the table was a piece of paper, folded like a pup tent. He went to the writing desk, held the paper to the light from the lamp and read "You looked like you needed rest more than company," and the note was signed, "Laura."

He ran outside and shouted her name three times, but no answer came, and as the last twilight glow faded from the sky, Morgen gave up, and went back inside the cottage.

The covered stew pot had been moved to a cooler part of the stove top, but when he lifted the lid, the stew inside was still hot. There was a ladle and a fair-sized wooden bowl on the counter top, so he ladled some stew into the bowl, found a spoon in a drawer, sat at the kitchen table, took a bite, and knew at once why it was called ambrosia.

It was neither broth nor gravy, but something in between, and delicious. In addition to cut up potatoes, carrots, and onions, it contained celery, barley, and chunks of at least three kinds of tender, delicious meat; lamb and beef, and a mystery meat that might have been venison. Famished, he wolfed it all down, and as he came to the bottom of his bowl, without any of the hesitation he had when he first saw it, broke the loaf of lady bread in half, sopped up the rest, and ate it, too.

Morgen had no trouble pulling the cork on a fresh bottle of Fiona's nectar, but knowing first-hand how potent it was, sipped it rather than drinking it down. Assuming he had taken sole possession of the cottage at, or around, 10:00 a.m., if sunset was around 8:30 p.m., he'd probably slept at least ten hours straight, and if it was 8:30 p.m. here, it was only 3:30 p.m. in Boston. When they played gigs there, they rarely started before 8:00 p.m. and sometimes ran as late as one o'clock in the morning, which might explain why, even after taking into consideration how little he'd slept the day before, he felt fully rested, wide awake, and ready for action.

Rested, well-fed, but alone, and still concerned about having gone AWOL the night before, Morgen stepped outside for some fresh air. The moon was bright, and from the cottage, he saw gray rocks protruding above the dark stream, offering a series of stepping stones that he might use to cross it.

Up close, he had no doubt that the rocks were deliberately placed stepping stones, and in no time at all, he was standing on the far bank, but unaware of any trails but the one that brought him there, Morgen had only two choices–return to the cottage, or follow the trail back to see the shrine by moonlight. He set out up the dark path, without seeing the barn owl, hidden in the foliage of a large, nearby tree, take flight and silently go on ahead.

The moonlight filtering through the treetops was barely enough to light his way, but he climbed steadily until, from the hilltop, he beheld the stone circle, bathed in moonlight in the clearing below. He followed the trail downhill, until, about level with the dolmen, then moved off the trail, away from the dolmen, into the brush on the rocky hillside.

Morgen found a perfect spot in line with the monolith standing in the center of the sacred ground, directly opposite the principal trilithon, two large upright stones, bridged by a third, horizontal stone, like a displaced section of Stonehenge.

He squatted to line up the shot he would take if he had a camera capable of capturing the magical effect of the moonlit structure, but his calves began to cramp, and he plopped down between the thick, gnarled roots of a tree, and there discovered he'd found a more perfect angle for his imaginary photo.

A cloud scudded across the face of the moon, blocking its glow, turning his world black until it passed, and again bathed the stone circle in its light. Alone, staring at the ancient stones, he experienced a sense of kinship with those countless generations who had venerated the shrine before him, seen it by moonlight, and gazed in wonder at the spectacle.

An arpeggio played through his mind, and a canto of melody and lyrics emerged, reflecting his thoughts and feelings. He closed his eyes to listen to the song, repeating over and over, capturing the emotion of the moment, better than ever could a photo, fixing it, deeply and forever in his memory.

"It's not clear, and I can't be sure.

I get the strange sensation that I've been this way before.

The feeling is elusive. It's like trying to pick up sand.

The more you try to hold it, the less stays in your hand."

Morgen was still meditating when he heard the choir begin to sing, and at first, thought they were his inner voices.

"*In This Place*, where I am,

Those who seek me shall find me here."

But when a second section began singing over the first section's last note, he opened his eyes.

"If they seek me here!"

Below, torches burned along the perimeter of the irregular circle of stones, casting shadows that leaped and danced about the sacred ground where the central monolith stood, draped in a dark cloak and crowned with an antlered headdress.

Outside the circle, a choir of women, clothed in gossamer gowns and wearing floral headdresses, were conducted by a choir mistress, wearing an embroidered cape who stood beneath the trilithon, and accented their song with strokes on her hand-held bell tree. The two choir sections combined to sing the eerie harmonies louder, stronger, and richer together.

"If they see, with their eyes closed,
They will surely find me here, *In This Place!*"

The harmonies sent a shiver through Morgen, and a final bell tree stroke signaled a drum beat, too close for comfort, where a string section began establishing a rhythm.

Slowly, he turned his head toward the orchestra gathered near the dolmen, all wearing Renaissance Fair costumes. One played a melody in an eight tone diatonic scale, and no longer concerned by their proximity, Morgen looked back at the choir, below, recognized Fiona, the choir mistress, her eyes fixed on the cloaked monolith, and realized if she looked up, he was in her line of sight, above and beyond the antlered headdress, and dared not move, lest he attract her attention. She seemed to be addressing the monolith, but he couldn't hear what she said.

The orchestra began a second movement in a five-tone pentatonic scale that in his present circumstances, Morgen found threatening, but the orchestra played on, oblivious to his presence. In the choir below, the women squirmed and struggled to raise their gowns, dropping the excess fabric over their belts, turning their long, gossamer gowns into triple-layered short skirts. Fiona, again with her back to Morgen, held up her arms, calling her choir to order, and in the next orchestral movement, a flute played the melody in a different, more novel pentatonic scale.

Below, at Fiona's signal, she and the ladies donned masks. From the hillside, it was difficult to see, but their masks appeared more fanciful than grotesque. Again, Fiona raised her arms, calling for order, and the choir watched for her signal, anticipating the orchestra's next movement.

That's when Morgen realized everything he observed was orchestrated. The music he heard underscored the activities he witnessed. If this was Laura's Spring Festival, he wondered when and where she would make her entry.

He hadn't long to wait. The next movement, carried by the strings, seemed a recapitulation of the original diatonic melody, but quickly evolved, adding two or more independent melody lines in the contrapuntal horn parts, and the choir fell into step with the solemn processional, undulating up the hillside toward the orchestra, but Fiona, nowhere to be seen, no longer led them.

Morgen looked back toward the trilithon entrance, but Fiona was gone. Suddenly, a barn owl flew out from under the trilithon, glided away and disappeared around the far side of the hill. Looking back at the choir, Morgen watched as the women, smiling wickedly, emboldened by the anonymity provided by their masks, begin moving provocatively through the orchestra, shamelessly baring thighs, shoulders and sometimes more, flirting indiscriminately as they promoted their charms, to any and to all.

With the return of the largo, pentatonic march, they slowly abandoned their teasing and turned to witness the goings-on at the stone circle below as carnyx horns called and answered, announcing the arrival of the main attraction, and Fiona, hidden behind an owlish mask, but easily identified by her embroidered cape, came into view around the outside of the shrine, leading Laura's pony cart toward the trilithon entrance.

Laura stood alone in the cart, wearing a golden, gossamer, multi-layered gown and floral crown, escorted by Amy, Barbara, and Calypso, one on each side and one at the rear of the cart, holding tall garland wrapped poles, connected at their apex to form a pyramid over Laura's head. At the trilithon entrance, the girls stopped to let the cart move on through, then stacked their attached poles together against the trilithon, and took positions between two torches burning outside the uneven stone perimeter.

The choir women made their way out of the orchestra, and hurried back downhill to take positions outside the stone circle, from where they could see most of the sacred ground within. The music became polyrhythmic as Fiona led the pony cart widdershins around the dark robed, antler-horned monolith. It appeared that as she completed her circuit of the monolith, she would lead Laura and the pony cart back outside through the trilithon, but as she came full circle, Laura sprang from the pony cart and began to dance upon the sacred ground within the stone circle. All eyes were riveted on Laura, surrendering herself to the music, dancing around the monolith, inspired by the panpipes, as Fiona led the pony cart away.

On the hillside above, Morgen became caught up in Laura's dance and the music, surprised to feel it flowing in and through him, excited by the seductive sensations the panpipes conveyed, and allowing them to influence his attention, much as they influenced the dancer in the sacred space below.

The tempo had begun to accelerate, and with it, Laura began stripping away layers of her costume, and Morgen became aware he had become one with the music. With nothing more than a sudden, involuntary shudder, he raised the tempo and introduced the growling electric guitar he heard within, to the music being played by the local orchestra. And he saw Laura react, increasing the tempo of her dance to keep pace with the new, accelerated rhythm.

Morgen saw that the orchestra played to his rhythm, and realized that it was not *he* who was caught up in their performance, but *they*, the choir, and the dancer, who were now caught up in his, and to prove it, with a second shudder, introduced a second electric guitar and accelerated the tempo, again. Now, he conducted the orchestra, directed the dance, and added still another electronic instrument, again increasing the tempo, and watched as both the orchestra and the dancer responded.

Laura continued to strip away layers of her costume, dancing ever faster with each circuit of the sacred ground, sometimes hidden from Morgen's view by the irregular stones supporting the hillside, and sometimes by the monolith that stood between them. Her dance carried her out of view as she discarded what was left of her costume, but he saw her hands grip the dark cloak, and cling fiercely to it, as she wrapped her legs around to embrace the monolith, and the tempo, no longer under his control, slowed as he watched her hands, one after the other, slide ever lower on the cloak, as did her legs until, on the far side of the monolith, she collapsed on her back at its base, and her hands fell away from the dark cloak.

Morgen was startled by the nearby shriek of an owl, a shriek that sent the masked choir, screaming, and running away into the surrounding darkness outside the stone circle. With a roar, the orchestra casted off their instruments, and charged down the hill, some snatching torches from the stone circle to light their way, pursuing the women.

Back inside the stone circle, the scowling Furies guarded the sacred ground, as the Muses, mostly hidden by the monolith, helped Laura to her feet and wrapped her in a doeskin.

To Morgen's surprise, when Laura stepped out from behind the monolith, she did not appear exhausted by her dance, but smiling happily, holding her doeskin covering tightly closed around her, hurried through the trilithon, and started up the dirt trail leading back over the hill toward the cottage.

Morgen stood, screened from discovery by the tree that had cradled him, watched Laura go out of view, then set out after her, unaware that the Fates, above and behind his sheltering tree, followed him with their blind eyes, weaving his destiny.

Morgen loped through the moonlit night toward the crest of the hill, a song stirring within him, a throbbing, lustful song of power and passion, and he held nothing back, wanting Laura to sense his desire, and share her own with him.

"I love the way you play your role,
A proper lady fair,
But when you take an evening's stroll,
It's not to take the air!"

Ahead on the dirt trail, Laura smiled, playing peek-a-boo with her doeskin, swirling it around, celebrating her naked freedom and Morgen's lustful attraction to her.

"It's no use your denying
What you do. I saw it all,
For I was out there spying.
Now, you're up against the wall."

Morgen sent his song silently into the night, sure it would reach the object of his desire, and she would embrace the inevitability of their mutual attraction, never realizing his unbridled passion conveyed a threat as well, and as his last line reached her, Laura frowned, wrapped her doeskin around herself, and began walking faster.

"I know your darkest secret. I was witness to your rite –
Your erotic transformation. I saw it all tonight!"

Laura drew her doeskin closer, as she hurried down the wooded trail.

"I knew if I were clever, no one need ever know,
So, I was there, my lady fair. I sure enjoyed the show!"

Laura heard him drawing nearer, and trailing her doeskin, bolted from the trail, into the deep woods.

"Unbidden, hidden, I watched you.
I viewed the whole charade,
Your beauty rare, all pink and bare,
Before me all displayed!"

Morgen slowed and paused to listen.

"I have witnessed your diversion,
Know your wanton appetite,"

He heard her moving through the woods, and grinning wickedly, abandoned the trail to follow.

"Your erotic recreation,
I was watching you tonight!"

Within the stone circle, the Muses danced and sang their chorus to Morgen's song.

"*Peeping Tom! Peeping Tom! Peeping Tom* peeping!"

Morgen frowned, hearing these lyrics, not of his making, come into his song, wondering what they might portend.

"*Peeping Tom! Peeping Tom,* keeping out of sight."

Laura, crouched behind a tree, heard it, too.

"*Peeping Tom! Peeping Tom! Peeping Tom* creeping."

On the hillside above the stone circle, the Fates wove their tapestry that hung down, covering the entrance to the Tomb of Every Hope, and sang along with the Muses.

"Can't go on, *Peeping Tom,* peeping in the night!"

And the Furies, standing in front of the entrance to the Tomb of Every Hope, sang triumphantly as the growling mastiff burst from behind the tapestry raced across the stone circle, leaped over the outer wall, and disappeared into the darkness beyond.

"Creeping through the night!"

Laura, crouching behind the trunk of a tree in the deeper woods, listened to Morgen's lyrics as he took back his song.

"The passion in your nature, so craftily concealed,
Has now been exposed, my love,
Your secrets all revealed.
What's done is done. You had your fun
And now you'll pay my price."

Morgen, searching the thick dark woods, came steadily closer to Laura's hiding place as his song continued.

"You'll come to me, prepared to be a carnal sacrifice.
There's no use in your pretending
You're some humble acolyte.

I observed your dedication.

I saw everything tonight!"

Laura burst from hiding, and clutching her doeskin robe to her, ran as fast as she could, Morgen loping after her, following the sound of her headlong flight through the dense woods, and in the excitement of the chase, as he steadily gained on her, Morgen didn't worry that his song had once again become the provenance of the goddesses.

"*Peeping Tom! Peeping Tom! Peeping Tom* peeping!
Peeping Tom! Peeping Tom, keeping out of sight.
Peeping Tom! Peeping Tom! Peeping Tom creeping.
Can't go on, *Peeping Tom,* peeping in the night!
Peeping Tom! Peeping Tom! Peeping Tom peeping!
Peeping Tom! Peeping Tom, keeping out of sight."

And then, with Morgen hot on her heels, Laura's doeskin snagged on a branch, nearly tearing it from her grasp.

"*Peeping Tom! Peeping Tom! Peeping Tom* creeping."

Laura laughed as she pulled her doeskin free of the branch and dashed past a large, thick-trunked tree.

"Can't go on, *Peeping Tom,*"

Morgen passed on the other side of the tree, expecting to cut her off, but it was a doe, not Laura, that sprang through his arms, and sent him tumbling into the chilly stream below.

"Creeping in the night!"

Morgen splashed to his feet, stunned by the cold water, bewildered as he watched the doe bound away. Then, responding to a menacing growl, he turned to confront the mastiff, on the cottage side of the stream, and froze in place afraid to make the slightest move.

"What brings you here?" the first Fury asked in her typically nasty tone.

Morgen turned slowly, hoping not to spur the growling mastiff to action, and seeing the Furies on the other bank, replied, bitterly, "As if you didn't know. . ."

"That is boldly spoken," said the second Fury.

"Like a challenge, spoken," snarled the bloodthirsty third.

"Intended, perhaps, to provoke?" concluded the first Fury.

"I'm the one who's been provoked," Morgen snapped back, instantly regretting it when he heard the soft, menacing growl from behind, that stood his hair on end, and not daring to turn to look at the mastiff again, for fear the dog might think it a challenge and attack, froze in place.

The second Fury looked disturbed by the dog's menacing growl. "Abandon reason," she said.

"Before you is a mystery," the equally disturbed third Fury clarified.

"A wonder not attained by reason," the first Fury concluded.

Before he could answer, the mastiff barked a deep-throated, blood-chilling warning, and Morgen spun to face it, and fully expecting the dog's attack, his back to the Furies, shouted at them, "There must be some reason!"

There was no attack, and no answer from the Furies, either. Morgen saw the mastiff tentatively wag its tail.

"Go away!" Morgen commanded. The huge dog's tail drooped, and to Morgen's surprise, it turned and trotted off.

Morgen stole a glance at the spot where the Furies had been, and were no more. Cold, wet, and confused, Morgen sloshed out of the stream and squished his way up to the cottage, never noticing the barn owl that watched from the tree above the stream, then silently took flight, and disappeared into the dense woods.

Inside the cottage, by the faint glow from the kerosene lamp, still lit on the writing desk, Morgen removed his shoes, and leaving wet footprints from his stockinged feet, carried them from the front door to the kitchen, and emptied them into the sink. He peeled off his wet socks, wrung them out, and placed them out on the still warm stove top. He then pulled his shirt off over his head, wrung it out, and smoothed it over the back of a chair, rescued his I.D. wallet, wrung out his pants, smoothed them with his hands and hung them over the back of a second chair, and finally, cold and shivering, placed both chairs closer to the front of the stove.

Morgen fetched the kerosene lamp from the writing desk, and went through the door at the back of the main room, and by its light, went to an open door, to his left, and saw inside the room, the bed made up for him. Placing his wallet and kerosene lamp on the small bedside table, he blew out the lamp, climbed into bed, pulled the covers over himself, curled up in a fetal ball, and shivered himself to sleep.

Some hours later, Morgen awoke, warm in his fetal cocoon, as long as he didn't touch any part of the cold bedding surrounding him. The room was as dark as his mood. He'd made a fool of himself the night before, and had no idea what time of day or night it was, only that he was dry, awake, and determined to find his way back to civilization. He got up, groped his way to the foot of the bed, stood erect, and stretching his arms out in front of him, moved cautiously to where he thought the doorway would be, and found a wall.

If this was the wall opposite the foot of the bed, the doorway he sought should be only a few steps to his right, and keeping one hand on the wall, moved that way until he ran into a door, facing him, at a right angle to the wall, not at all the way he remembered the layout of the room. He ran his hand down the door jamb to the doorknob, took a step back, and opened the door to the great room at the front of the cottage.

The interior was dimly illuminated by a source of light that filtered into the room through the window by the writing desk, but he could make out his clothes by the stove where he'd left them, and dry enough to wear, he put them on. His shoes were still damp, but he put them on anyway, stood up, took inventory by patting himself down, realized he'd left his

ID wallet and the kerosene lamp on the nightstand in the dark room, and fetched the matches from over the fireplace.

The hall in the back of the cottage was still completely dark, so he lit a match at the doorway and returned quickly to the bedroom on the left, saw the ID wallet and kerosene lamp where he'd left them, but had to blow out the match before it burned his fingers. He struck another match, but couldn't light the kerosene lamp while he was holding the match, so he snatched up the lamp and hurried back into the kitchen, where he could see well enough to light the wick with a third match, and then, with the kerosene lamp lighting his way, returned to the bedroom for his ID wallet, turned to take a final inventory of the room, and noticed, for the first time, illustrations and a text describing Morningstone, hanging on the wall. Recognizing the Bridge Across the Stream of Consciousness, where he'd crashed into the ditch, he turned up the wick, examined the illustrations and text, and realized he could not be far from the bridge, he had no way to calculate the exact distance, but knew water flowed downhill, and reasoned that following the stream would be the fastest way back to the bridge.

Morgen, now missing for more than a day from what he considered the real world, embarrassed by his churlish behavior the previous night, was in no mood to try to explain himself to the natives, so he set out in the pre-dawn twilight to follow the stream, from whence, he reasoned it couldn't be much more than a mile back to the well-traveled road he'd left when he swerved to avoid the doe, and should be able to return to civilization in no time.

Daybreak was nigh, and he wanted to get out of town before a hue and cry could be raised. With no luggage to slow him down, he set off at a fast pace, and remembering his military training, after his first hundred paces or so, decided to run a hundred, then march a hundred, swapping intervals until he got to the bridge.

Not only was it mostly downhill, but following the narrowing stream as it dropped steeply over rapids, he arrived soon at the bottom of the hill, where the stream widened and flowed more gently, under the bridge he sought, and the sun was just beginning to peek over the horizon when he arrived.

He scrambled up the embankment to the road and went to the crown of the bridge for a last look at the sports car, and discovered, to his dismay, that it was gone. Had the side of the ditch collapsed leaving the car hopelessly on its side in the muddy bottom? He hurried over to look, but there was no trace of the car. Even the collapsed side of the ditch was restored. He wondered if it might be another bridge, but found the Morningstone sign was exactly where it was before.

Morgen's heart sank. Had it been stolen? Would a thief take the time and trouble to try to conceal the crash site? Not likely, with him still around to testify to the contrary. If Smythe had his tractor together and towed it out sooner than he thought he would, would he stop to restore the ditch, and if so, how, and with what?

Morgen had planned to return to the main road on foot, but if Smythe had managed to get the car out, and it was drivable, it would be better all-around if he drove it back to civilization, and there, dealt with the powers that be. And if Smythe didn't have it, the first thing he'd have to do when he got back to civilization was fill out a stolen car report. No doubt, Rodney would read him the riot act, but *All's Well That Ends Well*, and as far as any scandal his disappearance might have caused, it would blow over, once he got back to work.

CHAPTER NINE

Morgen set out running and marching along the path back to Morningstone, and as his endorphins kicked in, he began to feel stronger and more clear-minded. He didn't know exactly how long it took him to get to the hillside above the village, but he wasn't particularly tired, and almost decided to run the rest of the way down to the village. Instead, he walked, so he wouldn't be out of breath when he arrived at Smythe's Forge and Auto Repair.

The big doors were padlocked shut, and banging on them didn't produce Mr. Smythe, so Morgen crouched down and tried to pry the doors open a bit with both hands, to see if the sports car was in the garage. It was as he was peering into the relative darkness inside the workshop, that a hand on his shoulder startled him enough to send him flying, like a criminal caught in the act.

It was Fiona, wearing her baker's apron, who stood before him. "Oh my! I didn't mean to startle you. I just came to tell you no one's here, now."

"Where are they?" Morgen asked.

"It's May Day," she answered. "Everyone's up at the shrine."

"Everyone except you," Morgen said.

"In a few minutes I will be," she responded. "I'm getting ready to leave. I only came down to bake the daily bread."

"I was hoping to find Mr. Smythe. I believe he towed my car out of the ditch sometime yesterday or last night."

"Oh? Well, I suppose he might have done, but if it's him you want to see, he'll be up there."

"I don't want to be any bother . . ."

"It's no bother. You can help carry the bread. Besides, I know a short cut."

"I knew there had to be a shorter way."

"You've seen the illustrations?"

"Yes. This morning."

"They were made by a visitor, ages ago. I put them up. I thought they would be of interest to our special guests."

"They are, as far as they go."

"My sentiments exactly," she said, and walking quickly back to her bakery, added, "The bread's done!"

Inside the bakery, Fiona went straight to her oven, pulled out a tray of several loaves of fresh-baked bread, and using a wooden shovel, began removing them and placing them to cool on a marble counter top. "Oh, just right," she cooed.

Morgen ventured a glance to see what constituted just right.

"Yesterday they were naked ladies," he muttered.

"Today, they're owls," she replied, merrily.

"I suppose that's significant," Morgen observed.

"Of course," Fiona replied, not bothering to explain why.

Morgen watched as she loaded the loaves into what looked like a laundry bag, pulled a string at the top to close it, swung the bundle over one shoulder, and indicating another bundle for Morgen, merrily intoned, "Shall we be off?"

"Lead the way," he said with a grin, and so she did.

He was a little surprised at how quickly and effortlessly Fiona covered the ground, and more than a little surprised when it turned out her short cut, considerably shorter than going halfway around the hill to get to the more gradual incline of the pony trail, was a lot steeper to climb, and his leg muscles, which had easily endured his march-run-march routine from the cottage to the bridge and the same, again, all the way to the village, began protesting on the incline. He kept his eyes on Fiona, thinking she would have to slow her pace or take a breather somewhere along the way, but she seemed tireless, and only slowed when she reached a more level meadow, more than halfway to the shrine, by which time, Morgen's thighs and calves were beginning to burn.

"It's easier from here," she said. "How are you holding up?"

"I'm fine," he lied.

"We're nearly there," she promised as he drew alongside, and they set out, across the meadow, at a more leisurely pace.

"Your coming to Morningstone was no accident, Morgen."

"No?"

"Oh, look!" Fiona said, smiling happily.

Morgen saw the huge mastiff trotting toward them, its tail wagging slowly as it approached. Fiona saw the look of dread on Morgen's face, and laughed. He shot her a glance, and in that split second, saw something in her face that suggested she might be the sort of woman who would enjoy the spectacle of seeing someone torn to pieces. Whatever was on the monster's mind, it went directly to Morgen, and Fiona, seeing how petrified Morgen was, only laughed all the more, when the mastiff licked Morgen's hand.

"It seems you've got a friend," she chuckled. "There, you see? He's just saying hello."

"Or tasting me, to see whether I'm worth eating."

"He's being friendly. Pet him."

Morgen's licked hand was entirely too close to the monster's jaws. On its head, was better than in its mouth, so Morgen petted it on its head, said, "Nice doggy," and was relieved to see the beast begin to happily wag its tail.

Fiona set down her bundle of bread, crouched down face-to-face with sudden death, and clasped the dog's loose ruff in both hands. Perhaps he'd been wrong about her, Morgen thought, judging by the way she played with the monster.

"I wouldn't do that, if I were you," Morgen said. "He could easily take your head off."

"Don't be silly," she replied, and cooed at the dog, "You're a sweetie, aren't you?" And addressing Morgen asked, "Do you know what he is?"

"A really, really big dog," Morgen affirmed.

"He's a mastiff," she said. "A very ancient breed, indeed."

"You're going to get all greasy."

"Greasy?"

"He's got grease all over him. He looks like he's been rolling in it."

"That's not grease. That's his natural color. He's a brindled mastiff, aren't you?" Fiona purred, then turned her back on the beast to pick up her bundle of bread.

Apart from its huge, terrifying, black head, it did have sort of a golden-brown coat, all streaked with black, which to an untrained eye made it appear it had been rolling in motor oil, but once Morgen realized it was its natural coloring, he had to admit it was actually quite unique, a look that one might get used to, or possibly even attractive enough for an outdoor picnic in a meadow like this one. Morgen petted its head, and it continued wagging happily, until Fiona moved on.

The mastiff trotted on ahead, leading them across the meadow toward the entrance to the wooded footpath to the shrine.

As they fell in behind him, Fiona said, "Now, there's a gift. A natural way with animals. Always a good sign."

She laughed again, and Morgen began to feel more relaxed,

"As I was saying," Fiona continued, "your coming here to Morningstone was no accident. You, an enchanter . . ."

"Enchanter?"

"Song and chant meant the same thing, didn't they? And you set words to music and sing the songs. You're an enchanter by definition," Fiona insisted, "casting spells on all the ladies. And songs are spells, aren't they? Once you've heard a song, there's no telling when it'll come back and go 'round and 'round in your head, even when there's no music to hear. I'd say that's magic."

"I never thought of it in quite that way," Morgen admitted.

"You with the world by the ears. Who can say what mischief you might cause, or what good you might do?"

Suddenly, she blocked Morgen with her right arm. They both froze in place, as she pointed at the mastiff in the meadow ahead and whispered, "Look, Morgen."

The mastiff, big as he was, was stalking something, slowly lifting a paw, slowly moving it forward, then, leaning forward to put his weight over it when he brought it down to the ground, and one by one, repeating the action with each separate paw. As incredible as it was to witness, Morgen followed the mastiff's stare to discover its quarry. Again, it was Fiona who saw it first.

"Look," she whispered excitedly, "close to the ground."

He saw a struggling bird, pathetically dragging one wing.

"It's an injured bird," Morgen whispered back.

Fiona, caught up in the drama unfolding in the meadow ahead, whispered back excitedly, "It's a lapwing."

Sympathetically, Morgen whispered back, "It's been hurt."

Fiona laughed at the bird's plight as the huge dog continued to move slowly closer.

Morgen, indignantly reacting to her laughter, hissed, "It's got a broken wing."

"Never," she whispered back.

He was shocked by her feral delight, which could only result in the poor bird's horrible end in the mastiff's jaw.

At a distance, the bird looked to have a black crest, breast, and collar, a white belly and face, and sounded to Morgen almost like a child, crying for help.

Morgen set down his bread bundle and hurried forward to hold the dog. At his approach, the lapwing fluttered along all the faster, with increasingly shrill cries.

Fiona was still laughing when she called out to Morgen, "It's a lapwing, Morgen. There's a nest nearby."

"It's hurt," he shouted, determined to do what he could to save the bird, but as he drew near, the mastiff charged, and the bird took flight, its broken wing miraculously whole again.

Morgen watched the bird breast-stroking its way ever higher and more distant, its cries taunting, as it rose into the wide, blue yonder. With a bone-chilling bark of frustration, the mastiff gave up the chase, and facing Morgen, gave a bark that contained an accusation as well as frustration, for being cheated out of its morning snack.

Morgen waited as Fiona approached with both sacks of bread on her shoulders. He relieved her of one, then fell in beside her as they followed the mastiff onto the trail through the woods to the shrine.

"I tried to warn you," she said. "But never mind. It's a good omen. A secret will be revealed to you."

To which Morgen replied wryly, "I can't wait."

It appeared the entire population of Morningstone was waiting for Morgen's arrival, the menfolk wearing colorful tunics over their slashed-sleeve shirts, some topping it off with feathered caps; their ladies wearing garlands of spring flowers and lovely gowns of various colors and lengths; and their children, equally colorful, the boys dressed like their fathers, the girls, like their mothers, together creating an atmosphere suggestive of a Renaissance Fair.

Fiona, Morgen and the mastiff emerged from the woods opposite the trilithon entrance to the stone circle, and a hush fell over the celebrants. Still feeling guilty about his previous night's crass behavior, Morgen was, at first, daunted by the size of the crowd, but where he feared finding jurists, saw only fans, greeting him with admiration, hope and joy as those furthest from the stone circle began to converge on it, while those standing nearby, including the six teenagers Morgen recognized from the pub, parted to let him pass, then fell in behind to follow at a discreet distance.

As he neared the entrance to the stone circle, neither Mr. Smythe, nor Laura were anywhere to be seen, but the teenagers, his unofficial escorts, were proudly flanking him.

Noticing the mastiff stopped inside the stone circle by the central monolith, Morgen stopped outside, but the dark entrance to the Tomb of Every Hope beckoned like the entrance to a carnival ride through a carnival House of Horrors.

"Well, Morgen," Fiona declared, "here you are!"

"Indeed, I am," said Morgen. "But I don't see Mr. Smythe."

"I imagine he's here, somewhere," she replied.

"It's all more colorful in daylight," he admitted.

"It is, isn't it?" she replied, and relieved him of his bundle of owl bread. "I'll take it from here."

"Now what?" Morgen asked, surrendering the bundle.

Fiona, still smiling warmly, answered, "You go in, of course."

"Into the Tomb of Every Hope?" Morgen said.

Smiling, Fiona observed, "Your friend is waiting for you. Stay with him. He knows his way around."

Fiona disappeared into the colorful crowd. The teenagers began to softly chant "Mor-gen, Mor-gen," a chant quickly taken up by the impatient locals. Morgen was still searching the chanting crowd, looking for Laura or Smythe, when a "thump" caused him to look back inside the stone circle.

The Fates were now weaving on the hillside above the dark chamber, their unrolled tapestry covering much of its entrance. As the crowd continued to softly chant his name, Morgen considered his options, fight or flight heading the list, until he saw Billy, among the teenage boys, give him an encouraging thumbs up. Morgen returned the gesture, took a deep breath, and then stepped inside the stone circle.

No lightning struck from above, the earth didn't tremble beneath his feet, and no crazed mob assaulted him. The monument hadn't risen on its own. It had been designed, erected, and come to be venerated by people like himself.

Morgen went to the mastiff, standing by the monolith, and to reassure himself, and make sure the dog remembered him, petted it and said, "Good dog. That's a good boy,"

The dog led Morgen toward the half-shrouded entrance to the Tomb of Every Hope, but stopped when the Furies emerged from the darkness behind the tapestry.

The crowd's chanting stopped. In the silence, Morgen became aware of the sound of the gentle breeze that blew past his ear. Predictably, the first Fury was first to speak.

"What brings you here?" she asked in a challenging tone.

The mastiff came to heel at Morgen's side, and everyone held their breath, waiting for Morgen's reply. The mastiff nudged Morgen with its huge head, as if prompting an answer.

"That all depends," Morgen said.

Morgen saw his remark had found a chink in the Furies' armor. While they considered their response, Billy, outside the stone circle, grinned broadly and held up two thumbs.

"That is shrewdly spoken," said the second Fury.

"Like a riddle spoken," said the third.

"Intended, perhaps, to beguile?" finished the first, regaining her hostile poise.

Morgen thought a moment before answering, hoping to keep whatever advantage he might have won.

"Beguile?" he asked, "with simple songs?"

The second Fury countered, "Simple magic may deceive."

"A dangerous dependency," agreed the third.

And the first added, "A thread both short and thin."

In that instant, Morgen knew what to say, and smiling at his teenage fans, answered confidently, "It calls for skill."

Out of the corner of his eye, Morgen saw Billy raise and jerk a fist, showing his enthusiastic approval of Morgen's correct answer. Morgen smiled, somewhat smugly, as he turned his attention back to the Furies. The second Fury stood aside, and said to her sister, "Wheels within wheels."

"Tread softly, fool," warned the third Fury as she withdrew.

"The world without is not the world within," said the first, pulling back the tapestry, to allow Morgen to enter.

The mastiff slinked forward but a sudden, unexpected crash of thunder caused Morgen to jump, and the mastiff scooted past the first Fury into the darkness. The sky grew darker, and up at the top of the hill, Morgen saw Mr. Smythe, huge and shirtless, gleaming in a flash of lightning, looking like a sculptor's vision of Vulcan, and nearby, another man, just as large, just as gleaming, holding a huge, slender, dragon-headed horn to his lips, a horn that rose straight up, high over his head, then peered back over the crowd below.

A nearby man cried out, Smythe struck his anvil, a woman screamed, and the second giant blew two notes on his tall, dragon-headed Celtic war horn. More screams and cries arose as if from the depths of hell, and the people of Morningstone began to wail their chilling, whole-moan incantation, summoning supernatural aid to open the Tomb of Every Hope, accompanied by crashes of thunder and more cries and screams as Morgen entered the dark chamber.

The Furies pulled the tapestry closed, blocking all daylight but not blocking out the sound of the screams, moans, whole-moan incantation, or rolling thunder heard outside.

In the utter darkness, Morgen could not see his arms stretched out before him, and only his weight on the ground beneath his feet, provided a point of contact with the world he knew. He felt the dog rub past against his leg, and grabbing it by its tail, followed it until he collided with a wall of stone, that the dog passed through, and only the receding sound of the animal's claws, scraping on stone prevented him from panicking. Groping his way down the wall, he discovered a low opening, and feeling around inside, discovered two walls, a ceiling, and floor of stone slabs, a reinforced shaft which he then entered, following the dog on his hands and knees.

As he crawled forward, inside the dark shaft, the sound of the incantation quickly faded, making it possible to hear the dog's progress ahead.

"Slow down, big guy," he called, "I'm coming!"

As he advanced, the shaft became lower and he hit his head against the stone ceiling more than once before he gave up and dropped down to crawl forward on his belly.

"If you can fit, so can I," Morgen muttered, but now the immediate sound of his own exertions made it difficult to hear the dog's progress, and Morgen stopped several times to listen, to be sure he could still hear the dog, ahead.

In that total darkness, Morgen had no sense of time, no sense of distance, and when last he stopped to listen, could not hear the dog leading him on.

He bellowed, "Yo, dog!" but the shaft was so close, it sounded to him as if he shouted inside a closet. . . or a coffin.

All at once an enormous bark rang out, echoing from a near and obviously much larger space.

Morgen began to crawl forward as fast as he dared, not wanting the dog to get any further ahead of him. "This better lead to something more than a bowl of dog food," he muttered, and suddenly, the floor seemed to fall away at the same time the mastiff rose before him and slobbered all over his face!

"Ahhh! Down! Get down! Sit!" he shouted, and the dog obediently sat. Filtered light dimly illuminated the cavernous Tomb of Every Hope, but compared to the shaft, it was like finding himself in Times Square. The shaft ended some two feet higher than the new floor. Morgen pushed himself out of the shaft and tumbled head first onto the floor of the huge chamber. He wrestled himself free of the mastiff's greeting and rose to take in his surroundings.

The interior was cavernous, easily as large as most man-made cathedrals he'd seen in Europe when he was in the navy.

Its floor was made of irregular stone slabs, and down the center of the floor, a swift shallow brook flowed through it. Its irregular walls provided balconies and walkways, and dim light entered through a natural oculus high overhead.

A torch ignited, lighting a ledge high on the far wall of the underground chamber, illuminating the Fates and their tapestry of destiny, that reached all the way to the floor below, where all its past ages lay in a crumpled heap. The first Fate, spinning, without looking up from her work, spoke normally, but her voice clearly reached Morgen's ears.

"She's yours, to do with as you may. Behold!" she said, and a torch ignited on a stone wall formation closer to Morgen. By its light, he saw the mastiff, sphinxlike, guarding a wretched nude figure curled up in a ball and chained to the wall.

"Before you is a mystery revealed," said the second Fate, as she wove thread from the first Fate's skein into the tapestry.

Whatever the locals were playing at, Morgen decided they'd gone too far. The question was, how should he deal with it? Were they planning to ruin him, blackmail him, or worse? He addressed them, while his mind was racing, still trying to fathom a way out of the mess.

"I must admit, you put on quite a show," he said, disgusted by the fact that he had become part of it. He tried to dismiss the idea that he'd been deliberately targeted, because they could not have known he'd go for a drive, get lost, and crash into their ditch . . . unless, of course, the Fates were really Fates, and if so, did that make everything better, or worse?

"Go," said the third Fate, derailing his train of thought.

"Look you close upon your former love, whose limbs embraced you; kisses brought you joy," said the spinner.

"Here, fettered, scourged, polluted by your lust," finished the weaver.

That never happened, he thought, as he moved toward the chained figure, determined not to do anything that might compromise himself. The mastiff backed away as he approached the chained figure. In the flickering torch light, Morgen saw the tortured woman, covered with welts, her nudity hidden in part by her long, golden hair.

104

"Laura?" Morgen said softly, but the figure didn't respond. Abandoning his resolution to stay away, he went to her, wincing sympathetically, as he gently parted her hair and saw her bruised face.

"Laura?" he said, his voice beginning to tremble with anger. She opened her eyes and looked up, apparently without recognizing him. As he leaned in closer, Laura's face twisted into a mask of rage. She screamed and launched herself at him, teeth bared. Morgen leaped back, out of her reach.

The mastiff leaped to its feet, the fur on its neck and back on end, barking furiously. Her charge arrested by her shackles; Laura began to laugh maniacally.

Horrified, Morgen staggered to his feet and shouted, "What the hell is this?"

"Is she not Nature, harnessed to your will?" the third Fate asked. "Through your abuse, unbalanced," added the spinner.

Suddenly, torches ignited on both sides of the stone slab shaft that had brought him there, and by their light he saw it was now guarded by the scornful Furies.

"Now hear us!" shouted the first Fury. "His perverse nature, Nature now perverts."

"And courts annihilation!" howled the second.

"He must die!" shrieked the third.

And the first, calling on the natural forces of creation and destruction, held her hands before her, curled like talons about to seize their prey, and raged.

"Now, let the mountains quake and spew forth fire,

That by the Earth he scorned, he'll be consumed."

The stone slabs beneath Morgen's feet began to slide apart, revealing molten rock below, and the brook that ran through the tomb flowed into the fiery chasm raising a column of steam, and fiery blast that cast weird shadows on the walls as the slab tilted down, threatening to tip him into the molten pit.

Morgen clung to a nearby rock formation, and as the frightened mastiff slid by him, instinctively grabbed it by the scruff of its neck with his free hand, saving it from a fiery end.

"This is a trial," the third Fate said, and cut the thread the second Fate had been working into the tapestry.

"Let cooler heads prevail," said the spinner, and the floor of the chamber was restored, sealing off the fiery chasm, re-establishing the course of the brook.

"Such cooler heads bring icy thoughts to mind!" screamed the defiant second Fury.

"In deathly cold, we'll see his race entombed," and a freezing cold wind howled into the chamber through the stone slab shaft, its icy vapor instantly freezing Morgen, the mastiff and the brook.

"And what of other creatures?" the weaver responded, indicating the mastiff, and drew that thread out of the tapestry.

"Nature weeps," said the third Fate, and as Laura sobbed below, the howling wind subsided, and the frustrated Furies watched as Morgen, the mastiff and the brook all thawed.

The mastiff shook itself from head to tail, while Morgen rubbed his arms to restore his circulation. The first and second Fury's sentences, summarily dismissed by the Fates, made the third Fury more thoughtful, as she addressed her sisters.

"Lest every living creature share his doom, might we not work a pestilence for Man?" she suggested.

The first Fury quickly embraced and expanded upon the idea.

"A plague, specific to his hateful race."

"That other creatures spared whose lives are lived
Obedient to law," came the second Fury's endorsement.

Having experienced Robert Frost's fiery ending and icy entombment, Morgen realized, however unjust, he was on trial for all the transgressions of humanity, and within the tomb, he was no longer in the real world, but somewhere apart from objective reality, wherein gods and demons held forth.

He saw the Fates had stopped weaving. Horrified to think they might consider the Furies' final solution, he dared not take a chance that the third Fury's option might carry.

"What law is that?" he raged. "Does no one speak for Man?"

And his rage summoned the Muses from the shadows within the Tomb of Every Hope, and they stepped out into the pale light from the oculus, high above.

"You loved her, once," the first Muse said.

"Her scars and angry wounds may yet be healed," said the second.

"Through your devotion, Nature be restored!" said the third, and the spinner said, as she threw him a key, "The chains are yours."

Morgen caught the key and stared at it. Did they mean for him to set unbridled Nature free? And if so, was it a key to humanity's survival or destruction?

"To do with as I may?" Morgen asked.

"Divorce from Nature is a strange conceit, indulged by Man, alone, and to his shame," said the weaver as she, her sisters, and the torches that illuminated them, dissolved in a veil of silvery moon dust, leaving the grim Furies, steadfast in their hate, and only the Muses to assist Morgen.

CHAPTER TEN

The first Muse told Morgen, "It's not too late. Your vows you may renew."

"Your husbandry attune to Nature's law," the second Muse volunteered.

The third Muse begged him to "Release her! Dedicate your life anew, and sing her song for everyone to hear."

Laura rose and held her shackled arms out to Morgen.

"Let Nature take her course? Am I a fool?" he asked.

"An honor rare bestowed on mortal head," Laura replied.

Believing Morgen had failed his test, the second Fury addressed the Muses.

"Nature's balance is a sacred trust," she said, and the third said, as the Furies vanished, "Survive or die, the outcome will be just."

Laura stood in the light of the single remaining torch, a dark silhouette, still holding out her shackled wrists to Morgen.

"The thread is short and thin," the first Muse echoed.

"It calls for skill," said the second, and the third said, her voice filled with sadness, "We've done all that we may. Do what you will," and the Muses, too, dissolved away.

The mastiff whined, but Morgen continued to stare at the key, weighing his fate, and the fate of humanity, should he fail the test. And Laura stood, holding out her shackled wrists, as the final torch dimmed.

For millennia, humanity had sought to harness Nature to its will, domesticating animals to supply food, hides, wool, fur, or feathers, and now, farming the sea.

Humanity also dammed and redirected rivers, cleared woodlands, and hunted creatures to extinction that threatened its livestock or crops, destroying less-desirable strains, preserving or artificially enhancing more desirable ones. If Nature was unfettered, what would happen to his world?

He'd witnessed Nature's fury in avalanches, blizzards, tornadoes, hurricanes, floods, droughts, wildfires, earthquakes, tsunamis, and volcanoes, and seen their horrific aftermath, admittedly on TV, but now, within the Tomb of Every Hope, he had been selected, for reasons still unknown, to represent humanity and must now answer for all humanity's crimes against Nature, but as he considered the pros and cons of action and inaction, the sound of Laura's shackles hitting the floor echoed through the Tomb of Every Hope.

Morgen turned quickly to her, holding out the key, but she was already walking away, deeper into the darkness of the underground chamber, and from what he could see in the dim light that entered through the oculus, her scars and angry wounds were gone, her beauty, fully restored.

Morgen and the mastiff followed as she led them deeper into the cave, to where dying embers glowed beneath the Cauldron of Inspiration, and where she took up its ornate ladle, and began stirring its contents. Still some distance from the glowing embers, the mastiff stopped and sat, and Morgen approached the cauldron alone, staying respectfully on the side of the cauldron opposite Laura, who gazed into the cauldron she stirred.

"I would have freed you," he said.

"I know," she replied.

He peered into the cauldron, and could not discern its contents, only that it appeared to be a cloudy, swirling liquid, punctuated with flashes of light, as if, within the cauldron, a storm was brewing.

"What's in it?"

"Inspiration," Laura answered, and looking into Morgen's eyes, lifted the ladle and held it out for Morgen to taste. No steam rose from cauldron or ladle, but still Morgen hesitated, fearing the liquid hid a fire within.

"Are you afraid, Morgen?"

As Morgen cautiously considered his answer to her question, she said, "Only a fool wouldn't be," and began to withdraw the ladle, but Morgen grasped the ladle's bowl, cool in his hand, and sipped from it.

Face to face, across the cauldron they stood, Morgen watching the swirling storm and lightning-like flashes he first saw in the cauldron, now dancing in Laura's eyes, and only slowly coming to realize the storm he thought he saw there, was the reflection in her eyes of the storm raging in his own.

He slumped, and Laura moved quickly, cradling Morgen in her arms, and lowering him gently to the floor. He felt the coolness of the stone floor on his back, and in the gathering darkness, felt her kiss upon his forehead.

It began as a pinpoint of light, growing brighter until he recognized the splendor space revealed as his own. He fended off the mastiff's wet attempts to revive him, and rose to his feet, enlightened, at one with himself and the universe. Beside him stood the Cauldron of Inspiration, before him was a massive oaken bed, and everywhere, musical instruments, many gloriously decorated, inlaid with gold, silver, ivory, and brilliantly colored enamels, were on display.

The mastiff stood on its hind legs, put its great paws on his shoulders, and licked his cheek. He turned his face away, ordered the monster down, and it sat, staring at him with its adoring eyes, awaiting further command. And Morgen, seeing his visage reflected in the gleaming side of the cauldron, wagged his head and softly murmured, "Bemused, again."

He went and sat on the edge of the huge oaken bed, petted the mastiff's head and muttered to himself, "Laura Webster. Oh, the webs you weave. Laura, for the laurels presented to honor a bard . . . or mock a fool." He sprang to his feet.

"Come," he commanded, and he and the dog followed the brook that flowed through his underground domain, until it came to a hole in the bedrock through which it cascaded into the deeper flowing Stream of Consciousness. Summoning music from thin air, he embraced his role in the mysteries yet to come, and sang his credentials loud and clear.

"I am Truth. I am Reason. I am Magic.

Harmony of the Carnal and the Mystical. I am Man!"

Morgen and the mastiff emerged from a cleft in the hillside, and were welcomed by a fanfare from the local orchestra and cheers from its choir.

With an acknowledging wave, Morgen continued his song, leading all down the steep, stony path to the sacred pool.

"I lived in a cave for a year and a day,
Fathered by a sun ray.
Once I was a bull. Now I can't say.
You'll have to find your own way.
I was once an eagle, strong and free.
There's nothing that I can't be.
Once I was a Word. Now I'm a key.
You'll have to learn to trust me!"

Mr. Smythe and the equally huge man lifted him onto their shoulders, and as the choir joined in the chorus, carried him past where the stream emptied its waters into the Sacred Pool. The enlightened Morgen, knowing the outcome of being so honored, quickly pulled off his boots, and tossed them aside.

"Chief bard of the ancients am I,
Anointed in the sacred pool.
My ancestral home is the sacred grove.
Honor your mentor, *The Fool*!"

Smythe and his companion threw Morgen into the sacred pool, and as the mastiff began barking, the giggling ladies of the choir fled up the wooded hillside path.

Morgan surfaced in the chest-high water, and continued singing his credentials, as he waded ashore.

"I've been around the universe several times.
Wine flows from my grapevines.
I've taught your musicians. I've taught your mimes.
Poets learn from my rhymes."

Morgen stripped off his shirt as he came ashore and was hidden by the mastiff and orchestra who crowded around him, as he stripped off his pants, Billy pushed through the orchestra, bearing the antlered headdress and dark cloak.

"At home on land, in sea, or sky,
When I pass the trees sigh.

You knew me before, well I never did die
I merely transmogrify!"

Morgen moved through the crowd, wrapped in the dark cloak, carrying the antlered headdress, and though no longer present, the choir's voices joined were heard in his chorus.

"Chief Bard to immortals am I.
O'er fantastic realms do I rule!
There's none to whom I need bend my knee.
Honor your leader, *The Fool*!"

The mastiff set out ahead along the narrow footpath that led to the hilltop, and Morgen followed, carrying his antlered headdress, continuing to sing his credentials, followed by the teenage boys and the orchestra.

"Multiple mysteries to me are known,
Everywhere the wind's blown.
Revealed thus in monotonous tone,
Lord of the standing stone.
I am a rock in a stormy sea.
Goddesses have loved me.
Some would protect me by Royal Decree.
Others would revile me!"

When they crested the hill above the shrine, the welcoming choir again joined Morgen in his chorus.

"Chief Bard of the ancients am I
Wit is my singular tool.
Beloved am I of the Ninefold Muse,"

Finally, as Morgen finished his song, he placed the antlered headdress upon his head, embracing his fate, completed his symbolic passage from mortal to supernatural surrogate.

"And still, you call me *The Fool*."

Nigel and Kevin each handed Morgen one of his boots. He put them on, preparing for what must yet come to pass. A number of drums in unison sounded a single beat, then three more, the choir entering on the third, accompanied by harp, a bed of strings and woodwinds sharing the melody, and below, Amy, Barbara and Calypso appeared outside the stone circle, strewing flowers before Laura, riding side-saddle on her unicorn-horned pony, her right leg curled around the saddle horn, providing a nest for the hare she carried in her lap, her left foot dragging the ground, her long golden hair combed down over her, held in place by the weight of a golden fishnet, wearing her floral crown, and with Fiona leading the pony.

Morgen quickly jumped to his feet as the choir sang.

"Freya! (Freya.) Janu! (Janu.)
Ishtar! (Ishtar.) Danu! (Danu.)"

During the instrumental release, which Morgen recognized as a thematic of "Morningstone," he moved part way downhill to meet her, stopping slightly below the dolmen. As Laura drew nearer, the choir sang the next line, during which Laura dismounted, freed the hare that scrambled away, capturing the attention of the mastiff that watched from the hillside above, but did not give chase.

"Life-giver, Ageless miracle! Love!"

Accompanied by a descending arpeggio, Laura shrugged and her golden fishnet fell to her feet, leaving her standing before Morgen wearing nothing but her floral crown and covered only by her long golden hair. She parted her hair as a single drum sounded, and they embraced as the choir sang.

"All Conceiver, Joyous Harmony!
(Freya! Janu! Ishtar! Danu!)"

Fiona led the unicorn back down the hill. Laura took Morgen's hand and led him toward the blossom covered dolmen as the choir continued to sing.

"Freya! (Freya.) Janu! (Janu.)"

Amy, Barbara and Calypso, joined the singing choir.

"Ishtar! (Ishtar.) Danu! (Danu.)"

Approaching the flower-covered dolmen, Morgen drew Laura back into his arms.

As Laura looked over Morgen's shoulder, her happy expression turned quizzical when she recognized the Muses celebrating inside the stone circle, alarmed when she saw the cynical Furies looking on in amusement, and above, the Fates, as the cutter, reached out, knife in hand, and cut the single thread upon which all depended. Horrified, Laura saw the untended unicorn rear and begin its charge uphill toward the flower-covered dolmen.

"Gentle Deceiver, Eternal Weaver!

(Freya! Janu! Ishtar! Danu!)"

The mastiff leaped to its feet and dashed downhill, to intercept the charging unicorn. Laura clung to Morgen, trying to pull him out of harm's way, but Morgen, hearing the mastiff's excited baying, fearing the mastiff misread Laura's intent, tried to get between Laura and the mastiff's charge.

In the blink of an eye, it was over. Morgen saw the mastiff throw itself against the unicorn, deflecting its charge enough to keep Morgen from becoming impaled by its horn, but unable to stop its forward momentum as it thrust between Laura and Morgen, knocking Laura down and away, crashing into Morgen, and throwing him headlong into the flower-covered stone dolmen where his antlered headdress shattered and the crescendo in the music faded away.

In the morning twilight, the ambulance sped along the country road, lights flashing, siren wailing. Inside, Morgen lay, strapped to a stretcher, a watchful paramedic by his side. When Morgen opened his eyes, the paramedic noticed.

"Back with us, are you?" he asked.

"Is Laura all right?" Morgen asked.

"Who?"

"The lady who was with me."

Fearing they might have missed a second victim, the paramedic pressed Morgen for more information.

"There was a lady with you?"

"The unicorn knocked her down."

The paramedic sighed with relief as he replied, "A unicorn, was it?"

"A pony dressed up like a unicorn."

"Had a bit to drink, have we?"

"No."

"Away day?"

"What?"

"Tripping? Hallucinogens?"

Losing patience with the paramedic, Morgen replied, "No. What about the lady?"

The paramedic became concerned again. "Was there someone with you in the car?"

"What car?"

"The one you wrapped around the tree."

"I never hit a tree. I went off the road into a ditch."

"Tall, leafy ditch, was it?"

Morgen didn't answer.

"All right. Stay with me now. Do you know where you are?"

Morgen still didn't answer. He was thinking back to that otherworld where important thoughts were couched in music, where music and lyrics merged and became spells that informed the thinker, and suggested courses of action.

Later, he remembered being wheeled into the emergency room, the doctor shining a penlight in his eyes, blood samples being taken, the sudden painful manipulation of his left ankle, and being asked to count backwards from ten. And the next thing he remembered, was waking up in the private hospital room, sometime between 3:30 and 4:00 p.m., on Mayday afternoon with Rodney, looking terribly uncomfortable, napping in a chair.

Morgen let him snore a bit longer, until Rodney woke up when the middle-aged emergency room nurse entered.

"He's awake!" the E.R. nurse said accusingly, then, turning her attention to Morgen, continued, "You're all right, now. You're in hospital. I'll ring for doctor."

"How're you feeling?" Rodney asked.

"Beat all to hell," Morgen replied, hoping Rodney would take pity and cut him some slack.

"You look it. Two black eyes. A broken ankle."

"Two black eyes?"

"You should see the other guy."

"What other guy?" Morgen asked, fearing the worst.

"There is no other guy. I'm told it's not unusual when an airbag blows up in your face."

"Two black eyes?"

"You want a mirror?"

Morgan sighed, and shook his head, "No."

"The police will want to have words with you."

"Why?"

"How do I know? Maybe you're going to be sued for damage to the tree."

"Damage to the tree?"

"They said it was just a formality. You were tested, by the way. Lucky for you, drugs and alcohol were ruled out."

"They tested me for drugs?"

"It's one of the conditions in the rental contract. You totaled their car. In the event, if you'd tested positive, they could have sued you for damages."

The E.R. nurse reappeared, and announced the doctor was on his way. Morgen and Rodney both heard her, but engaged in conversation, failed to make an appropriate response to her announcement.

Morgen looked at the cast on his left leg, propped up on a pillow, and asked Rodney, "So, what's the damage?"

"You broke your ankle. The rest is mostly minor cuts and bruises," he replied.

The nurse interrupted, and repeated, sternly, "Doctor's on his way. He'll be able to tell you all about it."

"How long was I out?" Morgen asked, but the nurse only said, "Doctor will be along in a minute."

Answering Morgen, Rodney replied, "Eight or nine hours."

Morgen sank back into his pillow, and the nurse sternly told Rodney, "You're not being helpful. I really must insist you wait for doctor."

"Fine!" Rodney snapped, told Morgen he'd be waiting outside, and took the chair with him as he left the room. Alone and awake, Morgen struggled to make sense of the disruptions in his concepts of space and time. It didn't seem possible that it was only a dream, particularly since, as he tried to mentally retrace his steps, he heard the music again, and remembered the lyrics. Had he somehow crossed a threshold between objective reality and a subjective realm of fantasy? If so, what did that say about all the great thinkers and creative artists that came before; the inventors, philosophers, mathematicians, and physicists whose works had shaped his world?

And as he mused, a melody and lyrics came to him.

"Is it real, or just in my mind?
Is it all coincidence, or has it been designed?
There's something that's still missing,
And I still don't understand,
If it is some kind of magic,
Will it be mine to command?"

The music that placed him under its spell slowly began to fade, and all he knew for certain was that he had to record his impressions, the music, lyrics, and revelations of his mystical journey, before he forgot them.

The door to his private room opened and Rodney, chair in hand, reentered, saying, "I can't sit out there. There are reporters prowling the halls, and I haven't figured out how to play this."

"Tell them what happened," Morgen suggested.

"You mean tell them that Morgen is an irresponsible, inconsiderate shit who, rather than show up at a previously scheduled press conference held in his honor, chose to leave everybody hanging while he went joyriding in a rented sports car, that was obviously more than he could handle, and now the widely advertised, Beantown Home Cookin's First European Tour has to be canceled."

"I'm really sorry," Morgen said.

"Sorry?" Rodney snapped. "You're sorry?"

"I don't know what happened," Morgen confessed. "All I know is that I went elsewhere."

"Elsewhere?" Rodney yelled.

Morgen continued. "While I was there, I heard music and lyrics no one has ever heard before, at least not in this world."

"I can tell you where exactly where you went," Rodney bellowed, "You were about four miles from where you were supposed to be, slumped over the wheel of the sports car you wrapped around a tree, still wearing your safety belt . . ."

"Then it must have been an out-of-body experience."

"How would you know? You were unconscious, knocked cold by the exploding airbag."

"I heard music . . ." Morgen countered.

"I can believe that. I've seen it in the movies: a flock of tiny tweeting birdies flying around your head."

"You're not listening!" Morgen complained.

At that moment the E.R. nurse returned with the doctor, and hearing Morgen's angry complaint, pushed past the doctor into the room.

"Here, here!" the nurse said firmly, addressing her remarks to Morgen, "Whatever it is, it can wait! It's a miracle you're alive!"

"It's a miracle any of us are alive," Morgen said, falling back on his pillow.

"Am I interrupting?" the doctor asked, and when everyone fell silent, he took out his penlight, moved to Morgen's bedside, and raised one of Morgen's blackened eyelids.

"I'll just take a look, shall I?" the doctor asked.

CHAPTER ELEVEN

That same day, Rodney called everybody together and announced he'd be sending them all home first class on non-stop flights to Boston.

"I'll cover your per diem until your departure dates, but since I had to cancel all our performances, you're back on your contracted maintenance pay schedule, effective immediately."

Stateside, Maggie would take over payroll. A few asked if they could extend their stays. For most, it was their first trip abroad, and so close to Europe, it was an excellent opportunity to do some sightseeing. Rodney had already considered that.

"I've paid for first class, non-stop flights to Boston from Gatwick or Heathrow. The travel agency I chose will refund you any money you save if you choose a different return date or other-than-first class accommodations.

"If you choose to fly business class or coach, that's your call, but when you collect that difference from the travel agency, your per diem stops.

"You might consider booking a coach flight home and use the money you save for sightseeing, but you are all due to report to my place on the morning of the 15th, and this being the start of tourist season, I suggest, if you plan to stay a while, you book your flight to Boston ASAP, and be sure not to miss it!

"If you're not home and ready to get back to work on May 15th, you'll be in breach of contract, and subject to termination. Those are the best terms I can offer. Any questions?"

Rhoda, one of the Trashbabies, wanted to be on the first flight home. Her fiancé was getting his M.S. at M.I.T., and she wanted to be there. Rodney promised she'd be first in line.

As for the rest, the questions raised mostly had to do with flights home from destinations outside the U.K. Rodney allowed that they could originate anywhere in the world that the U.K. ticket price would cover the airfare, and furthermore, his arrangement with the travel agent included the travel agent recommending places to visit, both in the U.K. and on the continent, and booking their flights back to Boston, and told them all that he and Morgen were booked for a flight back to Boston, a little more than a week later, after Morgen's final checkup with the English doctor.

Morgen had to stay off his foot, and generally keep his ankle elevated, to which end he was issued a wheelchair, and Rodney hired a male nurse named Gerald to help him get around, and arranged for Alan, the A&R man, to send over a laptop, auxiliary sound system, and Officejet printer.

For Morgen, all the medical attention brought back tragic memories of his mother's last days. She'd been ill for some time, and Morgen knew she was slowing down, but didn't realize she was painfully slipping away. Her breast cancer had metastasized, spread to her lymph nodes and beyond, before it was discovered during a routine checkup. They operated and she endured an intensive course of chemotherapy that seemed to help, but the medical bills kept piling up. His father's retirement and her social security weren't enough to cover their expenses, and he'd sat with her when she refinanced the house that had been mortgage free since his father died, several years earlier.

The entire year after Morgen graduated from high school, he stayed by her side, cooking, cleaning, and looking after her, convinced that with the medical attention she was receiving, it was only a matter of time until she'd recover.

Some of his memories were unbearable, and he tried to turn his thoughts back to the good times they had together, when his Dad was alive, and when it was just him and his mother, but not since his mother's funeral, had he felt such an overwhelming sense of loss and loneliness.

Her insurance was barely enough to cover her burial beside his father. The unpaid medical bills were ruinous, he couldn't make the mortgage payments, so he had to sell the house, and it had to have a number of upgrades before it could go on the market, during which time, he was hit with capital gains taxes. Ultimately, when he turned it all over to an attorney, most of the bills were either paid or forgiven, but he was left virtually penniless, and that's when and why he joined the navy.

His happiest memories, and his most devastating, were both tied to his beloved adoptive parents, neither of whom were there to comfort him now, when he was feeling so foolish and downhearted. If Beantown Home Cookin' had been there for him, it might have been more bearable, but Rodney, who dutifully paid for his medical care and hired the male nurse who looked after him, was too busy, or too disappointed in him, to give him much time, so Morgen suffered through that most depressing first week of recovery. The music, mysteries, and memories of Morningstone were all he had to lift him out of the debilitating doldrums of despair.

Now, more than ever, he understood what George meant when he said that music was why he was put on Earth, why he was born with the gifts he had, and with each recaptured melody, his spirits rose—not enough to dispel the guilt he suffered for causing the cancellation of Beantown Home Cookin's European tour, but enough to give him some hope that good might come from it.

While Morgen busied himself by writing out the lyrics and transcribing the music, Rodney was putting out fires caused by the sudden cancellation of their summer European tour, and with considerable input from the distributor, was beginning to sketch out a new schedule for a fall tour.

At the end of that first week of uncomfortable readjustments, hard work, and self-imposed isolation, Rodney and the male nurse went to Morgen's room.

"Well, today's the big day," Rodney said.

"It sure is," Morgen said, saving his work and shutting down the laptop.

Gerald pushed Morgen's wheelchair to the elevator, and they all rode down to the hotel lobby.

A limousine was standing by outside. Gerald lifted Morgen out of his wheelchair, set him on the backseat, then placed the wheelchair in the boot. Rodney went around to the other side of the limousine, climbed in next to Morgen, Gerald climbed into the front passenger seat, and they left for the hospital.

Rodney and Gerald sat nearby, watching Morgen, sitting on a metal table his leg stretched out in front of him, as the orthopedic technician removed the cast with a cast saw.

"Do you want me to cut this any special way to try to preserve all these autographs?" the orderly asked.

"No," Morgen answered. "Let 'er rip."

"You're the boss," the smiling orderly answered, and added, "Don't worry. The saw won't cut you."

"I'm not worried," Morgen replied, "if the foot falls off, I'm already in the hospital."

The tiny buzz saw went to work, cutting right through all the signatures and well-wishes of the band, the Trashbabies, and a few other notables Morgen had met since the accident.

"Do you want to save these?" the technician asked, offering the two halves of the cast to Morgen.

"No, but I don't want to see them on eBay, either."

The technician gave them to Morgen, then explained he'd wash his leg, put a sock on it, and then apply the walking cast, but Morgen had to stay off it until it was completely dry.

"At least it's warm," Morgen commented.

"It's warm going on," the orderly explained, "but it can get cold fast as it dries out."

He then held what looked like a rubber heel against the bottom of the cast, fastened it around with rolls of hot plaster to hold it in place, and then added more plaster to the cast.

"I see what you mean," Morgen said. "It's already starting to cool down."

The doctor stuck his head inside the door. "You know to stay off it today?" he asked. "I've brought you these crutches. You won't need the wheelchair any more, but don't put any weight on that cast until the plaster's dried hard."

"I've never seen crutches like those before," Morgen said. "Do they come with an owner's manual?"

"As a matter of fact, they do!" the doctor replied, smiling as he handed Morgen a printout. "They're Ergoactive Ergobaum 7G Royal Ergonomic Forearm Crutches, the latest in comfort and support for the walking wounded, and they're adjustable."

"Can he take them on the plane?" Rodney asked.

The doctor had never been asked that before, and replied, "I don't see why not. People with crutches fly every day. I'm sure the airlines will know what to do."

He then shook Morgen's hand. "Have a good trip."

"Thank you, Doctor."

As the doctor was leaving the room, he paused in the doorway, turned and said to Morgen, "Drop in to see me when you come back. I'd like to see how you're coming along."

"Thanks, Doc," Morgen said, and the doctor left.

The technician finished applying plaster to the walker and told Morgen to sit for a minute, while he cleaned up, and he'd adjust the crutches for him.

May 9th, the day after the walking cast was put on, was Gerald's last day, and even with the new walker, Morgen was glad to have him around to help him get used to the crutches.

The walking cast was heavier than the first one, but now, no longer in the wheelchair, Morgen could sit more naturally at the desk, which was easier on his back. That same day, when Rodney called Alan to find out which carrier he trusted to have him send the laptop back to him, Alan said he'd send one of his people out to pick it up that afternoon. When Rodney told Morgen, he immediately began saving all the music files he'd created during the previous week, to multi-gigabyte USB files, and when he'd finished, downloaded his Brindled British Mastiff Screen saver.

Then, with everything packed except the things he'd need for tomorrow's flight, he really had nothing more to do until he and Rodney went out to dinner that evening, so he sat and talked to Gerald, who'd been a Royal Army Medical Corpsman, but that was old news by then. Instead, they talked about Beantown Home Cookin's first hit album, and traveling with the Trashbabies. Gerald left a few minutes before five in the afternoon, and still, the messenger hadn't arrived.

The conversation with Gerald had helped to pass the time, but Morgen was peeved that he'd lost so much work time. If he had known the messenger wouldn't get there until after five, he might have gotten in another four hours on the laptop.

That evening, he and Rodney dined well at a great Italian restaurant, enjoyed a fabulous lasagna and a surprisingly excellent chianti, but their conversation only dealt with the dinner, their plans for the following morning, meeting for breakfast, taking a cab to Heathrow, and their BOAC flight to Boston, boarding shortly before 11 a.m., and scheduled to arrive in Boston around 1:30 p.m. local time, giving them plenty of time to get home and settle in.

Home was Rodney's 5,000 square foot estate outside the city. When they met, more than three years earlier, Morgen had been renting an apartment in town, with little privacy, and neighbors constantly complaining about his late hours and loud music. Rodney, a successful stockbroker with a prestigious firm, quit to become Beantown Home Cookin's manager, and since Morgen was having trouble with his neighbors, said it only made sense that Morgen should move into a bedroom on his estate, and for the same rent he'd been paying for his apartment, he'd have no aggravation from neighbors. Rodney's house was on a large lot, with plenty of parking in front of its two-car garage, on its circular driveway, and later, on the driveway that extended to the soundproofed, mirror-walled carriage house dance studio Rodney had built for the Trashbabies. The Trashbabies were Rodney's idea, based on his happy childhood memories of watching TV's *Solid Gold Dancers*, and he made sure their studio had a fantastic sound system, showers, restrooms, lockers, and a relaxing lounge area, all inside the carriage house.

Maggie fielded all the calls to Rodney's home office, and they conducted business on the premises, but the main floor of Rodney's mini-mansion was a full ten feet above ground level, and the lower level, main floor, and second floor Master Suite were all served by a walk-through elevator to the right of the garage and left of the stairs to the main entry. With the growing popularity of Beantown Home Cookin', Rodney made alterations to the unused 1,260 square foot lower level where, even with its two-car garage, walk-through elevator and utility room, there was plenty of space for restrooms, a soundproofed band rehearsal studio, and fully equipped control booth for recording new songs and arrangements.

Rodney managed the business end brilliantly, and now, alterations in place, the house was home to Morgen, a welcome buffer between him and the outside world, allowing him to concentrate on his music and choreography with the Trashbabies. But, since his unfortunate escapade, Morgen and Rodney seemed to no longer share the same goals and dreams.

Morgen had apologized, and Rodney had officially accepted his apology, but their relationship had become strained.

Rodney insisted the empirical evidence proved Morgen had never gone anywhere after he wrecked the sports car, except to the hospital, and was openly hostile to Morgen's attempts to bring him into his fantasy world. Not knowing how to overcome the barrier between them, Morgen continued to quietly develop the material he'd discovered during his out-of-body adventure. If Rodney's assessment was true, Morgen reasoned, whatever music he "imagined" he'd heard, came from his subconscious, so unless he was plagiarizing something he'd heard earlier in life, forgotten, and was now dredging up from memory, it was all his creation, coming from a dream-state where copyright law didn't exist, and until such time as a genuine copyright proved otherwise, he registered them all as his original works.

On Monday, May 15th, as previously agreed, everyone gathered in the Grand Room at Rodney's estate. Maggie made sure everyone was comfortable, and Rodney appeared.

"I hope you all enjoyed your vacations," he said, "and I'm glad you've all made it back!"

Rhoda, one of the Trashbabies, announced, "I'm not back."

"How's that?" Rodney asked.

"I'm getting married," she said, her voice rising to a happy squeal at the end of her announcement.

There was a moment of silence, and then the Trashbabies all began screaming and squealing with delight, happy for one of their own. Rhoda went on to explain that she and her fiancé had put off getting married until after the European tour, but since it had been canceled, and her fiancé was getting his master's degree in Aerospace Engineering from M.I.T. at the end of the month, and he'd already taken a job in Portland, Oregon, they didn't want to put it off any longer.

"We're getting married in June, and moving to Oregon," Rhoda said, and pulling a stack of elegant wedding invitations from her handbag, continued, "and you're all invited! I'm announcing it now to give you plenty of time to replace me."

Rhoda would be missed, of course, and not easy to replace, but there was no arguing with her position. She and her fiancé had thought it through, so after hugs, Rhoda bid everybody farewell, and fled before everyone started to cry.

Rodney's gathering, intended to set rehearsal schedules to prepare for the recording sessions in the U.K., the fall European tour, and now including finding and breaking in a new singer-dancer to perform Rhoda's dance and vocal roles, had little effect on Morgen's schedule. On Mondays and Wednesdays, he'd work with the band, Tuesdays and Thursdays, since he wasn't up to working on choreography, he'd work with the Trashbabies on vocals, or check in to see how their choreography was coming along, and what they had planned for him, when he could start rehearsing again.

Fridays, he'd make himself available wherever he was needed. As far as he was concerned, weekends would be their own, at least for now, but they were all welcome to come in on their off days, if there were parts they needed to work on.

Morgen had a soft-cushioned stool brought to the band rehearsal room, and stood to sing and record his vocals, without putting weight on his left ankle, by placing his left knee on the stool. He did the same thing the next day, when he had the Trashbabies in to learn their new vocals to a rough mix of the songs he'd recorded with the band the day before.

Upstairs, Maggie, excited about Rhoda's wedding, suggested Rodney host a wedding shower for the couple, on the back lot of his property. Although they all had invitations, the cold reality was, if they showed up at her wedding, they would draw attention away from the bride on her most special day, and that would be awful, whereas, if they held a wedding shower, it would be an ideal way for Morgen, the band, the Trashbabies, Rodney (and Maggie, of course), to share in Rhoda's happiness, and who better to host it than Rodney?

Rodney appeared to be considering the idea, so Maggie explained that bridal showers were for the bride, her female friends and relatives, and a bachelor party, if there was to be one, would be thrown by the groom's friends, but a wedding shower would not only be appropriate for Rodney to host, but include both the bride's and the groom's families and friends, and if Rhoda so desired, could also provide Rhoda with a final performance with the Trashbabies, and maybe even feature her fiancé as the object of their "Witchy Stew." Rodney smiled as he imagined that scenario, so Maggie forged ahead.

"We could hire professional photographers to capture the event for Rhoda's Wedding Scrapbook, and the invitations could be designed like concert tickets that had to be shown at the door for admission!"

Rodney said he'd talk to everybody, but if they decided to go for it, Maggie would have to be the one to get all the permits and whatever else they'd need to do it, including a stage, concert lighting, P.A. system and crews.

It turned out everybody was thrilled with the idea, which didn't surprise Maggie. Knowing the Trashbabies were Rodney's pet project from the start, she'd been pretty sure when she made her pitch, but she was beyond ecstatic when Rhoda called to say she and her husband-to-be were honored and thrilled to accept Rodney's gracious offer, and couldn't wait to have the wedding shower at Rodney's rural estate. Was there a limit to the number of guests they could invite?

Maggie hadn't given that a thought, but quickly countered with "How many have you invited to the wedding?"

"A hundred and twenty to the wedding and reception,"

"With us, that would make it about 135, if everybody comes," Maggie said, thinking it over.

"Oh no," Rhoda blurted. "Not that many. I wouldn't invite the older cousins, aunts and uncles on either side. I'd say around a hundred, max."

"No problem," Maggie said. "I just wanted to be sure we weren't expecting the entire M.I.T. student body. What do you think of my idea of sending out flyers for invitations, and including concert tickets for admission?"

"We love it," Rhoda said, "and I'm looking forward to my final performance of 'Witchy Stew.' I can't wait to see how Warren will handle that!"

"I'll order the tickets and flyers as soon as we get off the phone," Maggie replied. "Send me your list, and I'll get the invitations out right away."

Rhoda emailed her list to Maggie before day's end, and that was that.

The upcoming wedding shower also seemed to thaw out the chill between Rodney and Morgen. Whenever they met over breakfast or supper, Rodney would start by talking about the fall tour arrangements, but inevitably, end up talking about the first marriage "in the family," and, caught up in staging the production, began to sound more and more like his old enthusiastic self.

The one hitch in Maggie's plan was that Rhoda's husband's new job was in Portland, Oregon, and they were planning to fly out right after the wedding, to set up housekeeping, which precluded gifts of antiques, furniture, appliances, or automobiles large or small. Cash would be most appreciated, because they wouldn't know what they needed until they got to Portland and found a place to live, but Rhoda had already made her choice of silverware and china known, so if either was chosen as a gift, the guests should check to see if the store where they were planning to place their order had a retail outlet in Portland, and arrange for the newlyweds to pick up their gifts there.

Maggie's list of stores began in Portland's Washington Square Mall, featuring JCPenney, Nordstrom, Macy's, Pier 1 Imports, and Pottery Barn, and concluded with a number of separate retail outlets including Bed, Bath and Beyond, Lowe's Home Improvement, Walmart, Home Depot and Target, all with stores in Greater Boston, too. It was too late to add all that to the wedding shower invitations, so Maggie typed up an addendum, and included it, folded, inside the flyer with the tickets.

Meanwhile, the Trashbabies held auditions, and the most promising candidates were invited to return on Friday for Morgen to listen to them sing parts in songs from Beantown Home Cookin's first album. Rodney tried to drop in on as many of the Trashbabies auditions as he could, but deferred to the ladies on their choices for who would go to the second round.

Trish, the newest candidate, was an accomplished and talented dancer, but had never sung professionally, and at her vocal audition, her intonation was great, but she lacked vocal presence, so Morgen had her come back on Saturday, to decide whether to keep her or let her go, and she must have known it, because after trying to sing her parts to his satisfaction, just about the time he thought she wouldn't be able to handle the vocals, she asked if she could try something different. He consented, and to his amazement, her voice suddenly had both power and confidence.

"Was that better?" she asked.

"Where and why," Morgen asked, "have you been hiding that voice?"

"I was trying to fit in with the other Trashbabies," she nervously replied, "because when I was young, I was thrown out of the church choir for singing too loud, and calling more attention to myself, than to the words in the hymn."

"I'm not a choir master, Trish," Morgen said, "and the Trashbabies are no choir. I have to know what you can do, so I can put you where you'll do us all the most good. I want you up on that stage with us, shining like the star you are!"

"Yes, sir," she replied, looking happily dewy-eyed.

"On Tuesday, at rehearsal, what are you going to do?"

"I'm going to sing my ass off!" Trish shouted.

At Tuesday's rehearsal Morgen then played his demo recording of "The Fool" for the Trashbabies for the first time, and was surprised by some of their reactions.

"You've read *The White Goddess!*" Alice exclaimed.

"I don't think so," Morgen replied.

"*The Historical Grammar of Poetic Myth,*" Alice embellished.

"Nope. What made you think I had?" Morgen asked.

"It's *The Battle of the Trees,* It's *Taliesin.*"

Sylvia joined in, saying, "I've read it. Alice is right. 'The Fool' sure sounds like some of the early Welsh poetry Graves explored in his book."

"Who?" Morgen asked.

"Robert Graves," Sylvia and Alice said, almost in unison.

"Sounds like something I should read," Morgen said.

"I found it difficult to understand," Sylvia said.

"Morgen won't," Alice promised. "He'll probably get more out of it than any of us."

"I don't know about that," Morgen said, "but 'The Fool' you just heard, I transcribed word for word, and note for note, exactly as it was in my so-called fantasy adventure."

Theresa, one of the quieter Trashbabies, said, "Then maybe it will show your adventure was never a fantasy, but a genuine mystical experience."

"Have you read it, too?" Sylvia asked.

"I've seen it," Theresa replied.

131

"I'll get you a copy, Morgen!" Alice exclaimed. "I'd really like to talk to you about it after you read it."

"Well now, I have to read it, don't I?" Morgen said.

"Would the library have it?" Trish asked.

"It might," Sylvia answered. "I've seen it in bookstores."

"Where have you seen a bookstore?" Sophie asked.

Morgen raised his voice enough to get their attention. "Ladies," he said, "Can we discuss this later? You've got your parts. Shall we listen one more time before we try to sing it?"

Poppy, the lovely Asian-American Trashbaby pleaded, "At least one more time, please."

Fully engaged, the Trashbabies' rehearsal went surprisingly well, especially the tricky parts, where Morgen had deliberately dropped a beat, or where the Trashbabies had to anticipate and come in before the chord change.

Fortunately, he'd worked it all out with the band during the demo recording, and the Trashbabies had little trouble with any of it. At their Thursday rehearsal, Alice presented Morgen with a hard-bound copy of Graves' book. That weekend, Morgen read it, reread the early Welsh poetry in translation that validated the forms he'd transcribed in "The Fool," and in gratitude, wrote a report he titled *The Fool's Mystery Revealed*, written in the style of Robert Graves' book, which he copied and presented to the Trashbabies at their next Tuesday session, warning them, jokingly, that there'd be a quiz at Thursday's session.

CHAPTER TWELVE

At first glance, Morgen's comprehensive report, composed in the same style as Graves' *Historical Grammar of Poetic Myth,* was almost as daunting as Graves' original *White Goddess,* but considerably less so when one realized it only dealt with

Morgen's song, "The Fool," and copies of it, originally only intended for the Trashbabies, were later distributed to the band, some were eventually leaked to the media, and some, signed by Morgen, even became collectibles.

THE FOOL'S MYSTERY REVEALED

In *The White Goddess*, Robert Graves suggests *The Song of Amergin* is an ancient Celtic calendar-alphabet summarizing the prime poetic myth, an incantation claimed to be made by the chief bard of the Milesians as they landed in Ireland around 1268 B.C., which makes me suspect it was a charm against hostile natives, cast according to an ancient formula by which the bard subsumed all the elements, seasons, and letters by which anyone could ever name any such elements or seasons, unto himself, and if nothing was omitted, gave him invincible armor against hostile conjuring. *Saint Patrick's Lorica* is a better-known example, in which the saint ascribes creation to the Almighty and invokes Christ as his armor.

In *The Romance of Taliesin*, the 13th century poet Little Gwion, challenged by the college of royal bards, presented his credentials in verse. "Primary chief bard am I to Elphin," he began, and listed an impressive catalog of the "I am, I was, I know and I shall be" variety, similar to verses I wrote for "The Fool," also a credential song, couched in apparent nonsense, but clear enough for those who know the formula. Like Little Gwion, I have no degree from an institution of higher education, but I've learned a lot in my adventures and independent studies. My understanding is often unique, because I have not been exposed to the potential for institutionalized error, but that also means I have no one to blame for my errors but myself. My reading of *The White Goddess* suggests "The Fool," on the surface little more than clever nonsense, is in fact his arcane résumé.

"I am Truth! I am Reason! I am Magic!
Harmony of the carnal and the mystical, I am Man!"

In the intro, the Fool claims he embodies Truth, Reason, and Magic, and then goes on to claim he represents all humanity. This is not simple hubris. If he is to expiate humanity's crimes against Nature, he must represent all humanity. But is he enlightened, or merely a fool? What are his credentials?

"I lived in a cave for a year and a day.

Fathered by a sun-ray."

The cave is the womb of the Earth. The 'year and a day' refers to an ancient calendar of 13 months (lunar cycles), of 28 days, yielding 364 days, one day short of a solar cycle, to accommodate which, a day had to be added to bring it up to the full 365. That day was dedicated to the Lord of Misrule, "The Fool." This line establishes "The Fool" as born on Earth, where these cycles exist, and is clearly a reference to Earth Mother, suggesting "The Fool," despite his subsequent claim to immortality, is a mortal, possibly annual Fool, rather than a perennial one, which, in ancient times, might have had tragic consequences for this 'king for a day.' His clearly stated lineage reveals him to be born of Sky Father and Earth Mother, godling, maybe, but Earthling, definitely.

"Once I was a bull. Now I can't say.

You'll have to find your own way."

Zeus was a bull when he carried off Europa.

"I was once an eagle, strong and free.

His claim to have been an eagle brings Zeus back to mind, for it was in this guise that the father of the gods carried off Ganymede to be his cup-bearer, and his following claim of shape-shifting ability also suggests the Olympian association.

There's nothing that I can't be."

"Once, I was a word. Now, I'm a key."

Here, "The Fool" may be invoking the Gospel according to John. 'In the beginning was the Word, and the Word was with God, and the Word was God.' "The Fool" is not so great a fool as to claim to be God, so there must be more to his riddle.

In fact, a reexamination of the Bull and Eagle references, coupled with his claim to be Man, presents us with three symbols for the Four Apostles typically found on the tympanum of the west portal of Gothic cathedrals, depicting Judgment Day, showing Christ enthroned, surrounded by Matthew, the Man; Mark, the Bull; and John, the Eagle; but Luke, the Lion is missing, and John has been cited twice, both as the eagle, and by his Gospel of the Word. But "The Fool" is also a key in the Major Arcana of Tarot decks, to which I turned to discover where Luke was hiding.

In the Major Arcana, "The Fool" is depicted as a youth at the beginning of his journey, an old man nearing its end, or a jester, depending on the deck, but the card is more a clue to discovering the answer, than the answer. In fact, there is a card in the Major Arcana, variously titled "Force" or "Strength," depicted variously by a Hercules overcoming a lion by brute force or as conceived by Arthur Edward Waite in his popular, *Rider Tarot Deck*, depicted by a woman, garlanded with flowers, taming the lion through love, and displaying the cosmic symbol for infinity or eternal life above her head, by which I understand she is a manifestation of the goddess, perhaps, with her garlands of flowers, the Queen of the May.

Rider Tarot Deck, first published in 1910, may not be the original source of that image. It may have evolved from an earlier deck that suggested Waite's card, but the message the key in the Waite deck conveys is that we must learn to create a balance between our spiritual and carnal natures. And therein I found the answer to the riddle. In the intro, "The Fool" claimed to embody harmony of the carnal and the mystical.

"You'll have to learn to trust me."

Or not. That's entirely up to you. I'm not completely sure I trust myself.

"Chief Bard of the ancients am I,
Anointed in the sacred pool.
My ancestral home is the Sacred Grove.
Honor your mentor, *The Fool!*"

This chorus seems to owe much to Gwion's Riddle and suggests that "The Fool" may be using the formula used by Gwion before him, Saint Patrick before Gwion, and Amergin before either of them, by which he intends to subsume all the mysteries unto himself, even as he claimed to embody Truth, Reason and Magic, in order to establish himself as the authentic representative of humanity.

"I've been around the universe several times."

The Roman god, Mercury, is an excellent candidate. He invented the original 13 consonant alphabet after watching a flock of cranes in flight. When I wrote of the *Song of Amergin*, I submitted that subsuming all the letters of the alphabet that might form spells or names of power, afforded magical protection against the unknown demons of the opposition. Invoking this god, with his early alphabet that contained the names of the thirteen months of the ancient lunar calendar, secures protection for all the days of the year, except for the one day that already belongs to the fool, the day dedicated to the Lord of Misrule.

"Wine flows from my grapevines."

The orgiastic mysteries of Dionysus are well known, as is his association with wine and grapevines. The Latin *"In vino veritas,"* is now generally understood to mean if someone is drunk enough, he or she will tell you anything you want to know.

"I've taught your musicians. I've taught your mimes.

Poets learn from my rhymes."

Apollo claimed to be the god of mimes, musicians and poets, but before his ascendancy, these gifts were in the care of the Muses. If "The Fool" is indeed a chief bard, it is his responsibility to teach those skills to future generations.

"At home on land, in sea or sky,

When I pass the trees sigh."

To be at home on land, in sea or sky, is not just another use of the mystical number three. In fact, "The Fool" claims the three states of matter—solid, liquid and gas.

That this is one correct understanding of the line is made clear by the reference to fire making the trees sigh. This phrase does not refer to a wildfire. Fire is often used symbolically to connote inspiration, and the letters of the Beth-Luis-Nion alphabet correspond to tree names, so the line may refer to the ordering of these letters into verse, the principal task of an enlightened bard.

"You knew me before. Well, I never did die.

I merely transmogrify!"

All these mysteries, once widely known, were forgotten, but never perished, and are still found throughout the world under a variety of names and disguises.

"Chief Bard to Immortals am I.

O'er fantastic realms do I rule.

There's none to whom I need bend my knee.

Honor your leader, *The Fool!*"

Therefore, I suggest "The Fool" is the poet-priest of the immortals, ruling over fantastic realms—literally realms of fantasy, which is to say his rule is imaginary. He serves the gods and goddesses who populate those magic realms, but does not kneel before them.

It is he who orders their days through his compositions. He is honored by them, and they, by him, in the works in which he portrays them. There is also reference here to a worldly privilege once accorded a Fool, who served a king or nobleman, that he need not kneel before his lord.

"Multiple mysteries to me are known."

From the earlier examples, it is clear that "The Fool" is acquainted with many mysteries.

"Everywhere the wind's blown."

Graves might argue "The Fool" is invoking Cardea, the goddess who, until the classical period, controlled the winds. In January, she was known to her followers as *Postvorta* and *Antevorta*, 'she who looks both back and forward.'

In my song, "Sweet Mystery," she's Janu, not so much for her January ritual as her two-faced attribute, thus reclaiming it from Janus, the two-faced god who stole it from her.

"Revealed thus in monotonous drone.

Lord of the Standing Stone."

Referring to the song as a monotonous drone is a deliberate bit of foolery, by which the self-deprecating Fool intends to disguise the true meaning of his song, and especially his claim to be Lord of the Standing Stone, referring to the *menhir*, the monolith venerated in "The Fool's" stead, until he takes his rightful place in the spring ritual.

"I am a rock in a stormy sea.

Goddesses have loved me."

The rock in the stormy sea is "The Fool," himself, unswerving in his devotion. This would be true, even if the stormy sea was to wear the rock away to nothing, perhaps one of the reasons the Muses love 'The Fool,' and always will.

"Some would protect me by royal decree.

Others would revile me."

"Although New Year's revelries persist into this age, the Feast of Fools is no more, the royal protection, like most of the royalty who offered it, gone. No longer The Lord of Misrule, 'The Fool' today, is merely reviled."

"Chief Bard of the ancients am I.

Wit is my singular tool.

Beloved am I of the Ninefold Muse,

And still, you call me *The Fool*?"

"Neither god, nor king, nor sorcerer, the enchanter survives
by his wits alone, in a world that has little respect for his gifts."

Rodney worked day and night, because of the six-hour time difference between Western Europe and New England, and although concert venues were approached and referred to Rodney by the distributor, he was still responsible for making the necessary reservations for lodging, travel, and per diem. To date, the schedule called for the tour to start in November and run through the first two weeks of December, which would get everybody back home in time for the Christmas holidays, but also meant they'd have to be in England to record their second album immediately after the Fourth of July, to allow time to record, mix, and manufacture the album, due for release in September, prior to their fall tour.

Maggie took care of the invitations, tickets, wish lists, permits and hiring all the contractors needed to setup the wedding shower.

Morgen stayed busy polishing his lyrics and arrangements, and recording demos of the music from his out-of-body experience, ending up with three solid rockers, "The Fool," "Peeping Tom," and "Sweet Mystery," an adaptation he composed of the song the choir sang at his interrupted otherworldly nuptials. He notated and arranged the procession and dance he called "In This Place," based on the Morningstone choir's a cappella vocal introduction to it, beginning with the slow march, and ending in a frenzied, sensual dance, as a showcase for the Trashbabies. And Morgen had two new ballads, too. Laura's haunting "Morningstone," and "The Likes of You," the love song he co-created with and for Laura.

When Beantown Home Cookin' learned Morgen had written an interpretation of the lyrics to "The Fool," they wanted copies, which Morgen happily provided. With that interpretation in hand, the guys didn't feel the need to read Graves as much as the ladies had, but Jeff, one of the three keyboard players, an honors graduate with a degree in English Literature from Tufts, and only a year to go at Berklee, if he hadn't quit to join George's band, told everyone that Morgen's out-of-body experience fit the profile of the hero's journey in Joseph Campbell's *Hero with a Thousand Faces*, a book exploring the similarities of heroic protagonists in myth, folklore and religion, and discovered in dreams by contemporary depth psychology, with the result that a definable single archetype emerged. Few in the band were familiar with it, but some had heard of it, and when they started talking about Morgen's adventure in those terms, a new discussion of his out-of-body experience emerged.

To aid in his explanation of how Morgen fit Campbell's archetype, Jeff drew a diagram of a circle, dissected by a horizontal line he labeled, "threshold," that sent Morgen's memory rocketing back to The Owl pub.

"Put 'enlightenment' below the line, and 'hero' above the line," Morgen said. Jeff smiled and said, "You've read it."

"I've seen it before," Morgen replied. "Now put 'conscious' above the line, and 'unconscious' below."

Jeff wrote in the labels, as Morgen continued.

"Double the line above the one you've labeled threshold," Morgen said. "It isn't so much a line as a liminal zone between the two, sometimes narrower, sometimes wider."

"That's different," Jeff remarked. "It makes the space below larger than the space above."

"As it should be, based on my personal experience."

Frank, the bass player interrupted, saying, "I have a question. If I remember correctly, the hero's journey was always undertaken by some kind of misfit, an unhappy loser, or someone whose happiness has been ruined by an unexpected tragedy. That doesn't sound much like you, Morgen."

"Well, I was exhausted. We all were," Morgen said, "but with a choice between a media inquisition, or a spin in a shiny new getaway car . . ."

George, an unabashed fan of Morgen's said, "I read Campbell's book, and I've been convinced from the start that your story of your out-of-body experience is authentic. I can lend you my copy."

"There goes the weekend," Morgen lamented.

"You'll love it," George insisted.

"It's not required reading, is it?" Emery asked.

"Not for me, it isn't," Owen said. "If Graves says it's so, that's good enough for me."

Morgen had gone through Graves' book, cover to cover, reading and rereading sections of particular interest, and was impressed with Graves' chapter on Dog, Roebuck, and Lapwing, creatures that appeared in his out-of-body adventure before he learned their significance in bardic myth and poetry. Was the white stag he saw standing in the small clearing shortly before he approached the bridge over the Stream of Consciousness a roebuck? According to Graves, it meant "hide the secret," so whenever it appeared, there was a mythological secret hidden in what came next.

Had Morgen known its significance, he would have known he was entering the supernatural realm of myth and folklore, especially when, moments later, dog appeared, in the form of the huge mastiff.

Dog's bardic meaning was "guard the secret." Dog, the mastiff, guarded the threshold, independent of the Furies, and dog closely examined Morgen, and let him cross, and in so doing, may have prevented the Furies from taking any hostile action against him. Much later, when lapwing appeared, it was dog that called attention to it.

On Friday, June 9th, crews began working shortly after dawn at the back of the house, setting up for Rhoda's wedding shower on Saturday, but it was also the day Morgen's walking cast was to be removed, and he was ready to go, sitting at his computer that displayed the daunting stare of a Brindled English Mastiff, when he heard footsteps, grabbed his crutches and opened the door just as Rodney knocked.

"Well, today's another big day," Rodney said.

"I can't wait to get out of this thing," Morgen replied.

"I'll get the elevator," Rodney said, and went ahead to press the call button. Already on the first floor, the doors opened immediately and they entered. Rodney pushed the LL (lower level), button, the doors shut and the elevator descended accompanied by a strange, faint buzzing sound.

"Excited?"

"I'm getting there," Morgen replied.

The buzzing sound grew a bit louder on the road to the hospital in a hired limousine, but was loudest as the orthopedic technician at Boston's renown Mass General Hospital finished cutting Morgen's cast, and the cast parted.

The technician gently washed Morgen's foot, ankle and calf muscles, as Morgen began jerkily turning his foot this way and that. The youngish orthopedic specialist watching told him not to worry about the jerkiness.

"You've been in a cast for weeks," he said, "and your muscles have atrophied. I'll be giving you some exercises to do to rebuild them. Does it hurt to move it?"

"No," Morgen replied.

"Let me see," the doctor said, and scooted his wheeled stool over to where Morgen sat on the edge of the stainless-steel table.

"Just relax. I'm going to manipulate your ankle. You tell me if it hurts," he said, and began.

When Morgen offered no response to any of the doctor's manipulations, he asked, "How does that feel?"

"A little stiff."

"That's normal. No pain?"

"Not really."

"How long before he can go back to work?" Rodney asked.

"Doing rock and roll shows?" the doctor asked.

"We're supposed to go back to England to cut a new album next month," Rodney answered.

"That's really up to him," the doctor answered. "Will you be sitting or standing?" he asked Morgen.

"He'll be in a booth," Rodney answered.

"Excuse me, Doc," Morgen said, as he stepped down from the table onto his good foot. The doctor jumped up off his stool to steady Morgen and Morgen pulled the doctor's stool closer, stood erect on his good foot, and his left knee kneeling on the stool.

"How's this?" Morgen asked.

"That stool has wheels!" the doctor chided. "Are you trying to break your neck?"

"I've been rehearsing and recording the whole time I had the walker cast on, and this is how I did it." Morgen answered.

"Then, you already have your answer," the doctor said.

"I guess the question really is, how soon before I can start rehearsing with the dancers?"

"We'll probably know by the time you have to leave for England," the doctor said. "I'm going to schedule you for regular physical therapy in one of our facilities . . ."

"No Doc," Rodney interrupted. "He'll be recognized, especially around here."

"Our professional staff treats all kinds of people, including international celebrities. We have a no photos on the premises policy . . ."

"He can't exercise in any public facility," Rodney injected.

"I can't be held responsible for his recovery if it's not supervised by one of our therapists," the doctor said.

"You're not responsible," Rodney said. "If you need me to sign a release, I'll be happy to do that, and if you can recommend a therapist who will come to the estate to supervise his recovery, you'll be kept informed of his progress, and we'll be happy to pay you for consultation."

"I'm sorry, sir, but Morgen will have to sign the release, himself," the doctor said.

"I'll sign it," Morgen said.

"Well, you need specialized equipment, a weight machine, a whirlpool bath . . ."

"Write me a list. I'll rent it, and have it installed by tomorrow," Rodney said.

"I'm not sure the equipment is rentable, especially not on such short notice," the flustered doctor explained.

"Then I'll buy it!" Rodney said firmly, and turned to the astonished orthopedic technician, who was holding the two halves of Morgen's autographed walking cast. "Are those for me?" Rodney asked politely.

The technician handed the cast halves to him.

"Thank you," Rodney said, and winked at him. "We wouldn't want to see them showing up on eBay, would we?"

"No, sir!" the technician replied.

The flushed doctor, not used to being bullied, resented Rodney's attitude, but unsure of the support or lack of it he might encounter if the situation went any further, said, as he exited the room, "If you wait in the waiting room, I'll try to put together a list of qualified therapists who might do house calls, and a list of equipment and exercises, but I want to see him back here in three weeks."

"Three weeks!" Rodney confirmed. "Friday, June 30th!"

"Sooner," the doctor shouted, "if he starts having pain!"

"You got it, Doc!" Rodney yelled back as the door swung shut on the retreating doctor.

CHAPTER THIRTEEN

Forty minutes later, Morgen and his crutches were still waiting in the back seat of the limousine when Rodney came out of the hospital, with an adjustable-length cane, grinning happily, and waving a sheaf of papers.

Rodney climbed into the limo, and ordered the driver to take them home. Morgen said nothing, waiting for Rodney to tell him why he was so smug. Grinning, Rodney glanced at Morgen, said nothing, and looked away. Finally, proud of his achievements, Rodney informed Morgen, "The equipment will arrive today, and I've got resumes of four recommended physical therapists we can interview, so how's that?"

"Great!" Morgen replied, still weighing Rodney's tour-de-force performance with the youngish doctor, who was definitely out of his league.

"It is, isn't it?" Rodney said gleefully.

"You don't like doctors much, do you?"

"They have their place. Sometimes, you just have to remind them where it is."

"The wedding shower is tomorrow," Morgen said.

"You think I don't know that?"

"You're going to have a bunch of installers over to set up equipment during the party?" Morgen asked.

"Just the whirlpool guy, and he promised to be out of there by noon. As for the rest, we can look it over on Sunday."

On the way home from the hospital, for several minutes they rode in silence, but kept sneaking looks at each other, Morgen grinning as he replayed Rodney's dialogue with the doctor in his mind, and Rodney enjoying Morgen's smile and the admiration he saw on Morgen's face. With Rodney in such a good, receptive mood, Morgen decided it was time to try again to talk to Rodney about his out-of-body experience and the new music it inspired, but not wishing to spoil the mood by approaching it head-on, opened the conversation with a rhetorical question.

"The question was, 'What do the characters represent?' " he said.

"What question?" Rodney asked.

"The question put to the class," Morgen continued, "and what followed was all about what the characters represented. I can't help but wonder if it was all staged for my benefit."

"We're discussing your fantasy?"

"My experience."

"When you were unconscious," Rodney remarked, smiling indulgently, equally trying to avoid spoiling the mood.

"Or maybe when I was exploring the unconscious."

"Are we talking about *the* unconscious, or *your* unconscious?"

"They may be one and the same. Either way, I think I've unraveled the mystery of the dog."

"The Mystery of the Dog," Rodney echoed. "That has a nice ring to it. Sort of like *The Hound of the Baskervilles.*

"Do you want to hear it or not?"

"I'm all ears," Rodney replied, still smiling like his old self.

"Thousand years ago," Morgen began, "dogs were as wild as their cousins, the wolves, predators, hunting in packs, and like humans, following the animal herds that made up most of their diet until, somewhere along the way, canines and humans discovered that they hunted better together."

"Stands to reason," Rodney said.

Morgen continued, "That early, mutual interdependence resulted in the domestic dogs of today, selectively bred for behavioral traits most desired by humans in their canine companions – guard dogs, hunters, war dogs, and pets."

"True," Rodney agreed.

"But when I first saw that monster mastiff emerge from the Rhododendrons, I thought it was with the Goths, the three

145

ladies I later learned represented the Furies, goddesses whose mission is to defend Nature against human abuse, and it was a genuinely terrifying animal."

"Big, huh?"

"Huge! Well, the second time I saw it, was during another confrontation with those same Furies, but I've been thinking about the details. When its bark startled me, it was standing on the liminal side of the Stream of Consciousness . . ."

"An actual stream, like a river?"

"That's what the locals called it, and the dog was on the opposite side from the Furies, so it might as easily have been barking at them as at me."

"Why would it do that, if it was their dog?"

"Exactly!" Morgen said excitedly, "I assumed it was with the Furies, until I got this . . . flash of insight. One of the three bardic symbols, signifying that what's to come is not necessarily of this world, but belongs to the otherworld, is the dog, and its hidden meaning is 'guard the secret,' and if Furies are guardians of that supernatural threshold, so is the dog!

"Cerberus, the hound of hell, was the three-headed dog that guarded the entrance to the underworld, preventing the dead from escaping back to the land of the living."

"Three heads?"

"Three heads. And the ancient Egyptians had Anubis, the Jackal God of death and the afterlife, guardian of that mythical threshold."

"You're losing me," Rodney said, shaking his head as if it was all too difficult to follow.

"That's just some historical, mythical background for what I now believe was really going on," Morgen said."

"While you were unconscious."

"All that's important is I now believe the dog, standing on the liminal side of the stream, may have been protecting me from the Furies.

'When I think of it now, the first time I saw it, it walked up, looked me in the face, and let me pass. That second time, when the Furies seemed bent on mayhem, it might be that the dog thwarted them!"

"Thwarted them?"

"Yes, and after, when I told it to go away, it did."

"Lucky for you."

"The dog and I cautiously became friends, and by the third time the Furies confronted me, the dog was by my side, and led me past them into the Tomb of Every Hope, the deepest, darkest test of my out-of-body adventure, where I represented humanity, and was put on trial for crimes against Nature."

"Some friend."

"It gets better!" Morgen said.

"It better get better soon," Rodney warned, losing patience.

"Inside the Tomb of Every Hope, the Furies finally launched their attack, but with the dog by my side, they failed.

"When the earth opened up, revealing a molten, fiery pit below, I grabbed the rock wall with both hands and held on to keep from falling in, but when I saw the dog sliding toward that hellish pit, I grabbed him by the scruff of his neck held on until the Fates pulled the Furies' thread from their tapestry, the earth closed over their fiery pit, and we both survived."

"I think I've heard enough," Rodney said, and turned away.

"The second Fury froze us both, but again, the Fates intervened, because that final solution for humanity would have destroyed all the rest of Nature's living creatures, too."

"And all they really wanted was for you to give it a rest."

"Maybe they only intervened to save the dog, but I was spared too, and with me, all humanity."

"So, you saved the dog, the dog saved you, and together, you saved the world! Sounds like a comic book."

Morgen continued, ignoring Rodney's sarcasm. "If the first Fury represented fire, and the second represented ice, the third, most cunning and dangerous of all, suggested a plague, specific to humanity, that other creatures spared whose lives were lived obedient to Nature's law."

"Nature's law? What's that? Survival of the fittest? Kill or be killed? I wonder if the prey considers itself obedient to Nature's law, or does the law of the jungle just apply to the hunter-killers?"

"By befriending Man, Dog is doomed to share our destiny."

Rodney yelled, "If you want a dog, just say so!"

Morgen sighed, and stared out his side window, and neither spoke to the other again, all the way back to the estate. As they rode up on the elevator, Rodney said, "I expect I'll see you at supper?"

"I expect so," Morgen answered.

In fact, dismayed by Rodney's refusal to credit any part of what he called Morgen's fantasy adventure, Morgen crawled into bed to think, for the first time in six weeks without a plaster anchor pinning him down. Before long he dozed off, slept through to the early morning hours, and missed supper altogether.

It was nearly five-thirty Saturday morning when Morgen rose. He'd been lying in bed, awake, for more than an hour, thinking about the challenges ahead, and Rodney's hostility toward Morgen's version of events was definitely a problem.

Rodney had been working steadily on arranging their fall tour, but seemed more concerned about Rhoda's wedding shower than the album they were scheduled to record, before the tour, which was especially troubling. Morgen had been in regular contact with Alan, the record company's A&R man in the U.K., keeping him up to date on the new concept album he'd been developing with the band and the Trashbabies, ever since the accident. He'd sent Alan demos of the new songs via email, and Alan had emailed back that the company expressed interest in Morgen's new, timely concept, and would consider shelving the previously approved album for the time being. But in all the time he'd been composing, arranging, and making demo recordings of the new songs, he hadn't told Rodney about it, because of his hostility to Morgen's version of the events that inspired it.

For Rodney's part, pulling together the fall European tour, even with the record distributor's help, was no easy task. Many of the venues booked for the summer tour, already had commitments for the days Rodney hoped to book for fall, and when the original venues couldn't fit them into their schedules, Rodney's plan B was to seek a deal with an alternate venue in the same general area, to try to keep all the logistical elements; hotels, travel, and per diem, on track.

Some alternative venues offered better deals than the others, no doubt based on the success of the internationally televised concert and attendant publicity following Morgen's accident, but others tried to take advantage of the late booking in their area, hoping to increase their profit margin at the tour's expense. And Rodney could not forget that it was Morgen's unprofessional conduct at the very start of the canceled summer tour, that created this mess in the first place.

One day, they'd have to tackle the issues head on, but after yesterday's confrontation, Morgen decided some things he'd admired in Rodney, may turn out to be negative attributes.

Rodney had been a successful stockbroker with a major firm, but had a keen interest in the musical end of show business–not the Broadway variety, but the marriage of music and dance he'd loved as a kid, watching *Solid Gold* on TV, and when Beantown Home Cookin' began capturing Entertainment Section articles in *The Boston Globe* and *The Boston Herald*, Rodney went to one of their concerts, where Morgen's original songs and theatrical stage presence floored him. After the show, he chased Morgen down, and they talked until dawn about what Rodney wanted to do for the band, and what he thought Morgen and the band could become, backed by his money, connections, and business acumen. Rodney's pitch was that he had both the wherewithal and the drive that could take them right to the top, especially if they had the *Solid Gold Dancers* on the same bill with them, and true to his word and his vision, a few months later, the Trashbabies were formed.

Saturday morning, with no cast on his foot, Morgen showered, shaved, dressed, and for the first time, walking with his new, adjustable cane, noisily clicked his way to the kitchen. The coffeepot was set to go, so Morgen plugged it in, put two pieces of dark rye in the pop-up toaster, fetched the butter dish from the refrigerator, a luncheon plate and coffee mug from the cupboard, a butter knife and spoon from the flatware drawer, pulled a chair over from the breakfast nook, and stood by with his left knee resting on the seat of the chair, waiting for his toast, while the coffeepot gurgled and dripped. When his toast popped, he buttered it, placed it on the luncheon plate, and with his free hand proudly carried it to the table in the breakfast nook.

He'd finished his toast by the time the coffeepot stopped dripping. He put his dish in the sink on his way to the coffeepot, poured himself a cup, added a spoon of sugar to it, took the creamer from the fridge, added some to his coffee, stirred it with his spoon and returning the creamer to the fridge.

He carried his hot cup of coffee to the breakfast nook, and drank it slowly, with great satisfaction. If that seems like *Much Ado About Nothing*, it was the first time in six weeks, Morgen, with his noisy new cane, had one hand free to carry anything from one place to another, and he felt empowered by accomplishing all the simple tasks on his own.

Maggie arrived in the kitchen at 6:38 a.m., laden down with shopping bags, surprised to see Morgen up and sitting alone.

"You're up!" she said as she put down her bags.

"So are you," he replied. "Are you doing the catering?"

"Me? Are you kidding? I came in early because the workers will be here around seven to finish setting up, and to let your therapist in. I don't suppose Rodney's up, is he?"

"He hasn't come down yet."

"You made coffee yourself?" Maggie asked.

"Yes. It was a challenge, but I saw the plug, and the cord reached the outlet, so I decided to risk it."

"You are feeling better today, aren't you?"

"You're looking at a man who not only plugged in a coffeepot, but buttered his own toast," Morgen boasted.

"Good," Maggie said, "No doubt your physical therapist will be impressed."

"Physical therapist?"

"Rodney interviewed a number of them over the phone yesterday, and one is coming this morning to get you started."

"That was quick," Morgen remarked.

"Well, you know Rodney," Maggie said. "The guy will be here this morning to install the whirlpool. Too bad, you missed the 'Witchy Stew' rehearsal!"

"I know the song and I'll be singing it from the wings."

"All I'm saying is Rhoda's last performance, as a Trashbaby, will be Trish's first . . . and Rhoda's fiancé is a hunk."

"Uh-huh," Morgen said, wondering what she wasn't saying.

"Now, about that whirlpool," Maggie said, "I don't suppose you'd be willing to share it from time to time."

"Is it big enough for two?"

"I meant when you're not using it," Maggie clarified.

"Oh," Morgen said, his voice filled with disappointment. "That's not so much sharing as loaning out."

"Well?"

"I don't expect to use it more than twice a day, and then for no more than 30 minutes at a time, so I suppose we could work something out," he replied with a smile.

The doorbell rang. Morgen's physical therapist, Marcel Aucoin, had arrived.

The garrulous therapist with a strong, French Acadian New England accent, told Morgen, within the first five minutes, about being from an Acadian family, expelled from the Maritime provinces of Canada during the French and Indian War, between 1755-1763, and after resettling in Massachusetts, a few years later, joined the rebel forces and fought against the British in the American War of Independence, making all the ladies of his line eligible to join the Daughters of the American Revolution, a matter of some pride to him.

Morgen noticed that the way he'd phrased his introduction, he didn't really expect anyone to comment on it, and never said any of his female relatives ever joined the D.A.R., but none of that diminished his historical references.

Morgen's therapy session didn't involve any of the unassembled exercise equipment. All it required was a high-backed chair and a sandbag, which Marcel brought with him. The chair served three functions. Morgen sat, holding up his left leg and trying to rotate his ankle in slow, smooth circles, which, in Morgen's case, proved to be a series of jerks, that Marcel promised would one day become slow, smooth circles. It gave Morgen something to cling to while he went up and down on tiptoe, several more times than was comfortable, and then, ankle all warmed up, he sat on it with his left ankle wrapped with the sandbag, adding weight to his foot as he raised and lowered it over and over.

To Morgen's chagrin, it turned out to be quite an intense workout, the best part being when Marcel helped him onto the platform over the hot, churning water of the tall whirlpool tub. When his calf, ankle and foot were fully cooked, Marcel helped him down, dried his leg, complimented him on how well he did in his first session, and promised to come back to continue torturing him on Monday.

By noon, the stage, lighting and sound crews had left. Morgen went out to see what they'd done and was surprised to see the stage with only two steps up across the front of it.

"What do you think?" Rodney asked proudly.

"I think the stage invites guests to swarm all over it."

"That's the general idea," Rodney said. "It's not a stage. It's the dance floor."

"Oh. In that case, it's brilliant."

"Did you see the menu?" Rodney asked, as he handed one to Morgen. It was on heavy white card stock, with embossed gold lettering, definitely intended to be considered a souvenir.

ARRIVAL CANAPÉS
Cold - Spiced Swiss Cheese Straws
Warm – Goat Cheese, Pesto and Tomato Crostini

BEVERAGES
J Vinyards Cuvee 20 Brut, California
J Vinyards Sparkling Rose, California
Still and Sparkling Mineral Water
Elderberry Cordial
Limeflower Cordial
Fresh Orange Juice
Assorted Soft Drinks

DINNER
Leg of Lamb roasted pink with Piperade, Basil Oil and deep fried Basil Leaves
Grilled Aubergine with leaf Spinach
Potatoes Puréed with Lemon scented Olive Oil

VEGETARIAN OPTIONS
Wild Mushroom Strudel and fresh Herbs in a rich Tomato Sauce
Aubergine Cannelloni

DESSERT
Apple Crisps with scoops of Blackberry Sorbet and fresh clotted Cream
Coffee and Assorted Chocolates

DINNER WINES
White – Marlborough Estate Reserve Sauvignon Blanc, New Zealand
Red – Yellow Tail Cabernet Merlot, Australia

Knowing very little about wine, Morgen assumed the wine list was impressive, but had to ask Rodney what Aubergine was.

"Eggplant."

"Eggplant?"

"Eggplant."

"Then why don't they call it eggplant?"

"Because they're notoriously expensive caterers," Rodney answered, "and how much can you charge for eggplant?"

"When do the guests arrive?" Morgen asked.

"It starts at 3:30 p.m. and it has to end promptly at 10:00 p.m., according to the permits."

"And what is it now, 12:00, 12:30?"

"It's lunchtime," Rodney said with a smile. "C'mon. Let's get something to eat, my treat. And I'm driving."

"Subway?" Morgen asked.

"Sounds good to me," Rodney said, and they took the elevator down to the garage and climbed into Rodney's Tesla Model S.

Rodney hardly ever drove, and since he'd gotten his Tesla, Morgen had only been in it twice, both times to go to lunch at the local Subway, but being in that car also served to remind him how much his current and future success depended at least as much on Rodney's financial backing and management, as on his own talent, and their good-natured camaraderie today, was welcome, but didn't quite erase the memory of Rodney's irascible attitude of the day before.

Rodney didn't bring it up, so Morgen didn't either. Lunch was simply lunch, tasty and satisfying to both, and when they'd finished, they went back to the Tesla, and started back toward the house.

"Too bad you missed the rehearsal," Rodney said on the way back, and for an instant, Morgen thought the axe was about to fall.

"You didn't get to meet Warren, Rhoda's fiancé," Rodney continued, "He's sharp, good-natured, and it goes without saying, he's a brain. Of course, he and Rhoda are nuts about each other, but for all that gray matter, he's not a bit stuffy, as you'll see, when you see their grand finale."

"We're still doing 'Witchy Stew,' aren't we?"

"Yeah, but Warren's in the show," Rodney said,

"I'll have it taped and keep the copyright and the master, but give them an edited show to play at their wedding reception."

"We're still doing it live, right?" Morgen asked.

"You bet!"

CHAPTER FOURTEEN

Back at the estate, the caterers took over the kitchen and back yard, but left the patio, with its breathtakingly beautiful wisteria-covered pergola, now in full bloom, untouched except for adding an extension to the built-in wet bar, which would, no doubt, be manned during the event. Four rows of tables with white tablecloths, white and gold cushioned, steel folding chairs, and high, white and gold canvas overheads, were set up on the back lawn, all cleverly arranged to provide unobstructed views of the dance floor.

The wedding shower was a huge success. The gift table had some gift wrapped items, but for the most part, the guests had followed instructions and deposited their gift cards in a "treasure chest" set on the table for that purpose. Everything the caterers did, from the food they prepared, to the wines they'd selected, was superbly memorable, which definitely made the menus collectibles, and for Massachusetts, in mid-June, the weather was less muggy than usual, and the uninvited mosquitos and flies either stayed away, or were quickly dispatched by cleverly placed, insect-killing electronics.

The Trashbabies were popular dance partners for the guys from M.I.T. who hadn't brought dates, but the guests, male or female, who did bring dates, were more interested in getting autographs, than worrying about competition. Of course, all the pre-recorded music was by Beantown Home Cookin', but everyone knew who put on the shower, and the music elicited nothing but support for the host. Sunset arrived at 8:20, and by 8:30, the Trashbabies began making excuses to go to the carriage house to change out of their party dresses and into the wardrobe for the finale. Trish, sitting by Rhoda and Warren, begged Rhoda to help with her costume, and Rhoda, a good sport, accompanied Trish to the carriage house to lend a hand.

Of course, it was part of the show, arranged to give Rhoda a chance to change into her new, white, gold-laced bustier, white panties, and white stockings with golden garters, over which she put on a tear-away dress that, to a casual observer, matched the one she'd been wearing. Warren had waited patiently, but appeared overjoyed when Rhoda returned.

The band's stage had been erected behind the dance floor. Sliding doors at the back of the dance floor hid the raised platform on which the band equipment had been set up and tested, into which Beantown Home Cookin', began plugging their guitar and keyboard cables, switching on amplifiers, "accidentally" drawing everyone's attention to the dance floor area, making it easier for the cloaked Trashbabies, now in their stage costumes, to get from the carriage house to the backstage areas on both sides of the raised band platform.

At last, the center doors parted, revealing Beantown Home Cookin', eliciting shouts of delight from the guests, but as Beantown Home Cookin' began to play the intro to "Witchy Stew," Rhoda pointed frantically at something left on the floor below the front of the raised band platform, and sent Warren to fetch what appeared to be an errant article of clothing that might distract and spoil the video recording.

Warren, knowing the piece was being recorded, crouching low to avoid appearing in the shot, scampered onto the dance floor and hurried to the front of the band stage, concentrating on the shiny, crumpled white robe. At the same time, Morgen stepped onto the stage, microphone in his left hand, cane in his right, and a still louder roar from the crowd as the costumed Trashbabies strutted from the wings onto the dance floor posing provocatively, displaying all the wiles and guile Morgen's lyrics described, effectively cutting off any attempt Warren might have made to get back to his dismayed fiancée.

"Look at their hair. The things they wear.

Oh, the things they do."

Rhoda watched in dismay as Morgen's vocal continued, and her hapless beloved, cut off from returning to his bride-to-be, displayed the shiny white *Million Dollar Baby* satin bathrobe he'd recovered.

"Designed to please, they strut and tease,

And brew their *Witchy Stew*."

One by one, as each Trashbaby sang her verse, they turned to confront their accuser, Morgen, and in so doing, pretended to discover Warren, trespassing on their dance floor, making him their object and target of choice.

"High heels. Short skirt. I'm dressed to flirt!

Does this look all right?

I want to dance! Always a chance,

Tonight, may be the night."

Suddenly, they turned sharply, challenging Rhoda's guests.

"Yeah!"

Then, turning their attention back to Warren, the Trashbabies advanced like cats purring for their dinners, carrying tiny battery powered electric candles to illuminate their charms, trapping Warren at the back of the stage, where they caressed his cheek, ran their fingers through his hair, felt his muscles, and rubbed their bodies against his, all of which made

Warren appear terribly uncomfortable, especially with Rhoda watching. Too late for Warren, Morgen sang his warning.

"They hide their guile behind a smile.

They'll put a spell on you.

Late at night, by candlelight,

They're cookin' *Witchy Stew*."

His next line was supported by waves of loud sighs from the Trashbabies as they cast their spells, aggressively competing for Warren's attention. His distressed expressions conveying his need for rescue and understanding from his betrothed, were well done, intended for audience consumption, as Morgen finished singing part one.

"A woman dare not be so fair and not be wicked, too."

A short instrumental turnaround set up the next set of verses, during which the Trashbabies refreshed their intimidating arsenals by touching up their lipstick, mascara, and perfume, for their next barrage of spells intended to finally overcome Warren's resistance to their "Witchy Stew," and Morgen, acting as if Warren was no longer anything but an object lesson to all young men, continued his song.

"Lip gloss and scent, mascara meant

To set a snare for you.

All you see is in their recipe

For makin' *Witchy Stew*."

Flirting outrageously, posing provocatively, and with one Trashbaby even pulling down the zipper on her red brocade vest to briefly reveal her ample cleavage before she zipped it back up, the Trashbabies sang their verses, not only catching everyone's attention (including Warren's), but apparently infuriating Rhoda to the extent that she stood up and approached the dance floor, while the Trashbabies mercilessly continued teasing Warren.

"A little show just lets you know

I'm here to have some fun.

If you see a lot of me,
What harm has been done, huh?"

As Morgen sang the next lines, Rhoda stepped onto the dance floor, glaring at the Trashbabies, and with a quick, violent pull, threw open her Velcro fastened gown, shrugged it from her shoulders, and clad only in high heels, white stockings with golden garters, shiny, white satin panties and a strapless, white brocade bustier with gold ribbons, marched across the dance floor to rescue her intended.

"They hide their guile behind a smile.
They'll put a spell on you.
Late at night, by candlelight,
They're cookin' *Witchy Stew*."

Her guests were variously shocked, scandalized, or delighted, according to their proclivities, and as Morgen sang the last line, with her left hand extended to block away the Trashbabies on the left, and her right palm up extended to block away the Trashbabies on her right, Rhoda sashayed up to Warren, nervously clutching the white satin robe, grabbed him by his belt, and as the Trashbabies fled into the wings, marched him back across the dance floor.

"Women dare not be so fair and not be wicked, too."

Beantown Home Cookin' continued to play, letting the audio engineer fade the music tracks, and as the music stopped, Rhoda, nearing the front of the dance floor, made a very deep (and revealing), curtsy of appreciation to her audience, which snapped Warren out of his trance. He quickly covered her with the white satin *Million Dollar Baby* robe, scooped up her break-away gown, and escorted her to the carriage house, ignoring calls for an encore. The sliding doors closed over Morgen and the band, and Rodney sprinted out onto the dance floor, and with a hand-held radio mike, addressed the guests.

"I'm sorry folks," he said. "That was the finale, Rhoda's last appearance as a Trashbaby. But what a way to go, huh?

"Our permit says we have to knock off at ten o'clock, so this is the last call for the open bar, but Beantown Home Cookin' and the Trashbabies, when they put some clothes on, will be here to sign autographs for you until lights out. I want to personally thank you all for coming and making this happy event all the more wonderful by your presence."

Not long after, the wedding shower was over. Autographs were signed on the backs of menus and embossed table napkins, the camera crews packed up and left, and by 10:16 p.m. all the guests had departed in good spirits.

Morgen was exhausted, and went to bed as the caterers quickly and efficiently packed up all their paraphernalia, linens, tableware, tables and chairs rented for that night, and were gone before 11:00 p.m., followed by Maggie, who made sure the house was secured, and finally, Rodney took the elevator up to his master suite and retired for the night.

Everyone had Sunday off to relax and recuperate, but Monday they were all back to business as usual, except for Rodney, who left early to go into Boston to supervise editing the "Witchy Stew" footage and didn't get home until a few minutes after eleven that night, when, apart from Morgen, who'd already gone to bed, Rodney was alone in the house. He considered waking Morgen to show him the two different versions of the "Witchy Stew" performance: one, a DVD for the newlyweds to screen at their wedding reception, and the other, a DVD with Youtube potential, but decided since he'd been looking at it all day, he'd go to bed, instead.

The next morning, when Rodney came down for breakfast, Maggie was already in, and had been fielding calls from Europe, and the U.K., getting numbers where Rodney could call them back after regular business hours, if need be, and both she and Rodney worked the phones, email and fax machines until noon, when Rodney invited Maggie to go to lunch with him.

On their way to the garage, Rodney saw that Morgen had the band and the Trashbabies hard at work in the recording studio and excused himself to go back up and get the DVDs he'd made the day before. When he returned to the garage, Maggie was still patiently waiting by the elevator.

"Now we go to lunch," Rodney said and led Maggie to his parked Tesla. "We're going in that?" she asked, brightly.

"We are," he answered, "and you get to pick the restaurant."

"Chinese?" she ventured.

"Chinese!" he agreed, opening Maggie's door for her. And she was more than a little excited, knowing this would tie her with Morgen for rides in the Tesla.

At the restaurant, she ordered Vegetable Chop Suey, and Rodney ordered Pork Fried Rice, Sweet and Sour Pork, and a pot of Oolong tea. She shared some of her Chop Suey, and he shared some of his Fried Rice and Sweet and Sour Pork, which made it an entirely enjoyable luncheon. Rodney was seldom so relaxed and when he was in an especially good mood, he could be genuinely charming.

On the way back, she asked, "When we get back, shall I run up and check on the phones?"

"The phones can wait," Rodney said, flashing her a boyish grin. "I want you to see these DVDs, and especially, I want you to see the looks on their faces when they see them!"

As it turned out, when they returned the Tesla to its special lower level parking space, they could see that the band and the Trashbabies were all still in the recording studio.

Grinning, Rodney said, "This'll blow their socks off!"

The red light by the door that signaled they were recording was not on, so they walked right in.

"Hi, gang! Is everybody here?" Rodney asked, but before anyone could answer, Morgen entered from the control booth.

"Ah, Morgen! Just in time. I've got something you'll all want to see!"

"And you're just in time to hear the new song we've been working on," Morgen said.

"Great!" Rodney said, "but I want to screen these two DVDs first. One is for the newlywed's reception, and the other I had cut for Youtube, should we decide to go that way."

The idea of putting it up on Youtube was new, and everyone wanted to see how they looked in the show, so Morgen didn't mind putting his playback on hold to see how "Witchy Stew" came out. They watched the one edited for the reception first, cut to feature the betrothed, telling the story the way Rhoda and Warren wanted it told, looking like it was all ad libbed, when in fact, it was all rehearsed, including Rhoda's deep curtsy, and Warren's covering her with the Million Dollar Baby robe, and all agreed it was sure to be a hit at their reception. The Youtube version, kept the same highlights, but in shorter cuts, allowing for more coverage of Beantown Home Cookin', and highlights of the Trashbabies' antics. Both were showcase edits, although the one for the reception featured more potentially embarrassing moments, exactly the sort of spicy video wedding guests expected, along with embarrassing baby photos, at contemporary wedding receptions.

The surprise was the ready-for-primetime Youtube video, almost certain to run up huge numbers of viewers within minutes of being posted, if the newlyweds agreed that it could be released. Rodney said he'd never release it without their permission, but if everybody considered it as a "Witchy Stew" music video, featuring Rhoda's historic last show as a Trashbaby, and Trish's first, he thought they'd probably agree. The gang loved it, some suggesting that if they weren't allowed to put it online, they should hire actors and re-shoot it. In all, it was every bit as big a hit with them as Rodney had thought it would be, and he enjoyed basking in the praise heaped upon him for the production and editing.

"You said you had a new song for us to hear," Rodney said.

"We do," Morgen answered, as excited about his new song as he was about the "Witchy Stew" videos.

"It's called 'Flying Snakes'," Morgen said as he disappeared back into the control booth.

"Flying Snakes?" Rodney repeated, wondering what kind of song would be called "Flying Snakes."

"You're going to love it," Alice said, and Morgen's voice came in over the studio speakers, "Quiet please."

Everyone fell silent, and the introduction began with growling synthesizer effects. Then a piano entered, outlining the melody to come, and repeated more powerfully with the addition of drums and rhythm guitar, setting up the beginning of Morgen's double-tracked demo vocal harmony.

"I've seen snakes fly, trees cry, and holy men lie!"

Morgen sang the song, but when it came to the release, in addition to his double tracked harmony, the band and the Trashbabies both came in.

"Your after-life is groovy. I've seen it in a movie . . .
Yeah!"

Rodney had never seemed to be particularly religious, but when he heard everybody sing that line, it took him completely out of the song, and afterward, he couldn't comment on any of its other lyrics, because he didn't hear them. Maggie was obviously all right with it, the band and the Trashbabies were all smiling happily, enjoying their latest efforts, but Rodney thought it would be offensive, and said so.

"Your afterlife is groovy? I've seen it in a movie? Really?" he sputtered. "Are you deliberately trying to offend people of faith?"

Everyone looked equally bewildered by Rodney's reaction.

"Maggie?" Rodney prodded, "What do you say?"

"I didn't really find it offensive," she replied. It made me think of the movie, *A Life Less Ordinary*."

"It put me in mind of *Ghost*." George volunteered.

"Ricky Gervais in *Ghost Town*," Linda said.

"*Passengers*," said Poppy, her eyes wide open.

"Well if you're going to get serious," Grant said, "What about Clint Eastwood's *Hereafter*, with Matt Damon."

"*It's a Wonderful Life*, with Jimmy Stewart," Trish said.

"Or Alistair Sim and Jack Warner in *A Christmas Carol*," Theresa offered.

"I guess the point is . . ." Morgen began.

"My favorite is *Topper Returns*," Sophie interjected.

"The point is, we've all seen the afterlife in movies . . ." Morgen began, again.

"Or *Heaven Can Wait*, with Warren Beatty," offered Maggie, and looking at Rodney continued, "We both enjoyed that one."

"Okay, so everyone's good with it," Rodney said. "But I want to hear what Alan has to say."

"He loves it," Morgen said. "He said it fit right in with our Save the Environment, theme."

"You played it for Alan, before you played it for me?" Rodney asked.

"He said we needed more material to bring the record up to album length," Morgen said."

"I thought the album was already approved as it stood?"

"The earlier one was," Morgen replied, "but we've been working on a new one, a more timely concept album, especially now that everyone is talking about climate change."

"And what makes you think that will fly with the label?"

"They're already on board," Morgen replied. "I've been running it all by Alan, right from the start."

"You've been running it by Alan and never told me?"

Morgen replied, "We've been communicating through email. I've been sending him the demos as we recorded them, and he's been running them past the powers that be."

"Has he?" Rodney snapped angrily. "And when were you going to tell me?"

"I tried, but you were busy, and never wanted to discuss any music I brought back from my out-of-body adventure, much of which is featured in the new album, but if you'd like to hear the songs we've been submitting, I'll be happy to play them all for you."

George, one of the keyboard players interrupted. "Excuse me. Before you do that, can we go to lunch, now?"

"All right with me," Morgen answered.

"Go to lunch," Rodney said, suppressing his sense of betrayal, "I should be able to hear all the new material in what –an hour–hour and a half, long enough to form an opinion. How about everyone meeting back here at three o'clock?"

Morgen answered, "Three o'clock will be fine."

A few, on the way out, repeated the time by which they were to report back, but all were eager to be elsewhere, if Rodney and Morgen were about to get into an argument. Now that the issue had come to a head, it did seem odd that Rodney had never said anything about the new material and their progress so far, but they knew he'd been working hard to set up the Fall tour, arrangements for Rhoda's wedding shower, and if they'd given it any thought at all, had concluded he simply hadn't had the time to discuss their new direction.

"Maggie," Rodney said, "You stay. I know you'll want to hear the new material, too, and I want to hear your opinion."

Maggie was on the spot. She did want to hear the new material, but knew Rodney invited her to stay so she would be a witness, if the playback, resulted in a major blow-up.

"What about the phones?"

"You turned on the answering machine when we went to lunch, didn't you?"

"Yes, of course," Maggie said, and obediently took a seat facing the studio playback speakers.

"It will save time," Morgen said, "if I stay in the control room and set up the next track while you listen to the one playing. We can communicate through the talkback between songs, and you can let me know if you're ready for me to play the next one, or if you need to take some notes."

Morgen played them all the demos of the songs Morgen had first heard in Morningstone, and Rodney had Morgen pause while he dictated notes to Maggie between songs, and when he'd heard them all, Rodney asked Morgen if he would put them all onto a flash drive, so he could review them, along with his notes, and they could talk about them tomorrow. Having anticipated Rodney's request, Morgen had copied all the files as he played them, and brought the flash drive out to the studio and handed it to Rodney.

"So, what do you think, so far?" Morgen asked.

Suppressing his sense of betrayal, Rodney smiled, not unpleasantly, and replied, "You've given me a lot to consider, and I might need to listen to some of them again, before I can make up my mind, but as you know, each song has to stand on its own merit, and before I say anything about what I've just heard for the first time, if you don't mind, I'd like to talk to Alan, and hear what he has to say about them, but I'll definitely get back to you by this time, tomorrow."

"Fair enough," Morgen said, noting that it was nearly three o'clock, and relieved that Rodney hadn't thrown a fit. "We'll take it from there."

"You haven't had lunch, yet, have you," Maggie said, holding out a brown paper bag to Morgen. "I've got a doggie bag of leftover Chinese you can heat up in the microwave."

"Wow! Thanks, Maggie. I'm starving."

"It's delicious," Maggie promised.

"C'mon, Maggie," Rodney said, "We've got our work cut out for us."

"Go ahead," Morgen said. "I'll shut all this down."

Rodney and Maggie took the elevator up. Morgen went into the control room, shut down the systems, then called the elevator down to take him up to the kitchen, where he heated the Chinese food, and dined alone. It was about five after three when George, still the bandleader of Beantown Home Cookin', took the elevator up to the first floor and found Morgen in the kitchen.

"I brought you back some pizza," George said. "Pepperoni."

"Thanks, but I've just finished Maggie's Chinese."

"In that case, we can share it," George said with a big grin, and sat down at the breakfast table with Morgen.

"Looks good," Morgen said, taking a slice of the still warm pizza. "Is everybody back, yet?"

"We're all back," George said. "How'd we do?"

"The verdict is still out," Morgen answered, "but he didn't explode, so I hope that's a sign he's willing to consider it. He wants to talk to Alan, before he talks to me, but I think that works in our favor."

"Some of us talked at lunch," George said. "You should know we're all on board. Some of the Trashbabies were surprised that Rodney didn't know about it, but all of them appreciate that your new songs feature them more. But I'd keep in mind that they're Rodney's creations, so I really don't know if they'll all throw in with us if it comes to a showdown between you and Rodney."

Alice came into the kitchen and announced, "Everybody's waiting for you."

George scooped up the last slice of pizza and all three of them went to the elevator. Inside the recording studio, everyone was waiting anxiously, but all Morgen could do was give them the same "verdict is still out" report, tell them to carry on, and that they'd know as soon as he did, probably tomorrow, with the result that more than a few of them had trouble sleeping that night.

CHAPTER FIFTEEN

Breakfast was cordial enough. Rodney said he'd listened to the new songs several times, and compiled a list of notes they could go over together, in the studio, if Morgen preferred. Morgen agreed that would be fine, asked who else would be attending, and was told no one else. Rodney's notes were confidential, intended for Morgen alone, but if Morgen then decided to share them with the band and the Trashbabies, he was at liberty to do so. Morgen thought meeting in the studio control booth would be best, because if issues arose, they could go directly to the material in question. When both had finished their breakfast, Rodney excused himself to fetch his notes, and politely took the stairs to his master suite on the top level, so that Morgen could take the elevator down to the lower level, and turn on the sound system.

In little more than the time it took for the elevator to go up to the master suite and back down to the lower level, Rodney arrived in the control room, notes in hand.

"All set?" Rodney asked.

"All set," Morgen confirmed.

"First," Rodney began, "the music is unusual, especially coming from a rock group, but generally I liked what I heard. It demanded attention to get into it, but it also sounded better each time I played it, and had the kind of appeal I've heard in sixties music, made more for listening, than for dancing.

"That said, I don't know how well it will fit into the modern popular genre we've been working, and I found some of the lyrics . . . make that a lot of the lyrical references, not only obscure, but enigmatic."

Morgen managed a thoughtful sounding "hmm," but Rodney had more to say.

"Generalities aren't really much help," Rodney continued, "so let's concentrate on the ones I found most problematic."

"Please, Morgen replied.

"All right, starting with 'Morningstone'," Rodney said, consulting his notes. "The melody and the harmonies were strange to my ears, but each time through, it grew more compelling. You don't sing on this one. You leave that to the Trashbabies, which I'm sure made it a hit with them, and I get that the song is an invitation, but by whom and to what? Is it an invitation to your fantasy? What mysteries, what destiny are you planning to reveal, and who are the seekers with whom you hope to share it? Are you the key, and if so, where does the path you provide lead? What destiny are you predicting? If it is you and your dream, you're inviting everyone to explore . . ."

"Whoa," Morgen interrupted. "That's a lot of questions. Give me a chance to answer them."

Rodney lowered his eyes and yielded the floor to Morgen.

Morgen began, " 'Morningstone' is one of the songs I remembered entirely from what you insist is my fantasy, but I wasn't offering the invitation. It was being offered to me, and although I didn't realize it then, obviously I accepted it."

"Yeah, I saw the bump on your head," Rodney interrupted.

Morgen said without emotion, "May I continue?"

"By all means," Rodney said.

"I found myself in unfamiliar territory," Morgen continued, "a fabled land of myth and mystery, quite beyond my comprehension, but before my journey ended, everything I needed to know was revealed to me, and although at first it was more than a little obscure, it became clearer as it unfolded, and each mystery was revealed."

"Like the Mystery of the Dog," Rodney quipped, smiling indulgently.

"Exactly like the Mystery of the Dog, and all leading to our legacy and ultimate destiny, which is why I had the Trashbabies sing it, instead of me, because I was the seeker to whom it was addressed, and only now, having experienced it for myself, am I able to introduce it to others."

Rodney sighed. "And now you're going to save the world."

"I don't pretend to have the power to save the world," Morgen replied, "but I don't believe anybody or anything is likely to suddenly appear and do it for us. I believe that unless we start interacting responsibly with our environment, failure to do so will doom us all. That's the message of my 'otherworldly' adventure."

"Got it," Rodney replied, "Moving right along, since it's way too long for radio play, what's with 'In This Place'?"

"It's a dance showcase for the Trashbabies."

"And the record company is fine with that?"

"They like it, and it's a showcase for the band, too."

"And a showcase that will require a local hire orchestra."

"We can play it without one," Morgen said, "not necessarily for the recording, but we won't need an orchestra for concerts."

Rodney said. "Let's move on to 'Peeping Tom.' It's gutsy, powerful, and edgy, as they say, but it's offensive, too, and I think you should reconsider its lyrics."

"It's an honest rocker, one of the strongest in the album, and the Trashbabies didn't seem to find it offensive."

"Did you ask them?"

"It never came up," Morgen replied.

"Right," Rodney observed, "and moving right along, I'm still concerned about 'Flying Snakes'."

"Really?"

"Yes," Rodney replied. "When you sing 'I do believe you're clever, bound to live forever,' you're mocking belief in the promise of life after death."

"I'm not mocking anyone's religious belief. I'm simply suggesting that if 'God helps those who help themselves,' only good can come of it if we behave appropriately in the face of an environmental crisis from which, if a benevolent supernatural being fails to appear and fix everything with a word or a gesture, humanity will suffer dire consequences," Morgen replied. "If it takes a shock to motivate humanity to act in its own best interest, I say, let this song be that shock."

"I get it. I even agree with it, but I have concerns."

"Rodney," Morgen replied, "Alan and the record company's powers that be, the band, the Trashbabies, and I all agree. It's a rational musical approach to a genuine crisis."

"I don't deny it," Rodney agreed, "but I have reservations."

"Reservations duly noted," Morgen said.

"Thank you," Rodney said. "Please tell Linda I want to see what they're planning to do for 'In This Place'."

The Trashbabies had all thumbed through *The White Goddess*, including Cassie, the gorgeous African-American Trashbaby, who found the title off-putting, but along with the rest, understood Morgen's related interpretation of "The Fool," but "In This Place" was another matter.

Linda, the Trashbabies' choreographer, was their *ipso facto* leader. They'd been playing back "In This Place" and trying out Broadway-style, showcase routines, but nothing had really come together, and when Morgen told them Rodney wanted to see how "In This Place" was coming along, Linda, exasperated, complained to Morgen, in front of the entire troupe, "I get that there's a procession, and it devolves into a wild and exhausting *Le Sacre du printemps*, but we're not exactly a ballet company, so if you have any ideas about where this should go, now's a good a time to share."

Before Morgen could respond, Jasmine exclaimed, "Excuse me, Linda, but you said it! Sacred music. A spring ritual."

Linda asked, "What do you have in mind?"

"Nataraja Shiva is perhaps the most familiar representation of the Hindu god, Shiva, performing his cosmic dance that both creates and destroys the universe. He is also the lord of dance and the dramatic arts, frequently propitiated by dancers.

171

"You've probably all seen him depicted in bronze statuettes, dancing wildly in a torch-lit circle," Jasmine said, striking the statuette's famous pose.

"I know the one you mean," Trish said.

"So do I!" Sophie added, "My grandmother had one on her mantlepiece, but I never knew who or what it was until now."

"I'll bring one with me tomorrow," Jasmine promised.

"This isn't India, Jasmine," Linda said, "and I'm not totally unfamiliar with Shiva, but I don't think American audiences are ready for it."

"But it should do quite well with English audiences, and that's where we'll be recording and introducing it, before we ever bring it here," Jasmine countered, "because Spring festivals are universal, and the music to 'In This Place' would come with us, wherever we go in the world, and if we each wore something that ethnically reflected our heritage, the 'In This Place' procession should have strong international appeal."

"What about the dance?" Linda asked.

"The way I see it," Jasmine replied, "the wild energy the dance requires will be exhausting, and since 'In This Place' is a showcase for all of us, and we are nine, I see eight of us in a circle, representing the flaming torches around Shiva." Jasmine began to move sensually, conveying the movement of a flaming torch.

"The ninth will begin Shiva's wild dance, in the center of the circle, and before she is exhausted, the next dancer in line will replace the Shiva dancer.

"The first Shiva will then return to the outer circle, and become a dancing torch. That way we will each have our Shiva showcase moment, until the finale. For that, I'm thinking that as we sing 'If they see, with their eyes closed,' we may all sink slowly to the floor as the curtain closes . . . or the stage lights dim, depending on the venue."

172

"You'll have to show me the moves you have in mind," Linda said.

"I'd be honored to do so," Jasmine replied, with a sparkling smile.

"When shall I tell Rodney, you'll be ready to do a run-through for him," Morgen asked, blown away by the concept.

Linda smiled back at Jasmine and replied, "Tell him we'll have it ready for him to see before you leave for England."

But for all the smiles, a residue of palpable tension between Morgen and Rodney remained, even as all the songs and choreography came together.

On Thursday, two days before Rhoda's wedding. Morgen and Rodney jointly announced everyone would get the weekend off, which gave the Trashbabies time to get their hair done, and aware that wedding receptions sometimes run rather late, were given all day Sunday to recover. The Maids of Honor were all relatives of the bride and groom, so the Trashbabies would only be guests at the reception, but they'd also be seen with the bride and groom in the wedding shower video, so Rodney and Maggie also planned to attend the reception. The band considered attending, too, but rather than be a distraction, decided on a day or two down on the Cape.

Their general plan was to prowl the beaches and, with luck, meet some romantically inclined beach bunnies, so when Roger, driving his seven-passenger van, spotted six attractive young ladies playing beach volleyball in their bikinis, he sped into the closest parking space. Morgen was with George in George's car, and by the time they found a parking space, they had a bit of a hike to get back to the others, who had the coolers, drinks, blankets, towels, sandwiches, and snacks with them in Roger's van. George, eldest of them all, and a bit overweight, didn't mind staying with Morgen as they slowly made their way back to Roger's van, where the guys were playing beach volleyball against the beach babes.

Leaving the parking lot, George and Morgen walked out onto the beach to claim a place near the refreshments, where they could watch the action, but Morgen hadn't gone more than a dozen steps into the shifting sand before the pain in his ankle became intolerable, and he stopped in his tracks. George, walking beside him, immediately saw that he was in trouble.

"What happened?" he asked. "Did you twist your ankle?"

"No, but it hurts like hell. I can't walk in this sand."

"Hey guys!" George shouted, and Grant, about to serve, paused, seeing Morgen was in trouble. Roger and Frank, drummer and bass player, the other two "originals," so called because they had been with George since the beginning, left their side of the net to come to Morgen's aid.

"Is it the ankle?" Roger called.

"I just can't handle the sand," Morgen replied.

"Do you need help?" Frank asked?

"No," Morgen said, "I'll be fine when I get out of the sand."

"Go back," George added. "I can handle this."

"What are you going to do?" Frank asked.

"While you guys are getting sunburns, we're going to find a cool, air-conditioned theater and spend some time with *Wonder Woman*!" George boasted.

"You sure?" Roger asked.

George yelled back, "Go on! The team is waiting on you."

As George helped Morgen out of the sand and back onto the asphalt parking lot, Morgen smiled through his agony.

"I love it. An afternoon with *Wonder Woman*!"

"I can't see either of us playing beach volleyball?"

"You got a point," Morgen answered.

"Wait here," George said. "I'll get the car."

George and Morgen worked up Morgen's songs together, back when Beantown Home Cookin' had played Top 40 and old favorites, until Morgen began writing original songs, and reactions to their new playlist began getting write-ups in the papers. In those three years, they'd become close friends.

About six months and more than a dozen new songs later, Morgen and George met Rodney when he came to hear Beantown Home Cookin' in a concert sponsored by a M.I.T. fraternity. After the show, Rodney hunted them down, and by daybreak, had offered to financially back Beantown Home Cookin', and as soon as papers could be drawn up, he became their manager.

Soon after, Rodney introduced them to the Trashbabies, his newly-formed, spectacularly talented singing, dancing chorus, with the goal of transitioning from a rock dance band to top-notch, all-original showband.

Rodney set about showing and telling the world about Beantown Home Cookin', and George, ever a complete professional and by then, Morgen's biggest fan, seriously enjoyed his new role as mentor and co-arranger of all Morgen's material, and although Morgen couldn't read or write musical notation, happily handed the reins over to Morgen.

Morgen had been teaching the band his songs by singing all the instrument parts to the musicians. It worked, but it was slow going, so George introduced Morgen to notation, harmony, music theory, and orchestration.

Morgen learned quickly, relished George's input, and their songs kept improving as they went along.

Back on Cape Cod, George and Morgen located an air-conditioned theater where *Wonder Woman* was playing, but with more than an hour to kill before showtime, went to Spanky's Clam Shack & Seaside Saloon for a lunch of delicious whole belly fried clams and onion rings, served tender, crispy, and not at all greasy. Then, unrecognized by the locals, they ordered cold drinks, went outside onto the deck, sat under the shade of a huge umbrella, and enjoyed the cool salt air and the sight of all the pleasure crafts at anchor.

" 'In This Place' is dynamite," George said.

"Here, or the song?" Morgen asked.

"Both," George replied, "but what the Trashbabies are doing with 'In This Place,' it's sure to be a show-stopper."

"Spring happens all around the world," Morgen observed.

"We've been talking about adding some musical effects."

"Such as?" Morgen asked.

"Temple blocks to support the Asiatic mood of the second pentatonic movement, and Jasmine asked if we could introduce some sitar, as well, especially during the frenetic dance. I checked, and we've got the synth samples to do it."

"You'll have to let me hear what you have in mind."

"No problem," George replied happily.

"I told you about the pitch-black shaft I had to crawl through to get into the Tomb of Every Hope, didn't I?" Morgen asked.

"You did, and I told you I'd never do it. I'd freak, crawling through utter darkness for five minutes. Never happen!"

"Well, you never went through boot camp."

"They have that in boot camp?"

"No," Morgen answered, "but they have damage control. I was the nozzle man on the fire hose, leading the hose team up to a huge tank of flaming fuel. Everyone who goes through boot camp is introduced to fire-fighting, but nobody gets closer to the flame and heat from that burning fuel than the nozzle man, and by the time I heard the order, 'Fog on deck!' it felt to me like my eyelashes had curled and my skin was about to start blistering from the heat."

"I could never go anywhere near a flaming fuel tank."

"If you fail to put the fire out, the ship and its crew, including you, might be lost," Morgen explained. "Every nozzle man who went through boot camp did what you're being asked to do. It's really not much different than following the dog. In dangerous situations, I tend to be fatalistic. If it happens, and I'm there, I do the best I can, and hope it's enough."

"If you say so," George agreed, and looking at his watch continued, "It's getting close to time. We'd better get going."

They were on time. The Entertainment Cinemas in South Dennis were state-of-the-art theaters, comfortably cool, and not surprisingly, in a beach community on a summer weekend, only slightly more than half full for the first show of the day.

They both enjoyed the movie, especially the opening sequences on the Amazons' island, and enjoyed the humor as Wonder Woman, raised in an all-female world, came to grips with modern manhood at war, but they found the final showdown between Ares and Wonder Woman too much about special effects and not enough about the story. On a scale of one to ten, Morgen gave it a 7.5, George gave it an 8.5, but both gave the actress who played Wonder Woman a 10.

After the show, walking back to George's car, George told Morgen that Wonder Woman was created by a guy from Massachusetts named Marston, who graduated Phi Beta Kappa from Harvard with a B.A. in 1915, a law degree in 1916 and a Ph.D. in Psychology in 1921.

"I bet he was a lot like you," George suggested.

"I had one year at B.U., before I joined your band."

"But you know things," George countered, "all kinds of things, most of which aren't taught in any schools I know."

"When I was a kid, I read a lot."

"Yeah, but you see things differently. You have a unique perspective on just about everything. You see relationships between things that no one else even suspects exist."

"That may be more a curse, than a compliment. I once read a definition of sanity that said it was the ability to see things as others do, and it's only a few hundred years since seeing things differently might get you committed, tortured, hanged, or burned at the stake."

"The 20th century was kinder," George replied. "Marston and his family were only fired from their jobs and ostracized."

177

"I'm impressed, and if I'm ever asked who created Wonder Woman, I'll be sure to refer the interviewer to you."

"Don't," George squealed. "I memorized all that to impress you. Keeping up with you leaves no room in my brain for Marston or Wonder Woman, in the unlikely event they ever came up in a Beantown Home Cookin' interview."

"Well said!" Morgen exclaimed. "More important to store the final score of the New England Patriots' incredible come from behind, overtime victory over the *Atlantic* Falcons, when Tom Brady won his fifth Superbowl ring. What was that final score?"

"Thirty-four to twenty-eight," George replied.

"Really?" Morgen asked, stunned that George knew.

"Thirty-four to twenty-eight," George stated confidently. "If you don't believe me, look it up."

Back in the car, George asked, "Where to, now?"

"Home, I think, if we want to beat the traffic."

George agreed, and they began the long drive back in silence, until George got onto Route 6, the Grand Army of the Republic Highway, honoring the American Civil War veterans association, still the longest transcontinental highway in the nation, running all the way from Provincetown, Massachusetts to Long Beach, California.

George asked Morgen how he would compare the Amazons of *Wonder Woman* with the Furies of Morningstone.

"Well," Morgen began, "in *Wonder Woman*, the Amazons are the good guys, and in Morningstone, at least as far as humanity is concerned, the Furies are the bad guys."

"Okay, fair enough," George said, "but are the Amazons more beautiful than the Furies?"

"There are a lot more Amazons, so they have a lot more beauty contest candidates, and although the Furies were mean-tempered, I can't say they were ugly, but I never saw them really smile or attempt to look attractive, either."

"That's one for the Amazons," George said. "Who do you think would win in a knock-down, drag-out fight?'

"There wouldn't be one," Morgen said.

"But you said the Furies were dangerous and wore armor?"

"They were and they did," Morgen replied, "but they carried no weapons. They don't need any."

"How so?"

"Their powers came not from conventional weapons but from the forces of Nature they are able to wield like weapons," Morgen explained. "One caused the earth to open up, and tried to dump me into a pit of molten horror, another called up a freezing wind so fierce, it would have frozen all life on Earth, and the third proposed releasing a plague that would wipe out the entire human race, but leave all other creatures immune."

"Well, how do you fight that?" George asked.

"You don't. You can't. It leaves us where we always were, at Nature's mercy. I saw Nature, shackled, and was given a key to free her. If humanity's shackles are intended to harness Nature, and keep her in check, they don't work. Even shackled, or perhaps because she's shackled, Nature seems to have no trouble inflicting wildfires, floods, hurricanes, earthquakes, volcanoes, droughts, and diseases, at will.

"I was still thinking about whether or not I should free her, when her chains fell away. She set herself free to go where she willed, and do what she willed, with or without my consent or approval, and that's when I realized I wasn't a *test*. It was a *lesson*. Humanity's control over Nature is an illusion, and our civilization has come so far, we're dependent on technology. To survive, we must understand the world as it is today, accept it, and learn to live in harmony with Nature's Laws."

They rode in silence the rest of the way back to the estate, but as George pulled to a stop in the driveway, he asked, "What if it's already too late?"

"It's not too late," Morgen said. "The verdict is still out. Inside the Tomb of Every Hope, on trial for all the crimes committed against Nature, I wasn't condemned. I was allowed a sip from the Cauldron of Inspiration."

"So now you know how it will all end, right?"

"It doesn't work that way. It's not a vat of knowledge. It contains inspiration, which, in my case, encourages me to go on, and provides insights I never had before, and allows me to see things differently than most others do. My being alive proves to me there is reason for hope. But hope, without supporting action, is nothing more than wishful thinking, and that is why it is vital that we get the word out as far and wide as we can."

George countered, "Not discounting the Furies fire and ice, if the third Fury represents plague, it may be too late. Before I flew back from England, I heard about NASA reports that the melting permafrost was exposing carcasses of dead creatures, thousands of years old, exposing us to viruses that predate human evolution, and for which we have no immunity.

"We've had thousands of years to deal with the threats of fire and ice," he continued, "but have never encountered these ancient, super viruses before. And I can't help but wonder if the third Fury has already launched her attack."

"Our new album is an attempt, on both conscious and unconscious levels, to convince humanity there's still time to make the necessary adjustments to survive as a species. If it's too late, why was I sent back?" Morgen replied. "Doing nothing is a choice with terrible consequences for humanity, because by doing nothing it proves we're unwilling to compromise and deserve extinction, whereas by accepting the hope and the challenge, we might yet deliver ourselves from the dismal result of continued neglect."

"I don't know," George said. "I find it all rather bleak. Once, dinosaurs ruled the earth, and now they're gone."

"Dinosaurs never ruled the earth," Morgen countered. "They walked the earth, but never ruled it."

"And now, we walk the earth," George said, "and we don't rule it either."

"Never have, and never will," Morgen agreed, "but unlike the dinosaurs, we are aware of our danger, and unless there's an asteroid speeding through space on a collision course with Earth, if we have the will, we can learn what we need to know, and work out a joint-venture partnership with Nature."

"If it's not already too late," George concluded, and quietly drove away. It had been a long day, and Morgen was glad to finally climb into bed.

CHAPTER SIXTEEN

On Sunday morning, Morgen took his toast and coffee out to the patio. The wisteria's stunning floral display of two weeks earlier was fast disappearing, but the shade provided by the heavy canopy of thick foliage gave the patio welcome relief from the sun's hot rays, and kept the patio relatively cool in the early morning. Yesterday's conversations with George about the ever-growing environmental crisis had taken Morgen out of the excitement of bringing that otherworldly music into this world, and refocused his attention on presenting it. Was there magic in the songs? If there was magic in the music, was it strong enough to influence its audience, and prod them to appropriate action? He considered the new music as a call for action, but until his talk with George, hadn't considered what form that action might take.

Shortly after ten o'clock, Rodney joined him on the patio. Good morning, Rodney said. "Did you just get back?"

"Good morning," Morgen said. "I came back yesterday afternoon, and was in bed by eight o'clock. How about you?"

"I didn't get back until nearly two in the morning. I had to drop Maggie off."

"So, how was the reception?"

"Everyone kept calling it magical."

"How did 'Witchy Stew' do?"

"It was one of the highlights of the evening," Rodney said. "We had to play it three times, as some people left early and more people arrived late. What about you? What did you do?"

"George and I had fried clams and saw *Wonder Woman*."

"Any good?"

"The gal who played Wonder Woman was beautiful and fit enough to probably do a lot of her own stunts."

"Gal Gadot."

"What?"

"Gal Gadot is the name of the Israeli actress who played the role of Wonder Woman. She's a former Miss Israel, who served two years as a combat instructor in the Israeli army."

"Gal Gadot?'

"That's her name."

"I suppose I better write it on my wrist, in case it comes up in an interview."

"Good idea. Right along with Tom Brady."

"That's never going to go away, is it?"

"Probably not," Rodney laughed.

"It's nice out here, isn't it?" Morgen said. "Peaceful."

"It is," Rodney agreed. "I know this is officially a day off, but you should know I read your interpretation of 'The Fool'."

"And?"

"I borrowed Maggie's copy of Graves."

"I didn't know she had one."

"She talks to the girls. Anyway, I read enough of it to think you may be onto something, but I don't think Graves is widely read. He's not an easy read."

"Did you read the chapter on Dog, Roebuck, and Lapwing?"

"I must have skipped that one," Rodney confessed.

"You should read it. I'm writing a song about them, and it will make a perfect finale for our concert tour."

"I'll read it," Rodney said, "but I fear 'The Fool' will go way over the heads of the audience."

"In which case, it's simply a nonsense song."

"But we know better. It's your credential song, isn't it?"

"Yup."

"Some people may figure it out, especially people who've read Graves," Rodney conceded.

"Some probably will."

"You said you wrote 'Flying Snakes,' but you remembered 'The Fool,' and transcribed it, verbatim."

"True."

"I believe you, but have you considered the consequences if you announce it to the world that way?"

"What consequences?"

"Well, if you insist on telling people you had an out-of-body experience, and most of the new album is music you heard when you were out-of-body, some people will assume you were on drugs."

"I was tested for drugs and alcohol in the hospital, and none were found."

"That may be worse," Rodney said. "They'll probably decide you're a minion of Satan, or a changeling."

"Get serious!"

"I am serious, and your accusers may be more serious, so please, when you're talking about it, consider how little difference there is between a vivid dream and an out-of-body experience and go with the vivid dream."

"What difference does that make?"

"Exactly my point. The results are the same, but the associations are totally different. When you're asleep, whatever you witness, whatever you do, say, or hear in your dream, your body is still in bed, on the couch, or the car seat, wherever you fell asleep, and what you remember from it is just as real or unreal as anything you might encounter in an out-of-body experience. The big difference is in perception. Dreams may inspire twitches, groans, and cold sweats, and the memory of that dream can be as vivid as your imagination allows, and the phenomenon is totally acceptable. I suspect all of us, have experienced, or will experience, a vivid dream.

"You're no fool, Morgen, unless you're the genuine 'Fool' of your dream, so consider that while a vivid dream may be cause for envy, it's unlikely to raise a hue and cry against you. If you say you dreamed something, it's no less magical than what you describe as your out-of-body experience, but rhetorically, it's less diabolical sounding, more familiar to all of us, and no cause for alarm."

Morgen gave it some thought before suggesting, "If I say I dreamed I had an out-of-body experience, will that work?"

"Why not just say 'While I was unconscious, I dreamed' and go on from there?" Rodney asked.

Morgen smiled and said, "And if I preface it with that disclaimer, you'll let me tell you what happened, what I saw, what I heard, and how I learned the things I learned?"

"From time to time," Rodney said, smiling back, "if you promise to stick to no more than one psychic revelation at a time, and allow me time to digest it before you go on."

"I can do that," Morgen said, but I've been sitting out here in this beautiful Wisteria shaded pergola, and thinking about where our relationship has taken us.

With some trepidation, Rodney asked, "And where's that?"

"That first night, when we stayed up until dawn, talking about all the things you wanted to do for us, how we were too good to limit ourselves to dance bars, how we belonged in Carnegie Hall . . ."

Rodney smiled and said, "I remember."

"You said with the talent in Beantown Home Cookin', all we needed was financial backing, a few hit songs and the *Solid Gold Dancers,* and we'd be the top showband in the country."

"Is that what I said?" Rodney asked, "because if that's what I said, I apologize. I should have said was, 'in the world'."

"And instead of the *Solid Gold Dancers*, you gave us the Trashbabies."

"They're just as beautiful, dance every bit as well, and they sing, too. I don't remember the *Solid Gold Dancers* singing."

Grinning broadly, Morgen said, "I'm not complaining. I don't remember the *Solid Gold Dancers*."

"They were sensational, every one of them," Rodney said, "but you can't compare them to the Trashbabies."

"I'm not, Morgen replied. "What I'm trying to tell you is you did it."

"What did I do?" Rodney asked.

"You've made us one of the top showbands in the world," Morgen said.

"Not yet, I didn't," Rodney warned.

"The world just doesn't know it, yet," Morgen said, "but with this new music, with this new album, and the show we're putting together with our Trashbabies, who are, in my opinion, second to none, we're on the threshold."

"Your lips to God's ears," Rodney said, and Morgen was more than a little surprised to see Rodney make a subtle sign of the cross with his right index finger.

Morgen went online to do some research. He knew Satan was the bad guy who took souls to hell and had them eternally tortured and tormented by his minions, but when he looked up changeling, he learned that in Western mythology and folklore, changelings were believed to be troll or fairy children, substituted for stolen human children, carried off and never seen again. Infants born with a veil were sometimes considered changelings, and believed by some to be clairvoyant, or possess supernatural powers, but he was horrified to learn that some apparently healthy babies, later discovered to suffer developmental disorders, were believed by their parents to be changelings, were abandoned and died from exposure, or worse, were taken by wild animals.

To suggest he might be mistaken for a changeling seemed ludicrous, but given his unknown ancestry, at a time when people went around looking for excuses to be offended, even the Trashbabies had been vociferously attacked by marginal, self-proclaimed feminists, because of their name. And then, remembering the way Fiona put such weight on her assertion that "There's a lot in a name," he laughed out loud.

Later that day, he showed Rodney the repeated verse to "Dog, Roebuck and Lapwing." There were only two lines, but you could pretend there were four, or three if you tried to count them as four, since the last line was a repeat of the first, and that sort of came out to three lines.

> *"Dog, Roebuck and Lapwing,*
> Your nonsense song makes my ears ring.
> Between the lines I hear you sing,
> *Dog Roebuck and Lapwing."*

Rodney was almost afraid to ask, "Is that all there is? Just four lines?"

"Wait till you hear it?" Morgen teased.

"Can't I hear it now?"

"No. I still haven't taught it to the Trashbabies."

Rodney said, with a wry grin, "Yeah, that's a lot to learn."

"You said it," Morgen agreed.

In fact, Morgen embraced Rodney's disclaimer, and it dissolved the distrust that had been developing between them. Morgen and the band concentrated on refining their arrangements and preparing for their recording sessions. The Trashbabies took advantage of all the time Morgen could spare to practice their vocals with him, and walk him through their new routines, created especially for the new album and concert tour.

Before the band left for England, Rodney saw and was pleased by the Trashbabies' evolving "In This Place" showcase, and Morgen introduced them all to "Dog, Roebuck and Lapwing." Since he wouldn't be around to coach them, he and the band had recorded the three different melodies for their vocal parts on separate tracks, so each could learn all three and practice their timing by singing along with Track One, Two, or Three, until it would be recorded in the U.K., where their parts would be interwoven and mixed into the number he'd composed for closing their live shows. It was a song Morgen believed, when Alan heard it, would also become the last track on the new album.

Their recording schedule allowed a generous four weeks for recording the new songs with Beantown Home Cookin', starting July 10th, and carrying them all the way to August 4th. The Trashbabies, continuing to rehearse their choreography in the States, were booked to arrive in the U.K., on Saturday, the 5th of August, and August 7th through the 11th to record their vocal parts, and as they did, the producer would begin mixing continuing concurrently as each song was completed.

The art department was already working on the cover, and the distributor expected to be shipping albums by the end of September. Rodney and the record company had negotiated a U.K. promotional tour to showcase the new album before they left on their fall European tour, now scheduled to start on Friday, November 3rd, in Hamburg, Germany.

Morgen was chilled by the sight of the pale, white creature that perched, motionless, a miniature ghost, bold in the bright moonlight, black eyes staring. And then, the owl blinked, opened its black beak, and in a voice remarkably like Fiona's, said his name. Morgen sat bolt upright, sending sharp pain through his neck.

The owl awoke him just in time to hear the flight attendant announce, "Ladies and gentlemen, as we begin our descent, please make sure your seat backs and tray tables are in their full upright position, your seat belt is securely fastened, and all carry-on luggage is stowed underneath the seat in front of you or in the overhead bins. Thank you."

Coming to his senses, he opened the shade, saw cloud-covered daylight outside, and realized his painful stiff neck was the result of falling asleep with his head against the closed shade. He'd taken the long flight to England once before, but he'd never fallen asleep on an airplane, coming or going. His tray table was already properly stowed, and he was already securely buckled up, so all he had to do was raise his seat to its full upright position.

He heard the landing gear whine down into position and lock into place with a thud. Looking around, he saw everybody in First Class, wide awake, and preparing for landing. He'd missed the local time and temperature announcement, but knew they were on their final approach to Heathrow.

All the cabin lights were on, but everybody seemed to be opening their window shades and looking out their windows. The seat next to him was empty, which meant Rodney had found a vacant double seat somewhere else in First Class and taken it so he could stretch out and get some sleep. He saw George and Jeff in the two rows of aisle seats on the opposite side of the first-class cabin, but couldn't see, and didn't remember who was sitting next to them.

And suddenly, as if out of a thick fog, the landing strip appeared, the plane touched down, the engines reversed with a roar and the plane slowed, and taxied to its assigned gate.

They deplaned at Heathrow on Friday, July 7th, and were greeted by Alan Fuller and a security detail sent by the record company to guide Rodney and Beantown Home Cookin' through customs, gather them into vans, and deliver them to their undisclosed location, a little over two hours distant, somewhere north and west of the airport, so once on the ground, Morgen had no time to wonder whether his vivid barn owl wake-up call was a welcome back, or a warning.

Alan chaperoned them through customs, made all the necessary introductions to the obliging security team, wished them a relaxing afternoon at the secret location provided by the record company, and promised to meet with them tomorrow to discuss the recording schedule. He then excused himself, and hurried off to another appointment elsewhere.

The security team cleared all their stowed luggage and instruments through customs, loaded it all into one van, loaded Rodney, Morgen and the band into a large, comfortable bus, and drove them more than two hours northwest of the airport to their undisclosed location, which turned out to be a comfortable, good-sized establishment, hidden discreetly in the Cotswolds, fully staffed during the day, included laundry and dry cleaning services, provided beverage coolers in every room, breakfast, lunch or supper served in the dining room, and sandwiches that could be ordered and delivered to the room, any time between 10:00 a.m., and 10:00 p.m. It also had free Wi-Fi, free breakfast, a pub-like bar, a restaurant, complete with a carvery, and a swimming pool.

Lisbeth, an enthusiastic, well-coached teenager, happily greeted each of the band members by name as they entered, and showed them all to their rooms, in a semi-private wing, all on the same floor.

Except for Morgen, Rodney and George, who each had private rooms with double beds, the band members were berthed two to a room with twin beds, a writing desk, ample closet space and private baths for each room, all very nice, for the time being, and rooms reserved for the Trashbabies, when they finally came to town. Roger and Frank, drummer and bass player, were put in one room; Emery and Grant, the two guitarists, in another, and two of the keyboard players, Jeff and Owen, in another, across the hall from George's room. Morgen's room was nearby, as was Rodney's.

Morgen saw no rehearsal space, but was told arrangements were being made, somewhere nearby. Someone had put a lot of thought into who bunked where and with whom, and no one complained about the arrangement, which had the rhythm section (bass and drums), in the same room so they could quietly run through their arrangements, although no matter how much Frank turned down his amp, if you were in the same room, you could feel his bass parts and hear Roger's drum rhythms on the drum pad. Emery and Grant, the two guitarists, who swapped off leads and rhythms regularly, could practice on their acoustic guitars, but if you looked into George's room, with George, Jeff, and Owen's keyboards all plugged into an amplifier and listening in earphones, it was like watching a silent movie. You'd see them all bobbing their heads or tapping their feet in rhythm, but all you could hear would be the sound of their fingertips hitting the keys.

The record company also provided a hospitality suite on their floor, which Morgen thought was probably a bridal suite, converted especially for them to provide a living area where they could gather apart from any other guests, hold band meetings, snack and watch a good-sized collection of DVDs on a big screen TV, and where, the following morning at ten o'clock, they met with Alan to talk over their schedule.

"First," Alan said, "let me say how great it is to have you here to record this exciting new album on our side of the pond. We've lined up a top-of-the-line studio, with state-of-the-art facilities, and some of Britain's top talents to produce, record and mix the album, and you'll be recording in a fantastic room, where entire symphony orchestras have recorded, and the engineer's assistants know exactly how their room works, so they know which mikes to use, which baffles to use and where to place them, whether you're going straight into the board or through amplifiers, and they get what most of us in the industry recognize as the best separation of tracks, instruments, and sections, for today's multi-track mixes."

George held up his hand.

"George?" Alan asked.

"Will we be recording digital or analog?"

"Probably both. They have two, 2-inch, time-coded 24 track Studer's, and digital forever. The producer and engineer will discuss the variables with you as you get set up. I'm pretty sure they do all their final mixing digitally, but I'll ask and get back to you," Alan replied.

"Will you be there?" George asked.

"As often as I can."

"Will we always be in the big room?" Grant asked.

"Vocals will be recorded in the booths, but otherwise, that's the plan," Alan responded, "in order to be able to match the studio ambiance in your original recordings, when they bring in the session musicians."

"What session musicians?" Owen wanted to know.

"When your producer heard your demos, he stipulated a studio string section, brass section, woodwinds, and choir, for some songs, and the distributor immediately approved it!"

"There are three of us," Owen countered. "Together, our keyboards can play all of those instruments, live, and that's how we've rehearsed them."

Alan answered, "We've heard what you can do on your demos, and the sounds you achieved are excellent, but it's not the same as having those parts played, or doubled, with musicians playing live in the studio on authentic instruments."

"When we're on tour, we won't be able to match it," Owen protested, at which time Morgen spoke up.

"Owen," he said, "live, we never sound like our recordings.

What matters most is that when we're not playing live, fans and record collectors will hear our music played the best, most exciting way possible, and it's our recordings that convince people to spend the money to come to our live shows."

George added, "When you hear the final mix, you'll hear why having a studio orchestra augment our recordings really does make a difference."

"We've rehearsed this music," Owen said. "We won't need four weeks to record it. Two at the most."

Alan spoke up. "Owen, the sessions are booked. It's part of the deal with the producer. As for how much of what ends up in the final mixes, you will all have a say in that."

Morgen signaled Alan that he wanted to speak.

"Morgen?"

"I've put together a Trashbabies' piece I'd like to be the last cut on the album," Morgen announced. "It's their exit music for the end of our concerts."

Morgen handed Alan a sheet of paper, a USB flash drive, and continued, "I have it, instrumentally, on this flash drive, and I've made you a copy of the lyrics."

Alan looked at the four short lines, centered on the page.

Dumbfounded, he asked, "This is it?"

Rodney, grinning broadly, answered "That's it!"

" 'Dog, Roebuck, and Lapwing' are ancient bardic symbols, indicating that what follows, or immediately precedes their appearance, contains little known mysteries," Morgen explained. "Dog means 'guard the secret,' roebuck means 'hide the secret,' and lapwing means 'disguise the secret'."

George said, "With the vocals, it should sound reminiscent of the ending of Holst's *Venus*, from *The Planets*."

"The Trashbabies will know their parts by the time they get here," Morgen said. "Play the instrumental that's on the flash drive, and you'll get the idea. It belongs on this album."

"Well," Alan said, "Of course, I'll listen to it, and add it to the schedule, but I don't guarantee it will make the cut."

"Understood!" Morgen agreed, "but with the time you've booked for recording, we'll easily do it and stay on schedule."

"And," George added, "we don't want any genuine harps on the recording. We want to play them on our keyboards, and transition from harp samples to modern sounds, creating a musical timeline between the ancient and modern sounds of our world underscoring the magic as the Trashbabies exit."

"What he said," Morgen added, agreeing with George's impressive, if somewhat flowery description of the piece.

Alan concluded by giving them the producer's choice of which song he wanted to produce first.

"The producer wants to record 'Peeping Tom' first. It's upbeat, and will give you all something to sink your teeth into on your first day, and give the crew a chance to adjust their setups to best capture your performances, and as the man said, the sooner he gets some of the songs he wants to augment, the sooner he can get the parts worked out and start lining up the session players."

"Alan," Morgen interjected, "Who is the producer? If we're going to work with him, we'll have to know his name."

"I should have said this up front, and I apologize," Alan said. "Trust me when I say he's one of the very best in the business and has a reputation for only working with the best musicians on the most outstanding albums of the last decade. You may recognize him by sight, but even if you do, he wants you all to call him 'Bob.' When the album is finished, if it meets his approval, which is to say, enhances his reputation, he'll put his real name on it. If not, it will have been produced by Bob whatever last name he decides to put on the jacket. Our label never paid this much for a producer before, and we're very excited that he found you and your music exciting enough to take you on, but those are his conditions."

"Morgen," Rodney jumped in, "I knew of his terms and I agreed to them. He works this way with new talent . . ."

"Our first album went platinum," Morgen said. "We're not exactly new."

"Then let me make it clear." Rodney said evenly, "One of the reasons 'Bob' insisted on conditions, was your going off the reservation and blowing the deal for us last summer. He's a professional and won't work with unreliable amateurs. He said he'd do it, under the conditions he outlined, because he knew and respected Alan, liked what he heard in your music, and believed it might have a shot at album of the year."

Morgen looked at George, hoping to gauge his reaction.

"And one more thing," Alan said, "while we're on the subject. Bob is your producer. Please let him do what he does best. If he wants to add a brass section, woodwinds, strings, or full orchestra, please don't argue with him."

"But this is our new album," Morgen argued.

"And it's his new album, too," Alan replied, "and he will do everything he can to make it the best album of the year."

"I'm looking forward to working with Bob," George said. "Reliable sources have said he's the new number one, and I'm delighted he's decided to take us on."

"Bob sounds cool," Frank chimed in.

Emery added, with conviction, "I've heard Bob's the best."

"The man with the golden touch," Jeff said.

When he realized everyone in the room was looking at him, Owen threw up his hands in surrender and said, "I'm in!"

CHAPTER SEVENTEEN

Although not part of any of his academic courses, pursuing his personal interests as an independent scholar led Morgen to read Edith Hamilton and Bulfinch in middle school; Frazer's

Golden Bough: A Study in Magic and Religion, and Cox's *The Feast of Fools – A Theological Essay of Festivity and Fantasy* in High School; and Seamus MacManus' *Story of the Irish Race: A Popular History of Ireland*, while he was in the navy, and couldn't help but wonder how much of his new material might have been inspired by those arcane sources, but knew there were other elements in his adventure for which he could remember no Earthly source in his experience, which suggested if it wasn't real, it supported the ideas of a universal unconscious, or genetic memory, had validity, but of all his friends, which is to say, his co-workers, the band and the Trashbabies, there was only one Morgen trusted with his deepest ruminations, and that was George.

Sunday morning, after breakfast, with nothing on the agenda, George and Morgen took a walk around the grounds.

"You feelin' up to recording?" George asked.

"I'm fine," Morgen replied. "I just want to get started."

"I think it's cool that we'll be starting with 'Peeping Tom'." George said.

"It is the most controversial song on the album," Morgen said.

"That's why it's good Bob wants to start with it," George affirmed.

"It's an easy one for us," Morgen said. "And it will give us a chance to blow off some steam, and establish ourselves with the studio engineers."

"I think I know why he wants to start with it. It calls for hunting horns, and what we do, especially with the newest samples we downloaded, will sound fine in live performances, but real horns playing those calls will take it to another level."

"You're probably right," Morgen said, "but thinking about the Trashbabies' parts, he might want to get them down early. The timing is critical, especially when the 'Furies' come in over the others."

"The Trashbabies will have it down."

"Rodney still has reservations about the lyrics."

"I don't think Rodney's likely to pursue his reservations, especially if Alan and Bob like it," George said.

"I knew you were going to say that!" Morgen exclaimed.

"Well, that's my opinion."

"No! I mean I knew you were going to say those exact words, here, in a place neither of us has ever been before, with that idiotic garden gnome watching us," Morgen insisted.

"You mean like déjà vu?"

"And I knew you were going to say that, too!"

George said nothing, and Morgen laughed. "And I knew that's what you'd do. It's true. I had a premonition."

"So, now what?" George asked.

"We talk about streams of consciousness."

"What do I say?" George asked.

"Not much. You let me do most of the talking, but then you say something brilliant."

"What?"

"I don't know. We haven't come to it, yet." Morgen said with a laugh, and when neither spoke for a moment, added, "I think the moment passed. I have no idea what comes next."

"You start talking about the stream of consciousness."

"What do I say?"

George burst out laughing. "How the hell would I know?" he said. "You're the one with déjà vu."

"There's a stream of consciousness that flows through Morningstone," Morgen began.

"Really?" George said, smiling, "How's it work?"

"It flows downhill."

"Are we talking about a river or a concept?"

"Both, I suppose. We were following the brook that flowed through the Tomb of Every Hope," Morgen continued.

"I was there?"

"No, the dog and I, and we came to a hole in the bedrock, into which the brook emptied, and I heard running water, not from a hose or a faucet, but from a stream. The dog went right past it, but I went to the edge of the hole to peek in. I couldn't see much, but the sound of the water rushing by and the brook emptying into it was pretty loud. And there was something about that hole and that water roaring by, swallowing the brook, that was frightening, like, it might undermine and dissolve the rock I stood upon, that made me back away.

"The dog was waiting for me, so I went on and as the sound of rushing water diminished, I began singing 'The Fool,' and conjuring music to go with it, even though I had no idea what came next."

"This was after you'd sipped from the Cauldron of Inspiration?"

"Yes, but I sang a song I'd never heard before, melody or lyrics, and afterward, remembered it clearly enough to bring it back with me, and decipher its obscure references. So, how's that work?"

"You tell me," George said.

"Well, you know the song. Anyway, I come out into a lovely, sunny day, but when I entered the Tomb of Every Hope, on the other side of the hill, there was thunder, and the sky was darkening like an enormous storm was coming."

"But you don't know how long you were knocked out before you awoke in your fabulous digs," George replied.

"That's right, I told you about my lair, didn't I?"

"Well, maybe the storm had come and gone by the time you went outside," George suggested.

"Maybe," Morgen admitted, "but everybody was out there, waiting for me, all dressed the same as earlier, and nobody was soaking wet. And I saw Smythe, the auto mechanic, in the crowd, and another huge guy whose name I never heard, but recognized because he played the carnyx."

"Wait, wait, wait," George interrupted. "You say he was playing an ancient Celtic War Horn?"

"Well, not then. It was before, and maybe later, too, but then, when I came out, he and Smythe put me on their shoulders, carried me down to the Sacred Pool, and threw me in. And here's the next thing. When I resurfaced, I saw where the water was gushing out through a crack in the hill, and pouring into the Sacred Pool. And I guess the reason I'm telling you all this is because that pool emptied into the Stream of Consciousness that flowed all through Morningstone, sometimes above ground, like when it flowed past the cottage and under the bridge, but also underground, which suggests the subconsciousness. Does that make any sense to you?"

"Is it supposed to make sense?" George asked.

"Excellent question. I suppose, if it was a dream, it wouldn't have to make sense, not in the way we usually mean it. But on the other hand, out-of-body experiences defy logic, but may still make perfect sense under certain circumstances."

"I wouldn't say *perfect* sense," George asserted, "but they seem to communicate on some unconscious level."

"Two things strike me from that part of my experience. One is that the underground stream is fed by a tributary, a brook flowing through the Tomb of Every Hope, and if it is fed by one, why not by many, separate streams of consciousness? The other is that the Sacred Pool might be the repository for all human knowledge, vibrant and dormant, there mixed, or sorted, before being sent on its way out into the stream of consciousness that flows through all of us.

"One of the colorful, oversized books in my father's library was *Man and His Symbols*, conceived and edited by Carl Jung, copiously illustrated, two text columns to a page, and heavy going when I read it at thirteen, made more difficult because it had been printed and bound in Yugoslavia, and some of the columns on the pages were out of order.

"What I remember most is not the symbols but the methodology applied to their understanding of dreams, and what I understood of Jung's collective unconscious seemed to lump together the instincts, intuition, and collective wisdom inherent in all humanity.

"Recently, I researched modern studies of genetic memory, which title I believe wrongly suggests the need of a family tree to support its theory that all humans are born with innate knowledge, sometimes expressed before the individual could have acquired it through study or environment.

"But I have always known, or believed that what they're now calling genetic memory, which may seem strange, since I have no idea who my biological parents were, is genuine, by whatever name you give it. I have always known things I never studied in school or came across when I was pursuing my independent interests. You said, the day we went down the Cape, that I had a unique perspective and see relationships no one else suspects exist."

"And you pooh-poohed it," George interrupted.

"No, I didn't," Morgen countered. "I said it might be more a curse than a compliment, and I had no desire to be committed, tortured, or burnt at the stake.

"What I like most about these recent studies, is that the research includes both children and adults displaying savant syndrome. It seems that people with sudden or acquired savant syndrome have had diseases or injuries affecting their central nervous system, but approximately half of the savants being studied are autistic children, and their special abilities are often expressed, even before they develop verbal skills. Savant syndrome subjects are frequently especially gifted in mathematics or the creative arts, especially music, but also painting and sculpture. What they all have in common is their knowledge of things they never learned."

"Like 'The Fool'?" George observed.

"Yes. I'm not claiming to be a savant. All I'm saying is I've heard music where there was none, mentally created, arranged, and influenced musical performances and lyrics, and returned with knowledge of things I never knew before, which is why I've been reviewing things to which I have been exposed to determine if they may have influenced my Morningstone adventure. And the answer is, yes. My experience may have been influenced by my propensity for the myths and folklore involved, but applied and revealed in ways, and with means I've never known or experienced before.

"Which brings me to today's revelation. You and I don't do drugs, and that's probably one reason we work together so well. You know my talent is largely innate, but it hasn't hurt me to learn to understand it as others do. What I bring to the table is, I suppose, my musical intuition."

"I saw that right from the start. That, and your natural talent as a singer and entertainer," George said.

"Thanks, George, but I'm not fishing for compliments," Morgen continued. "I used to think I channeled the greats who went before me, and their subconscious input inspired my composition and performance, but ever since I was introduced to the *White Goddess*, and discovered the uncanny relationship between 'The Fool,' and Robert Graves' translations of the ancient Welsh poetry, I have been wondering.

"He was the scholar, not I. While in Morningstone, we may have drifted together in a bubble floating in the Stream of Consciousness, but in my quest to validate my out-of-body experience as authentic, I came to a disturbing realization.

"I searched for 'The Tomb of Every Hope' online, hoping to learn in what culture it originated, and where it might be found, and learned it was Graves' own colorful invention, which was fine, until I realized I first heard that name from the Furies, before I ever heard of Graves. How was that possible?"

"Frankly," George answered, "I see nothing unusual about it. You and Graves shared a bubble in Morningstone, where the Furies were first to mention 'The Tomb of Every Hope' to you. That you and Graves shared that bubble, does not convey a claim to Graves. He may have picked it up at the same time and place, invented by the locals, or coined by Furies, but once it existed, visited and revisited by many or few."

They were at the studio on time, but it was a few minutes after 10:00 o'clock when they finally were set up enough to do a run through, and after 11:00 o'clock when they recorded their first performance, and in the nervous excitement of actual recording, hit a few wrong notes along the way.

Adjustments were made, the band settled down while individuals played short passages to aid the engineer in making his presets. It was nearly noon when Bob announced that they had time for a run through, if the band was ready, or they could break, and start recording after lunch. The band wanted to record a few run-throughs before lunch. The first one sounded great, the second had two errors in a lead guitar part, but rather than punch it in, Bob said they should record another, so they did, and then, it was time for lunch.

The recording engineer announced they could order takeaway, and with two drivers and two vans standing by, the drivers would fetch it.

The band chose takeaway, and Alan arrived just in time to place his order from the four takeaway menus from the accommodating local area restaurants. It took fifteen minutes or so before all the selections were made, and another five minutes to place all the orders over the phone, and then the two vans set out, two stops each, to pick up the food.

Hot and cold drinks came from vending machines in the waiting room, and the office staff always kept plenty of coins on hand to make change for visitors. It was a lovely day, and there was a very nice shaded patio area behind the studio, so everyone decided to take lunch there, including the assistant engineers, chief engineer, Bob, Rodney, and the studio office staff who didn't have to stay inside to answer the phones.

Based on this first luncheon at the studio, it was clear the natives and visitors appreciated Papa John's Pizza, Subway Sandwiches, and more exotic Indian Tandoori Chicken, Chicken Masala, or Lamb Masala, and Chinese Sweet and Sour Chicken, varieties of Chop Suey, and Fried Rice.

After lunch, Alan joined Rodney and Bob in the recording booth as Morgen sang "Peeping Tom" four times through, after which Bob announced that among the four tracks, he had everything he needed.

Alan, Rodney, and Morgen were well pleased with what they'd heard, and Bob asked the band if they'd like to take a run at another song. George said, considering they were already set up for it, they should take a shot at recording "Sweet Mystery."

They ran through a rehearsal to give the engineer an opportunity to re-adjust the levels, equalization and tracking for the song, but Bob asked the guitarists, Emery and Grant, to turn off their amps and join him in the booth.

"Did we do something wrong?" Emery asked, as Grant closed the air-lock door to the control room behind them.

"Not at all," Bob said. "If you play it exactly the way you just did, when you're overdubbing, it'll be great. I want the guitars amplified for this song, but if you play as loud as I want you to play, you'll be bleeding into all the other tracks.

"Bass and drums are the heart of the rhythm section, and they're the only live instruments in the room, and naturally bleed into each other's tracks, but because of the way we mike them, we can still mix them so they sound great.

"The keyboards are plugged directly into the board, so we play it back loud enough in the earphones so they can hear what they're doing, but I have complete control over their tracks in the mix. You'll be playing in the same space that the orchestra will use later. When we record your parts, I'll record them both at the same time, so you can feed off each other, the way you do live, but I'll have control of your separate tracks, and be able to manipulate them for volume and placement in the whole, as long as you both stay in key. Based on what I've heard so far, I want you to play it together until you both nail it. Later, there'll be an orchestra and a choir recording in the same acoustic space you'll be inhabiting. Make sense?"

By then, both Grant and Emery were both grinning happily, and Emery said, "You're the producer . . . Bob."

"Thank you," Bob said with a grin, and into the talkback. "I'm ready when you are," and nodded to the chief engineer.

"Sweet Mystery, Take One," the engineer said into the talkback, and rolled the click track.

The first take was excellent, but he asked for a second, as a safety, and apart from a few tiny control panel adjustments, it might have been a playback of the first.

"Okay guys, come on back," Bob said into the talkback.

The guys in the main studio looked surprised, but happy as they started to walk toward the control booth. Bob turned to Emery and Grant and said, "Gentlemen, you're on!"

The drums, bass and keyboards accepted the congratulations of the guitarists as they passed each other, five coming in, and two going out. And George, who was the most experienced of them all, and knew what was going on, called after them, "Don't embarrass us. Show 'em what our axe men can do!"

They did, with a single run through to balance the tracks, followed by a rock solid first take and an equally solid safety.

And then it was Morgen's turn, again. Bob had him sing it twice in the first sound booth, twice in a second, and sent in an assistant to set up a mike in the Main Studio, so Morgen could sing it there, as well.

In the control room, Bob heard Morgen ask the assistant engineer setting up the microphone, if he could have a stool, and jumped on the talkback.

"Morgen, you can't sit down for this." Bob said. "Just do it like you did in the sound booths."

"I need a stool, or a chair, or something," Morgen said.

"Bob," Rodney interjected, "he doesn't want it to sit on. He needs something to kneel on. Something that preferably won't squeak."

Bob, without apologizing, said, "Okay, Morgen. We'll get you something that doesn't squeak right away. Do you want a cushion with that?"

"That would be great," Morgen said, smiling broadly. "As long as it's not made of leather and doesn't squeak."

The assistant engineer took one of a number of hard-backed chairs from a large booth off the main studio.

When Rodney saw him bringing it to the main studio, he took off his jacket, rolled it up and brought it out, too.

"Try this," Rodney said.

"Thanks," Morgen replied. "I hadn't realized I'd been standing so long, until I had sung this song four times, and I don't know how many times I'll have to sing it out here."

As the assistant engineer came back to adjust the microphone, Rodney smiled his big, friendly smile and told Morgen, "Whatever you do, don't break a leg."

"Say something, Morgen," Bob said over the talkback.

"Thank you," Morgen replied.

Morgen heard them laughing over the talkback, as Bob said, "Can you give me a little more than that? We're trying to get a level in here."

"Thank you, one and all, and thank you to all my fans in the control booth and all the people just waking up on the other side of the pond, with no idea what's going on over here, Good Morning, Massachusetts! And God bless Tom Brady!"

It worked for the folks in the control booth, especially the band members, who recognized Morgen's loud "Good Morning Massachusetts" as a spin-off of Robin William's portrayal of Adrian Cronauer in *Good morning, Vietnam!*

"That should do it," Bob announced through the talkback. "Sing the song the same way you said that line, by which I mean with the same volume and intensity, and I'll give you the rest of the day off."

"Okay, but I'll need to hear more in my headphones."

"Comin' at you. Slate it," Bob said, and the chief engineer bellowed "Sweet Mystery, Morgen's vocal, Take Five!"

It was an incredible, high-energy take, and left everybody in the control room stunned.

"Can you do that again, Morgen?" Bob asked.

"A safety, or did I overmodulate?"

"Your modulation is fine. I'm hearing playback from your earphones," Bob said, and asked, "How're you holding up?"

"So far, so good."

"Okay," Bob said, "Slate six."

Although the songs were quite different, the rest of the recording sessions went about the same way. The setup was established. Rhythm section first, sometimes with a scratch vocal to help everyone keep his place. Lead and rhythm guitars, next, made possible because all the improvised intros and exits had been predetermined during rehearsals, which isn't to say they were always played the same way, but that they always entered and exited at the same times. If the keyboard settings were noted at the start of the session, they were easily punched in and overdubbed if they made mistakes.

Beantown Home Cookin' recorded everything on their agenda within three weeks, allowing Bob to start recording the session musicians he wanted to bring in to punch up the recordings, so he gave the band the time off, which no doubt saved time and controversy as parts were added to the songs.

Morgen, as the composer-lyricist, was allowed to attend, but seldom did. Bob knew what he wanted, and Morgen wanted to save his opinions for the mixes, when all the tracks were recorded.

The Trashbabies arrived when expected, and it was great to see them all again. Morgen had continued his exercises, his ankle was coming along well, and he was looking forward to working with the Trashbabies on their routines.

As for the Trashbabies vocals, they'd nailed "Peeping Tom" and were going through the rest of their parts like they'd been singing them all their lives.

"Dog, Roebuck, and Lapwing," intended for a theatrical exit, was so beautifully performed, recorded, and evocative, that Alan went so far as to suggest it might make a hit single. The Trashbabies brought so much attitude, style and elegance to Beantown Home Cookin's music and stage presentations, they seemed to be on their way to stardom in their own right.

"If you keep writing stuff like this for the Trashbabies," George gleefully warned Morgen, "We'll all end up sidemen for them."

The record company execs, eager to hear the new material, asked Bob to meet them at the studio on Sunday, to let them hear the work in progress.

Bob loved "Peeping Tom," the first song completed and mixed, and strongly believed it had serious hit potential. He played it first, and was surprised and angry when, instead of praise, the infuriated Chairman of the Board, who had two teenage daughters, was outraged by a song he believed pandered to the worst kind of violent, sexual abuse, flatly refused to release it, and threatened to cancel the entire album.

Bob, deeply offended by the Chairman's outburst, replied that if the song was not on the album, his name would not be on it, either, and walked out before the contretemps spun completely out of control.

That evening, Alan called Rodney to bring him up to date on the fallout from the failed sneak preview of the recordings.

Shaken by the news, Rodney asked, "So, where's that leave us? Has Bob quit? Has he been fired?"

"That's still up in the air," Alan replied. "Bob left before it went that far. And as for someone getting fired, if it comes to that, I expect I'll be at the top of the list. We should meet tomorrow to discuss our options."

"Hotel or rehearsal hall?

"The rehearsal hall," Alan replied, "at ten o'clock."

"We'll be there," Rodney said, and turned off his phone.

CHAPTER EIGHTEEN

The rehearsal hall was a big, empty barn, with huge double doors, and an original rough-hewn plank floor inside over which a temporary tubular truss stage had been installed, and covered with seamless, interlocking tongue and groove flooring, concert lighting and a public address system powered by a manned, relatively quiet, mobile diesel generator parked outside. A smaller, low tubular stage for the drummer was setup at the center, rear of the eight by six-meter stage.

That Monday morning, twenty of the 36 folding chairs set up in front of the stage had been rearranged into a large circle, and the generator was only powering the work lights and electric wiring to the craft services table, where hot coffee, tea, and cocoa, a variety of cold soft drinks, and a very tempting display of fresh pastries beckoned. Quilted sound-proofing was all over the outside walls and could be slid along the horizontal poles to cover the double doors. Rodney, Beantown Home Cookin', and the Trashbabies were all present, and with Alan presiding, the meeting was officially called to order at 10:10 a.m.

Alan first brought everyone up to date on where matters stood, essentially as he'd previously reported to Rodney, then began outlining their options.

"Given that 'Peeping Tom' is scratched," Alan began . . .

" 'Peeping Tom' is Homeric simile. 'Even as' one person or thing is or was, 'so is' or was, someone or something else," Morgen interrupted. "It's at the root of all sympathetic magic, including the infamous Rite of Spring, where promiscuity is intended to increase the herds and provide bountiful harvests. One might argue sympathetic magic is at the heart of the Lord's Prayer in 'Thy will be done on Earth as it is in Heaven'."

Alan reddened, but carefully measured his reply. "One might," he agreed, "but one damn well better not! To compare The Lord's Prayer to some licentious heathen ritual may be more offensive than 'Peeping Tom.' And it doesn't matter how innocent or clever your motives may be, the song has to stand on its own, without you explaining it, and as of now, it comes across as celebrating, even encouraging, outlawed violent behavior targeting women."

"That's not…" Morgen began, but Alan cut him off.

"I'm your A&R man. My job, Morgen, if I still have it, is to develop you and your repertoire, and help you choose songs with hit potential.

" 'Peeping Tom,' or any attempt to defend 'Peeping Tom,' would be a distraction that might hurt all we've done so far."

Theresa, easily the quietest of the Trashbabies, said wryly, "I'm not really comfortable with it, Morgen."

Then Sylvia spoke up. "If we don't need it, why do it?"

Sophie added, "Especially if it's going to hurt us."

"Fine," Morgen said, his support falling apart, "Scratch it!"

"Thank you," said Alan, having achieved the first part of his mission. "Assuming they haven't severed their legal responsibilities to the production of this record, I think it would behoove us to present an alternative song to Bob."

208

"When we discussed it over the phone, you told me the powers that be had already approved this new material," Rodney countered.

"They had," Alan said, "and in the excitement of feeling like they might be doing something to preserve the environment, and the fact that I'd lined up Bob to produce it for us, they may not have scrutinized it then, as much as they are now."

"Now, they want to censor all my songs?" Morgen asked.

Faced with the concern and betrayal he saw reflected in their eyes, Alan replied, "I don't know that, Morgen. Please keep in mind, it's my head on the chopping block. I've been on your side since the beginning, charming, wheedling, and perjuring myself to put this deal together. If I don't find a way to salvage it, I'm finished."

There was a moment of silence, as everybody realized Alan's jeopardy.

"Okay," Alan said, "about 'The Fool'."

"What's wrong with 'The Fool'?" Morgen asked.

"Nothing," Alan answered. "I think the song has real potential as a novelty song, but I also think your interpretation is way over the heads of your audience, and I'm not convinced that a novelty song is strong enough to be your title track."

"I expect it to go to and stay in the Top 40 for a very long time," Morgen replied.

Alan answered, "You won't be able to go around explaining it to everyone, any more than you could with 'Peeping Tom'."

"I'll put the word out," Rodney said.

"Much appreciated, Rodney, but what makes you think that getting the word out will make any difference?" Alan asked. "Do you really think anyone will take it seriously?"

"Some will buy it as a simple novelty song," Rodney said, "But others, and especially Morgen's fans, will discover its mysteries, and spread the word."

"Possibly," Alan agreed, "but Morgen, I still want you to come up with a new song to try to convince Bob to stay with us, and to show the suits we're taking this all seriously."

"Any kind of song in particular?" Morgen asked, his voice dripping with sarcasm.

"I was thinking of something featuring the 'harmony of the carnal and the mystical,' you promised in the opening to 'The Fool'," Alan replied, "and if it was something that might lead your fans to desire greater understanding of 'The Fool,' I suspect it would be especially well-received by all concerned. Alternatively, if you wish, I can find a new song for you."

"I'll give it some serious thought," Morgen said.

Alan's voice sounded sincere when he shook Morgen's hand, and said, "Thank you, Morgen," before he left.

Rodney announced it was time for lunch, and after saying that they could vote for as many different cuisines as they wanted, called for a show of hands to decide whether to go Chinese, Indian, Italian, or to an English Pub. The pub won. Of course, with a sudden crush of an unexpected 25 extra customers for lunch, it had to be the biggest, most expensive pub in the vicinity, but one of the van drivers called ahead, made last-minute reservations, and their surprise luncheon visit was such a big success, that they didn't bother going back to the rehearsal barn at all, but called to tell the generator crew to wrap, meet them at the pub, and take the afternoon off, which everybody did.

Everybody, that is, except Morgen. After lunch, he took a cab back to the hotel, sat in front of his computer, and tried to come up with a new song. Unconsciously, picking at the keys, his fingers began playing the tune from that moonlit night above the stone circle that came back to him when he awoke in the hospital, but now was resolved with new lyrics recorded as they came to him.

"Seems so distant, but still so sublime.
It's not that place has been displaced,
So much as, maybe, time.
Could it just be inside of me,
Born of my hopes and fears?
A tale to tell? A magic spell?
The Music of the Spheres?"

No one was back, when Morgen had dinner from the carvery of the hotel dining room, and chose medium rare prime rib. He skipped dessert and returned to his room, kicked off his shoes, stretched out on his bed and shut his eyes.

Before she spoke, he felt her warm body roll over on top of him, her soft breasts pressing against his skin.

"You're not going to sleep, are you?" she asked.

Morgen looked up into Laura's beautiful eyes, her face framed by her long, blonde hair, staring down at him with an impish grin that suggested sleep was not on her agenda.

"I was just resting my eyes," he answered.

"When you could be looking at me?" she teased.

"They're all rested now," Morgen said.

"Good" she said, her grin widening, "I like the way you look at me."

She brought her face close to his, and as his arms embraced her, and held her close, she kissed him long enough to make her intentions clear. He tried to roll her over, but she resisted, and stayed on top, gazing down at him, and still favoring him with her naughty smile, said, "I like it when you look at me, and I like to look at you, too."

"And I love the feel of your skin on mine," he said.

"And what else?" she teased.

"Everything else."

"Everything?" she asked, her eyes narrowing, as she shifted slightly, and withdrew her right hand from his chest, caressing his skin as she ran her hand down over his body.

"Oh, yes," he replied, anticipating her target. "But what about singing your song for everyone to hear?"

"Your mystical encounter will soon be a matter of record."

Laura's impish grin became downright salacious, as she continued to slide her hand down and down, nearly derailing Morgen's train of thought.

Responding to her intimate caress, he gasped, "So, now, you're going to leave it all up to them?"

Straddling him, she raised her hips slightly, rocked back, sighed with satisfaction, and said, "It always has been."

He had an out-of-body moment, looking down at the two of them, on his huge, oaken bed, the medieval instruments inlaid with gold, ivory, and brilliantly colored enamels all around, and his great mastiff friend, watching, sphinxlike. He awoke instantly, and immediately regretted it.

He'd left his midi workstation on, and when he sat in front of it, the screen lit up, as if anticipating his input, but he couldn't remember what Laura said that woke him.

Morgen sat, staring at his keyboard for a moment, until he suddenly did remember, and repeated aloud, "Mystical Encounter' will be a matter of record!"

That night, at around 2:30 a.m., he began picking out a melodic opening, tentatively, at first, then with more certainty. He turned on his notation program, set an audible tempo click track, counted in the click track, then played his intro to "Mystical Encounter," that displayed on his monitor and began spitting out of his ink-jet printer as he sang the lyrics.

"Can this be defined as simple-minded superstition?"

"Just another sign, of some neurotic condition."

The next day, in the rehearsal barn, Morgen continued singing as he handed out the sheet music to the band.

"You say it's déjà vu and you, you trust your intuition."

Roger, the drummer, played a drum intro, and the other musicians joined in as their parts come up.

"I knew that's what you'd do, It's true.

I had a premonition."

George smiled and wagged his head, concentrating on his playing as he recognized the line from their conversation, and that afternoon, as the Trashbabies filed into the rehearsal hall, Morgen, sang as he handed them their sheet music.

"This is a *Mystical Encounter*, reality revised.

Everything required, recognized."

The Trashbabies, in groups of three, sang their background vocals into three separate mikes, as Morgen paced, sang, and conducted their separate entries.

"We maybe could ignore simple temporal dislocation.

But this is something more–more like predestination.

If this is second-sight, you can't ignore the implication."

Less than a week later, Alan sat with the recording engineer at the studio console, aiming his phone receiver at the studio monitors to share the sound with Bob over the phone.

"O, stay with me, tonight

And seek celestial confirmation!"

Bob, wearing an audio headset plugged into his cell phone, sat on the dock of his Thames river hideaway, gazing out over the water, and bobbing his head as he listened with ever-growing interest as Morgen, supported by the chorus of "ahhs" the Trashbabies sang.

"If the sun should rise in the west now,

I won't be surprised.

I can see the fire in your eyes."

Bob's voice was lost in the music as he shouted into his cell phone, "Horns. I'll want horns!"

Inside the studio, Alan nodded happily, and scribbled "Horns" on his note pad.

The following week, Bob and Alan both sat at the console, as a brass section recorded Bob's required horns.

The following day, Morgen was there, wearing earphones and singing in an isolation booth.

"I'm drawn to you. You're drawn to me,

"Like we were magnetized!"

Inside the control booth, Bob slowly increased the volume slide on Morgen's vocal track.

"Pulse rate ever higher. Feel it rise!"

On the afternoon of August 26th, Rodney was happily listening from where he sat on the sofa at the back of the control booth, as he punched in a number on his cell phone.

In her office at the TV station where her show originated, Angela answered her phone, and held it at arms-length until she realized what and who she was hearing, and then held it closer to her ear, to hear Morgen's vocal.

"You know that what I feel is real, not my imagination."

Rodney held the phone toward the monitors so Angela could hear it better.

"You're too close to conceal your erotic inclination."

As Angela listened, she smiled.

"I feel your heat. Oh, your subtle undulation."

The Trashbabies, wearing headphones, sang the backup, and although Morgen could not see them singing in the large room, he was able to see their reflections in the glass of his isolation booth as he sang.

"The feeling is so sweet. I tremble in anticipation.

This is a . . ."

The Trashbabies couldn't see Morgen as they sang their backup harmonies in the open studio, but they could clearly see into the control booth, where some watched Rodney, holding his phone toward the control room monitors, and the others watched Bob, Alan, and the engineer.

"*Mystical Encounter*. It cannot be disguised."

In her office, Angela was nodding appreciatively, tapping out the rhythm on her desktop as she listened to the song.

"Now feel my desire . . . localize!"

When Angela heard Morgen sing "localize," her mouth dropped.

She recovered quickly, looked around to be sure she hadn't been observed, and then laughed. And as the music began to fade, jotted "call Alan re Morgen" on her note pad.

On Tuesday, the 29th, it was standing room only in the control room, with everybody joyfully listening to the final mix of "Mystical Encounter."

On Thursday, the 31st, Rodney and Alan dropped in at the rehearsal barn and announced the record company accepted "Mystical Encounter" and was going ahead with the album.

"So, will Bob's real name be on the album?" Morgen asked.

Rodney answered, "That's still being negotiated."

Alan explained, "Bob wants more money for producing the additional song, and the company hasn't said either way. I expect they'll come back with a counter offer, but Bob is still pissed about them rejecting 'Peeping Tom,' so I don't know."

"They should just pay him," George said.

"When Bob had the Trashbabies sing their chorus, and then brought them in like waves on a beach," Morgen added, "that really put it over the top."

The band and the chorus agreed, but Rodney quickly quelled the potential uprising by saying, "That's between the record company and Bob. We should all stay out of it, unless specifically asked for an opinion. We've come too far."

"I know I said this before," Alan chimed in, "but Morgen, if you can write a song like that in one night on demand, the sky's the limit!"

"I wrote it for us, for this crowd, and I heard them and all their parts coming together as I knocked it out on the keyboard." Morgen said. "As for dreaming up a new song, it's not the first time I've been accused of that, is it?"

After supper, Rodney pulled Morgen aside.

"Alan's setting up a distributor sponsored U.K. tour to follow the album release, before we leave for Hamburg."

"Is he?" Morgen asked.

"It will be a promotional tour, paid for by the distributor," Rodney explained, "all very hush-hush. You won't be on the bill, except as mystery guest performers."

"How's that work?" Morgen asked.

"It's brilliant," Rodney explained. "It's too late to line up bookings in any worthwhile U.K. venues, but the record company has acts booked all over, and they can arrange to feature you in a special guest set, in whichever venue is the biggest and best for you to available showcase, by having their talent give up one of their sets."

"Do we get paid?"

"The distributor covers all the per diem, transportation, hotels, cartage, setup and breakdown."

"But we don't get paid." Morgen confirmed.

"I'll cover us," Rodney explained, "at our rehearsal rates."

"Rehearsal rates for live shows?"

"One set. A showcase to promote album sales," Rodney explained, "That, and radio play, sells tickets on your tours, and puts money in our pockets."

"But if 'pocket tour' isn't advertised, how does that help?"

"Give me a chance, and I'll tell you," Rodney said. "It won't be advertised in the media beforehand, but it will be covered by the media, after the fact. More to the point, your clearly stenciled road cases will arrive in broad daylight, your roadies will all be wearing embossed European Tour jackets, and select local media will be tipped off, so if some paparazzo gets photos, it might be too late for the papers, but it could end up online, and while calls to the venue or to ticket vendors can't acknowledge your appearance, they are allowed to say they don't know, but they've been getting calls hinting at a special guest appearance.

"They won't be told who the guest performers may be, or, if they show up, what time they'll go on, but nothing stimulates fan feeding frenzies quite like word of mouth."

"Is that legal?"

"Apparently, Alan and his crowd have done it before, and as far as venues are concerned, if a show isn't sold out, they love nothing more than seeing ticket sales skyrocket on the day of the show, which, incidentally, builds your reputation for sellouts for future bookings."

"We're not ready yet."

"It won't happen until the record is released and you're ready to go, both reasons why it has to be a stealth program."

"Well, it will give us a chance to get some audience responses to the new songs and choreography before we start our official European Tour."

"Not to mention opportunities for audience reactions for the European press. So, when will you be ready?"

"Musically, we should be ready in a week. I'm all that's holding up getting the choreography together, and I'm getting better every day, but it's all new, and I still tire quickly on some of the numbers."

"Just one show a night."

"One show a night."

"Not to change the subject, Alan thinks we should go ahead and schedule Angela Knight's, *Knight on the Town* for broadcast on the weekend of October 27th and 28th, which means she'll want to tape the show on Tuesday, the 24th with pick-ups, if necessary, on Wednesday, the 25th.

"Sounds good to me," Morgen said.

"Fine," Rodney agreed, "You've got the BBC costumers on Monday, the 23rd. Alan will not book you anywhere the following weekend, when *Knight on the Town* airs, but the BBC wants you all to do a walk-through at the ruined abbey on Monday, and Tuesday is the Halloween concert broadcast."

"We can do it," Morgen agreed.

George sang the songs during the band's morning rehearsals, running the sets in the order they were supposed to run in the concerts, sometimes arbitrarily cutting a song from the practice session, and usually, the second time through, not including "Flying Snakes," intended to be the encore, if one is required, or "Dog, Roebuck and Lapwing" the Trashbabies' exit, because they'd be running through both of them in the afternoon rehearsals with the Trashbabies. As for Morgen, most days he went to the Trashbabies' playback rehearsals in the morning, where, for his sake, they usually began by running through "In This Place" and "Dog, Roebuck, and Lapwing" first, both numbers that he didn't perform with them.

For "In This Place," they sang the introduction as they entered, marching as in a slow, wedding procession, circumnavigating the stage area, deliberately varying it to an oval to adjust to wide, shallow stages, or maintaining it as a circle, for narrower, deeper stages. Then each outside "flame dancer" took her turn as a soloist as the dances became ever more accelerated. Although Shiva was a male god, Morgen saw immediately how the routine related beautifully to the depiction of Shiva, as the cosmic ecstatic dancer, lord of dance and dramatic arts.

Morgen was so taken with the performance, that he was considering making it into a multi-media extravaganza, featuring projected images complete with glorious marching Indian elephants, and a projected image of a Nataraja Shiva bronze, but even without the multi-media elements, the piece already benefited enormously from Jasmine's introduction of Bollywood's exotic sensuality to the Trashbabies performance, and after playing it a few times in rehearsals, Roger introduced his temple blocks, and George, Jeff, and Owen added the synthesizer sitar elements that seemed to introduce music from all around the world–too late for the album, but dynamite for the stage show.

The Trashbabies used a spiraling march motif, going in the opposite direction, for the procession in their "Dog, Roebuck, and Lapwing" exit, that didn't feature dance but exotic, interwoven lyrics and melodies, that began with one voice, and added another for every half-line, and lost them, one by one, as they exited, until the last Trashbaby sang the last line, and the music slowly faded away.

As for Morgen's rehearsals with the Trashbabies, he insisted that once he started on a run-through, he didn't want to take a break until the entire set was run. His idea, and it seemed to be working, was to build up and restore his muscle tone and stamina, so that he'd be able to do an entire show without collapsing on stage.

At first, Morgen's routines were physically tough for him, memorizing his moves and timing, keeping on, even when he tired, and he was more than a little grateful to soak in a whirlpool bath at the end of each day. But the second week of his rigorous schedule, he put on a lavalier mic and sang the songs as he ran the routines, figuring out where and when to breathe, and discovered something that seemed humorous at first, but later became a serious matter of concern. Morgen had no trouble remembering any of the words, entrances or exits for the songs he'd brought back from Morningstone, but he missed entries, or flubbed lines in some of his newest original songs, and the more he worried, the worse it became.

"Relax," George told him. "You're trying too hard. You know all the words. You're the one who wrote them."

"It's not about knowing the words, George," Morgen snapped. "It's about knowing the order in which they come and go, and what comes next that eludes me."

"You'll get it," George said reassuringly. "Concentrate."

"Right," Morgen snapped. "Relax and concentrate. Got it."

Then they all got the word that the album was shipping, and would be released officially on September 26th, and their first performance was scheduled for Friday, the 29th, and the distributor was trying to set up another for the 30th.

Morgen didn't panic, but he did change his rehearsal schedule to rehearse the songs with the band every morning, and with the band and the Trashbabies every afternoon, which meant he didn't get to see any more of their rehearsals of "In This Place" or "Dog, Roebuck, and Lapwing," but he finally did get off the book, as far as his new lyrics were concerned, and by Monday, the 25th, he was no longer screwing up "Flying Snakes," "Mystical Encounter," "The Fool in Concert," "Sweet Mystery," "Bemused: First Canto," "Bemused: Second Canto," or "Bemused Third Canto."

On the morning of the 27th, Alan and Rodney came to the rehearsal hall with two cartons of albums. They opened both cartons to let everyone see them, but Alan explained that they weren't for them to keep.

"You'll all get yours delivered Stateside," Alan said. "These are for you to autograph before we send them out to our V.I.P. list, mostly radio Dee Jays, but a few to the venues we've been lining up for you."

As everyone signed albums, Morgen asked, "When, where, and what should we expect in staging, lighting, and sound?"

"Well," Alan replied, "I can tell you now, that your first two shows are surprise engagements in Leeds and Manchester, and the first is a week from Friday, so I hope you're all be up for it by then."

"We're up for it right now. What kind of venues are they?"

"They're rock show venues," Alan answered, "Leeds has a capacity of 2,000 plus and Manchester holds well over 3,000."

"Concert halls?" Morgen asked.

"Well, yes and no," Alan answered. "Officially, they're large dance clubs, but they feature up-and-coming talent in concert, and in both cases, they'll take you as surprise guests, which is about the only way we can book you this late in the day. And you'll be happy to know that the following weekend you'll have the same sort of surprise guest showcases, Friday night in Sheffield, which holds well over 2,000, and Birmingham, Saturday night, and it holds up to 3,000.

Morgen wasn't entirely happy, but they had to start playing somewhere.

He picked up an album, flipped it over to look at the credits and liner notes, and his frown deepened.

Seeing Morgen's expression, George asked him, "What's the matter now? Did they spell your name wrong?"

"They gave the producer's credit to some guy we never met," Morgen said.

"No. They didn't," George said with a really big grin.

Morgen's expression didn't change.

"C'mon," George chided. "You knew all along his name wasn't Bob."

When George's smile sank in, all Morgen could say, through his own big smile, was "No shit!"

Rodney approached. "Have you got a minute?"

George politely excused himself.

"In line with what I told Alan about getting the word out on 'The Fool'," Rodney said, "I promised to send Angela Knight an autographed album as soon as they came out, and I'd like to include a copy of your interpretation of 'The Fool'–give her a chance to check it out, maybe come up with some things she'd like to cover in the show, if that's all right with you?"

"Wicked brilliant," Morgen agreed. "It's all starting to come together, isn't it?"

"Damn straight," Rodney answered. "I just wanted to make sure we were on the same page with this."

"Make it happen."

CHAPTER NINETEEN

With a week before their first public performance of the new material, Morgen, George and Linda tried to anticipate the worst situations they might encounter, and come up with creative solutions to them.

Remembering their early dance hall days of 45-minute sets, the first thing Morgen and George did was work up a playlist that would present each song in an appropriate setting, and intersperse enough rock music to keep a dance crowd entertained. Linda was more concerned with the dance routines, and how much time the dancers would have to recover between songs.

For lack of the unilaterally cut "Peeping Tom," the playlist fell a little over two minutes short of the 45 minutes they'd been allotted for their performance. To make up the time, Morgen composed a two-and-a half minute dialogue in iambic pentameter, between a Bard (himself in a spotlight), and Mother Nature, (one or more of the Trashbabies), and on different nights, they would perform it in different way, always on a darkened stage, with Morgen, revealed in a follow-spot, freezing when the disembodied voice (or voices), of Nature spoke, his eyes searching the darkness beyond the follow spot, looking for the source of the omnipresent voice, speaking his lines into the void. Happily, even the hard-core rock crowds were enthralled.

> Nature: "Though the hour is late, I'm glad you've come.
> It's ages since you looked me in the face,
> But time is precious. There's much to be done.
> The days grow ever shorter for your race."
>
> Bard: "Are we, then, cast aside? Of use no more?
> Is this the scope and wisdom of the plan?
> To this, mad ending, all that's gone before?"

Nature: "When did I ever turn my back on Man?
Alone, of all my creatures, do you mock me.
Have I not satisfied your every need?
Still, nothing that you say can ever shock me.
Gall have you plenty, that, and glutton greed.
And have you grown so great that you don't need me?
The only change in Nature with you lies.
So, now you doubt my love. You needn't heed me,
But I, alone, will weep if your race dies."

Bard: "In all fairness, your harsh words assailed me.
I'd no idea the future looked so bleak.
Forgive me. It's my own strength that failed me.
We ask for truth, but miracles we seek."

Nature: "Like bards of old, go. Sway the mighty host.
Beloved poet, reach all that you can.
There are, among you, some wiser than most."

Bard: "In truth, I've little confidence in Man."

Nature: "I give all that I have, but make it do.
Obey my laws, even as I must.
Life is my gift. The living's up to you.
Succeed or fail, the outcome will be just."

They created a playlist for the BBC *Live Halloween Concert* broadcast related to their club format, based on the new album. Morgen suggested they introduce each band member, allowing 10-20 seconds to show off his skills, take a bow, and the same for all nine Trashbabies, a strut on, pose, exit that might run as much as 30 seconds each if they entered from the wings and worked their way across the stage.

If they ran short, he suggested they might even call everyone back on stage to hold hands and take a coordinated bow with him. If they could get away with all that, it should add about six minutes to their show. And if they did an instrumental "Peeping Tom" Entr'acte, that would give him another 2 minutes and 30 seconds, and with 8 minutes of Trashbabies' international "In This Place" that, with the BBC title sequence and an announcer, and the final BBC end credits, plus all the audience reaction footage, should do it, and presented his playlist to George and Linda.

> "Dialogue with Mother Nature" (introduction)
> "Witchy Stew" (to set a spooky Halloween Mood)
> "Morningstone" (to invite the audience into the fantasy)
> "The Stranger" (to introduce the Halloween tour guide)
> "Bemused: First Canto" (anticipating the adventure)
> "The Fool" (The first odd character met along the way)
> "Bemused: Second Canto" (reaction to The Fool's promises)
> "In This Place" (a musical sampling of ethnic diversity)
> "Peeping Tom" (Entr'acte instrumental)
> "Bemused: Third Canto" (the dawn of understanding)
> "Mystical Encounter" (harmony of carnal and mystical)
> "The Likes of You" (a hymn to the goddess of love)
> "Sweet Mystery" (invocation of Mother Nature)
> "Reprise of the Fool" (after all, only the messenger)
> "Flying Snakes" (a call for rational awareness and action)
> "Dog, Roebuck, and Lapwing" (universal secrets revealed)

"We can't play 'Peeping Tom'," George said.

"We won't sing it," Morgen said. "It will be an instrumental entr'acte, a sneaky intermission to give the ladies a chance to get ready for the next act after performing 'In This Place.' Allowing a full 2 minutes and 30 seconds for 'Peeping Tom,' and most of another minute when I sing 'Bemused, Third Canto,' and another minute or so before they have to come back on for 'Mystical Encounter,' they'll have a little more than four minutes to make the turnaround. Is that enough?"

"Not today, it isn't," said Linda, with a smile, "but with a little practice, it could be."

"We'd be better off cutting to a commercial," George said.

"I don't think they have commercials," Morgen replied.

"Maybe the BBC could insert a filler, some rehearsal footage, or even better, a short interview, or interviews with some of us, the way they do at sporting events, to cover the time you've allotted to the Entr'acte instrumental."

"Brilliant, George," Linda agreed. "We should talk to them and see what they think."

"Don't be surprised if they kill the idea of a six-minute parade to introduce us all individually. I'm pretty sure they'd prefer an interview segment for our intermission, rather than risk losing their audience," George added.

"Good point," Morgen replied. "I've been thinking about how to stage it live, rather than how they'd stage it for TV."

"We should talk to Alan," George suggested. "He'll know who we should talk to at the BBC. I have no idea what it will do to their budget, or who would make that decision."

"Either do I," Morgen admitted.

"We should all be part of that discussion," Linda suggested.

"I'm sure we'll be consulted," George offered.

"They'll have to consult us," Morgen agreed.

On Friday, October 6th, after brunch, it took more than six hours, with only one stop along the way, to travel by buses from their hideaway in the Cotswolds to the gig in Leeds, West Yorkshire, after which they were spirited off to Manchester, where the hotel expected them, checked them in after midnight, and allowed to sleep late the next morning.

Their roadies had stayed overnight in Leeds, and arrived in Manchester in the early afternoon of Saturday, the 7th, to set up for that night's surprise show. Both shows had been sold out, their performances were enthusiastically received by the crowds, and that night, at the hotel, they talked into the wee hours over their triumphs before going to bed.

Somehow, they managed to check out before 11:00 o'clock Sunday morning and were back in their Cotswolds' hideaway in time for supper, Sunday night. For an officially unannounced concert-oriented showband playing for surprised dance hall crowds, they were pleased with their performances.

Rodney hosted dinner for them all in one of the private banquet rooms, and told them about the venues that were coming on for their November-December European tour, due to begin in an indoor arena in Hamburg, which meant they'd have custom staging, lighting, sound, seating, and would be performing to an essentially concert audience, that motivated them all the more to learn how everything was coming together. Happily, with winter weather on its way, everywhere they were booked in all of Northern and Central Europe was either an Opera House, a theater, or an indoor arena.

Meanwhile, Angela Knight put their new "concept album" on her office turntable, read Morgen's in-depth interpretation of "The Fool," and uncertain of its arguments, but impressed by its composition, listened attentively to the entire album, following his interpretation as she listened to "The Fool."

Morgen's interpretation was self-contained, and, however obscure his references may be, both the song and his composition intrigued her, so she handed the album and the interpretation of "The Fool" to Nanette, her production assistant, a bright young Cambridge graduate, to check Morgen's references to Graves' *White Goddess*, and report back to her.

The following weekend, Morgen, the band and the Trashbabies were all in Sheffield, South Yorkshire, for their Friday, October 13th, surprise appearance, where they were every bit as enthusiastically received as in Manchester. On Saturday night, in Birmingham, the West Midlands, in another huge dance venue, some of their surprise performance was captured by newsreel camera crews, and they saw footage of their show Sunday morning on the telly, and while nobody actually said anything about an eventual gig in Wembley Stadium for fear it might jinx it, it was an idea never far from their minds, however deeply concealed, even from each other.

Monday morning, when they assembled in their makeshift rehearsal hall, Morgen showed them the only changes he'd made to his playlist, which now included an intermission for BBC interviews and rehearsal footage that brought the show up to the full one hour schedule, without "Peeping Tom" or Morgen's six minutes of introductions and bows.

Monday morning, October 23rd, the day before the show with Morgen was to be taped, Nanette reported to Angela.

"Good morning," she said, as she stepped cautiously into Angela's office, carrying a thin, zipped padfolio document bag in her left hand and a hardbound copy of Robert Graves' *White Goddess* under her arm.

Angela greeted her loudly and anxiously, saying "Good morning, Nanette! What have you got for me?"

"I spent a lot of time on this, Angela," Nanette said as she lowered herself into the leather chair opposite her boss's desk.

"I expect it will be well-worth it," Angela said, smiling brightly.

"I hope so," Nanette said, as she placed the copy of *The White Goddess* on Angela's desk.

"Well, let me have it," Angela prodded.

Nanette unzipped her padfolio document bag, took several typed sheets of paper from it, and reported, "To start with, I took Morgen's interpretation at face value, and considered my job to be verifying his assertions, based on Graves' book, and on the face of it, I did. It is what Morgen claimed it is, a credential song–*his credential song*, and that makes it a job application."

"A job application?" Angela wondered aloud.

"Some of his references are obscure, but judging by what I read in Graves, they're substantially accurate," Nanette continued. "More to the point, he's got a lot going on in the non-conforming couplets between verses."

"So, it's not really nonsense at all," Angela concluded.

"It's definitely not nonsense," Nanette confirmed. "The verses are all part of an impressive litany of his esoteric knowledge, but he finishes each quatrain with a couplet that reveals his true identity and motives."

"I'm listening," Angela said.

Nanette continued, "The first time he says, 'Chief Bard to the ancients am I, anointed in the sacred pool. My ancestral home is the sacred grove. Honor your mentor, the Fool.' When I read that, at first, I thought he was claiming descent from ancient Druids, and maybe he is, but the next time the couplet appeared, he claimed 'Chief Bard to Immortals am I. O'er fantastic realms do I rule. There's none to whom I need bend my knee . . . Honor your leader, the Fool'!"

"And . . ." Angela prompted.

"I had missed that the first time through," Nanette admitted, "but by stating clearly that he rules over realms of fantasy, that makes the Immortals who dwell there, fantasies, too."

"So, he admitted he just dreams them up!" Angela said.

"He not only dreams them up," Nanette observed, "he orders their days, and says so! In his third couplet, he writes, 'Chief Bard of the ancients am I. Wit is my singular tool.' And that's the real deal! Wit is his singular tool! He claims to be beloved of the Ninefold Muse, but we'd still call him a Fool. And that would likely be so. He claims to see things we don't see, hear things we can't hear, and experience things we'd fail to understand, and would probably reject as nonsense if he tried to share them."

"Covering all his bases, eh?" Angela observed. "So, whose job is he after?"

"Would you believe The Messiah?" Nanette asked.

"Oh, no."

"You'll feel better when I tell you about my irrefutable evidence that proves he's a fraud!" Nanette exclaimed.

"What's he done?" Angela gasped. "How is he a fraud?"

"He claims he composed 'The Fool' before he read Graves' book," Nanette continued, "but the references he cites are all in Graves' book, and there are far too many to be coincidental."

"I don't know," Angela said. "The way he tells it, he wrote his song before he read the book, and discovered a paradigm in it that applied to his writing, as well. I saw enough in that book to agree with him, and if such a paradigm exists, how can you say his work is fraudulent? You didn't see any of the footage we shot in Birmingham, did you?"

"No. I was buried in Graves' book all weekend, making sure I'd found what I thought I'd found," Nanette replied.

"Well, Morgen introduced his show with a scene he'd composed in iambic pentameter, clearly composed for current audiences, and its theme was definitely Morgen's own," Angela said, embarrassed to be defending Morgen against the red-faced research assistant she'd assigned to check him out.

"I didn't say he plagiarized Graves," Nanette said. "I only said he copied the formula he found in Graves, and then wrote his song based on that formula. And now, from what you just told me, he's done it with Shakespeare, too!"

"You can't accuse someone of fraud for adopting someone's style."

"I'm not. I'm saying that the song he supposedly composed for the Trashbabies exit," Nanette continued, "could only have been written by someone who'd studied Graves. Whether you use this or not, is entirely up to you, but he used little-known ancient bardic symbolism in 'Dog, Roebuck, and Lapwing,' which is the title of Chapter Three in Graves' *White Goddess*, and goes on to write, 'your nonsense song makes my ears ring. Between the lines, I hear you sing, Dog Roebuck, and Lapwing.' Those three creatures, when they appear in ancient poetic works, indicate that a secret is concealed in the text that follows. It may not be plagiarism, but it's derivative and proves he was familiar with Graves' work."

229

Nanette handed the book across the desktop to Angela, and said, "I marked the page for you."

"Thank you, Nanette," Angela said. "Really good work."

"I hope you'll find it useful. It was a lot to wade through."

"It's useful, Nanette," Angela said. "I couldn't get by without you."

Nanette knew that Angela was a fan of Morgen's, and she'd been upset by her revelations of Morgen's feet of clay, but Nanette also genuinely believed it was better to unmask a charlatan than let him carry on, and was proud of her part, however great or small it might be, in unmasking Morgen.

For her part, Angela read Graves' chapter on "Dog, Roebuck and Lapwing" twice, and could find nothing wrong with Nanette's logic. She played the record, listened closely to "Dog, Roebuck, and Lapwing," and without realizing when or how, fell completely under its spell.

How long she'd stared out the window, listening to the record click it's way around and around, taking her somewhere, anywhere, or possibly nowhere, before she finally snapped out of her trance, and then, as she did every night before taping a show, went home, heated up a TV dinner in the microwave, ate, and went to bed early, more than a little depressed.

As for Morgen, he reviewed his interpretation of "The Fool," assuming that since Angela had it, she might use it to steer their conversation, and he did not want to forget anything he'd written, or how he'd come to the conclusions he had, after his Tom Brady fiasco. The show taped in the early afternoon, he wasn't expected to show up until 10 o'clock, for wardrobe, makeup and hair, and that left him time to go over his set list.

Mid-morning, the following day, Morgen heard a knock on his door. He opened it to find Rodney, looking a little too serious for that landmark morning.

"Alan tells me the TV crew who took the footage of you in Birmingham works for Angela Knight," Rodney said.

"Who do you think tipped her off?" Morgen asked.

"It wasn't me, and it wasn't Alan," Rodney said. "She's Angela Knight, hostess of the biggest pop culture talk show on television, syndicated halfway around the world. She knows all the club owners, managers, musicians, too, for that matter, not to mention the roadies and teamsters who drive the vehicles, the security people, everyone. If she wants to know who's where, all she's got to do is make a few phone calls."

"Well," Morgen said, "I guess those are all good reasons to keep her on our side."

"She may not be on our side."

"Why do you say that?"

"Well, you did leave her hanging on May Day."

"That's a long time ago."

"To you, it is. But what if it's not to her."

"Well, then," Morgen answered with his famous grin, "I'll just have to charm her."

"Be careful," Rodney cautioned. "Listen carefully to what she says. Be courteous, and answer her questions politely."

"What's put the wind up with you?" Morgen asked.

"I don't know. Maybe it was that damned owl."

"What owl?" Morgen asked, shuddering.

"Last night," Rodney said, "I dreamt I saw a toy owl. The kind that looks real, but has a transistor radio in it. When I reached out to pick it up to see how to turn it on, it blinked at me and said your name."

"My name?" Morgen asked, trying to appear amused.

"Creepy," Rodney said. I had trouble getting back to sleep."

A voice interrupted. "Sir!" it said.

It was Morgen's driver, announcing it was time to get on the road if they didn't want to be late. Morgen definitely didn't want to be late, so they left, and Rodney called after them, "Stay alert!"

CHAPTER TWENTY

On the TV studio set of Angela Knight's *Knight on the Town*, Angela sat with Morgen, interviewing him for her show. The atmosphere was friendly, but charged, Angela probing and Morgen displaying all the wit, charm and charisma he hoped would one day make him a superstar.

"I'd only been out a matter of hours," Morgen said, "but for me, whole days had passed. And I recall all of it. I remember every word and all the music that inspired our new album."

"Prepping for this show, I listened to your new album more than once," Angela said. "I found it mysteriously enchanting, and not at all what I expected. This isn't really a rock and roll album, is it?"

"It's what we call a concept album, but we were never really a typical rock and roll band. We've always intended to be a showband. We play original rock and roll songs and ballads, but now, with the Trashbabies on board, I've begun composing music for their interpretive dances."

"Like 'In This Place'?" Angela asked.

"Exactly."

Angela said, "You're listed as the composer and lyricist on the album, but if this is all music you heard while in another dimension, you can't really claim them as original compositions, can you?"

"I'm glad you brought that up," Morgen replied. "It didn't all come from that other dimension, as you put it, but I did think, long and hard, about the music I brought back from my dream, and finally came to the conclusion, based on the empirical evidence, that I could, and should, claim it as my own."

"What empirical evidence is that?" Angela wanted to know.

"On that rainy May Eve, or the wee hours of May Day, when I crashed into the tree, I was knocked unconscious.

"I was discovered, a few hours later, still strapped into the vehicle, proving I never visited Morningstone, or anywhere else, in those hours before I was found, and in the hospital, where, thanks to some obscure clause in the rental agreement for that unfortunate automobile, I was tested for drugs and alcohol as soon as I arrived, none were found present in my system. That's the empirical evidence.

"But I distinctly remember spending most of two days in Morningstone, a parcel of apparently metaphysical real estate where I met Furies, Fates and Muses, a living, breathing goddess of love, and perhaps Mother Nature herself, and where I heard, arranged, and even sang much of the music and lyrics you heard on the new album."

"Your manager, Rodney Hazelton, when he sent me your album, also sent me your fascinating interpretation of 'The Fool,' reinforced by reference to *The White Goddess*, a book by Robert Graves, first published in 1948, subtitled *A Historical Grammar of Poetic Myth,*" Angela said. "I understand that book was first brought to your attention by one of the Trashbabies."

"Yes," Morgen replied. "Alice brought it to my attention when I introduced my new song, 'The Fool.' She'd read *The White Goddess* and was struck by similarities between my lyrics and some ancient Welsh poems Graves interpreted."

"But you'd never heard of it until Alice told you about it."

"That's correct. She even bought me a copy, and I saw, immediately, why she thought I'd seen it before."

"And that book inspired your interpretation of 'The Fool'."

"Yes."

"Morgen, you may not know, but Graves' *White Goddess* was rejected by the most imminent archaeologists, historians and folklorists of his time, and T. S. Eliot called it a 'prodigious, monstrous, stupefying, indescribable book'."

233

Morgen smiled and said, "Did he? T. S. Eliot, the man who wrote *Old Possum's Book of Practical Cats*?"

"You've read that?"

"No," Morgen said, with a chuckle, "but his name came up in my first BBC radio interview, the morning of our May Eve concert broadcast, and I looked him up on the internet. He came from a prominent Boston family, and ultimately settled in England. I wonder if the interviewer, knowing I hailed from Boston, was trying to establish some sort of link between us."

"I don't know," Angela continued, "but I found it amazing, that after just one read, you were able to so accurately ape Graves' style in your interpretation."

"It's innate," Morgen replied. "I've always been able to do it. When I started singing along with my parents' old records, I imitated the singers' voices, and when I read Shakespeare, I found myself speaking in iambic pentameter."

"Which you use in your introduction," Angela added.

"Guilty." Morgen admitted.

"But you never read *The White Goddess* until after you wrote 'The Fool'."

"True."

"And 'Dog, Roebuck and Lapwing'?" Angela asked.

"No, I was wide awake when I wrote that for Alice, a sort of 'thank you' note for introducing me to Graves. But, typically, it evolved, and now it's an exit song for the Trashbabies."

"So, you wrote that after you read *The White Goddess*."

"Yes," Morgen replied, "and when I said I read the book, I didn't mean every word, cover to cover. I focused on the ancient poems and thought I was done, until something clicked when I saw the title of the third chapter, 'Dog, Roebuck, and Lapwing,' I read the chapter twice, and took notes, which I almost never do. It was fascinating. I'd seen them all in my dream, but had no idea that they were bardic symbols, or their presence indicated what came next, or had just happened, was to be understood in mythological terms, or that there was magic between the lines."

"Do you believe you had a real out-of-body experience? Could Morningstone exist, perhaps in another dimension?"

Morgen gave it a moment of thought, before answering.

"We may have to redefine reality, but it was certainly real to me. You must have had a few particularly vivid dreams."

"I have," Angela replied, "but dreams aren't real."

"Aren't they?" Morgen continued. "Once you've dreamed them, they become part of your experience."

"Are you saying your adventure was nothing but a dream?"

"Not to me, it wasn't," Morgen replied. "But even if it was, it's now a matter of record."

"Do you believe Fates, Furies, and Muses really exist?"

For a moment, Angela thought Morgen wasn't going to answer, but he did, and his answer left her dumbfounded.

" 'Fragmentation of the goddess is merely a device of exposition, used to reveal the crisis dramatically through a confrontation between various aspects of her character'," he said. "In my dream, a teenage girl said that. It's another example of what I meant when I said all I needed to know was revealed while I was there!"

"If Furies, Fates, and Muses are just facets of a greater goddess," Angela asked, "who is she?"

"She's known by many names, in many tongues, and in every culture known to humanity," Morgen said. "She called herself 'Laura Webster,' a clue to her real identity. Websters were weavers, both attributes assigned to the Fates. As Laura, she's the prize awarded the bard best-beloved of the Ninefold Muse. I saw her as a beautiful woman, the incarnation of the goddess of love, a revelation of young Mother Nature. And later, within the Tomb of Every Hope, I learned that 'Divorce from Nature is a strange conceit, indulged by Man, alone, and to his shame.'

"And Angela, I suspect that's why we're in the mess we're in today. We talk a lot, but never get down to brass tacks."

"Brass tacks?" Angela repeated.

" 'Nature's balance is a sacred trust. Survive or die, the outcome will be just'," Morgen continued. "We've had a lovely chat, and you've asked me some excellent questions, but you didn't ask me the most serious question. You didn't ask if the human race will survive Nature's justice?"

Angela asked warily, "What would you have said, if I had?"

Morgen, normally upbeat, sighed before he answered, "I don't know. Once, music and magic were believed to go hand in hand. Enchantment was the way poets brought humanity into harmony with Nature. Their songs were spells meant to elevate human consciousness."

"That's asking a lot from a song, isn't it?" Angela asked.

"Maybe it's all a fairy tale, and no such music ever existed, but the idea that it might, that it could, is magical in itself. And the timing couldn't be better for casting a musical spell. Halloween is our one holiday devoted to magic and the supernatural, so don't you think it's worth a try?"

It was Friday night. Beantown Home Cookin', the Trashbabies, Rodney and Morgen had all gathered in the hospitality lounge to watch *Knight on the Town*. The screen showed a wide-angle shot of the *Knight on the Town* TV show set, a cozy armchair by a fireplace, a China teapot, teacup and saucer on a small table to one side of the armchair, a floor lamp casting a warm glow on Angela, sitting prettily forward on the edge of her seat, preparing to give her closing lines with earnest intensity.

The camera dollied in for a closeup of Angela. Looking directly into the camera, and therefore, directly at all her viewers, Angela said, "Wow! When Morgen gets down to brass tacks . . . but despite his exponentially expanding fan base, Morgen has detractors.

"He's accused of sexism by feminists who resent the name and on-stage antics of the notorious Trashbabies, and others object to the occult overtones they perceive in songs like 'The Stranger,' 'Witchy Stew,' and perhaps now, 'Flying Snakes.' These latest, candid revelations may just add fuel to the fires of their discontent."

At that, Rodney, watching along with all the rest, snarled "Shit!" was quickly hushed from all sides, and everyone's attention returned to the TV screen in time to see Angela smile graciously and say, "But I like Morgen. Oh, he's a challenge, but he certainly left me with a lot to think about. And if dreams do ever come true, why not this one? So, I say, 'Good luck, Morgen. It's nice to have you back'."

On TV, as Angela poured herself a cup of tea, the *Knight on the Town* logo appeared, and the voice over announcer began, "*Knight on the Town*" is brought to you, in part, by . . .'"

Back in the hospitality suite, Rodney turned off the TV.

Morgen, looking pleased with himself, said, "Thank you, Angela."

Alice said, "That was sweet, Morgen. Did you really write 'Dog, Roebuck and Lapwing' for me?"

"It started out that way, but then it grew and grew, and now, you all share it. But it really did start with you, Alice."

"I thought we'd see more footage from Birmingham," Jasmine said.

"We might have," Linda intoned, "If Rodney hadn't turned off the TV."

"If you think you missed something, tune in for the rerun tomorrow night," Rodney said, and left.

"Anyone want to play some cribbage?" Emery asked.

"I'll play you," Owen answered.

"I'm going to get something to eat," Morgen said, "if anybody's interested," and that signaled the start of a general exodus from the hospitality suite.

At breakfast, Rodney apologized for his reaction to the *Knight on the Town* program the night before as he and Morgen enjoyed a second cup of coffee and Danish pastries.

"I've heard from more than a dozen people since last night's broadcast," Rodney said, "and everybody thought you were great, and some were especially pleased that you'd put out the word about the environmental crisis of climate change."

"Without using any of those words," Morgen answered.

"I'm serious," Rodney said. "You were right on the money. It seems a lot of people are getting serious about the environment, and you were clever enough to identify and tap into their anxiety, so congratulations on a job well done."

"I was just telling it like it is," Morgen protested, but was secretly pleased that Rodney was coming around.

"And so, you know, I think 'Mystical Encounter' is a hell of a song. When I was talking to Alan, who was as amazed as I was, by the way, I wondered aloud how you managed to come up with a song like that, overnight, and he said it was a mystery to him, too, but he was thrilled that you did. Later, thinking about that conversation, I realized what I'd said, and I got to wondering if it was one of your mysteries. Did you just dream it up, or did you have help from 'the other side'?"

Morgen grinned and said, "I was alone, and wide-awake, in the middle of the night, when I wrote that song."

"Oh," Rodney said, sounding somewhat disappointed.

"But," Morgen continued, "It was inspired by a nocturnal visit from my lady friend on the other side of the veil."

"Inspired, you say?" Rodney replied, "Dare I ask how?"

"A gentleman would never tell," Morgen said, "but a fool might. I'd spent all afternoon trying to come up with something, but I'd never been so lost at sea, musically and lyrically, as I was that day, I 'diddled' as you call it, on the keyboard, and I'd written and discarded notes and fragments of rhymes, but in the end, everything I composed was rubbish.

In despair, I kicked off my shoes, laid back on top of my bed and rested my eyes, not wanting any outside distractions to interfere with my inner Muse, but nothing came. No music. No lyrics. Nothing. And then I felt a warm body roll over on top of me."

"Seriously?"

"Seriously enough to open my eyes!"

"Who was it?"

"It was my lady, and I'd be a liar if I said I wasn't turned on. It may even be that she came to turn me on, to reawaken my desire, and get my creative juices flowing again. I think she was giving me a choice—to be with her, or stay here to finish what I'd started. Frankly, I'd rather be with her, but didn't think I'd earned the privilege.

"That's when she assured me our 'Mystical Encounter' would soon be a matter of record. I think that's what woke me up. I hadn't written 'Mystical Encounter' yet, and apparently it had to be a matter of record before I could stay with her.

"Unfortunately, awake, I couldn't remember what triggered my awakening. I still had no new music. No new lyrics. Nothing. But I was wide awake, so I went to my midi workstation and began playing the short piece I now call 'Bemused: Second Canto.' It's the one that ends in a suspension, but as I played it that night, it came to a resolution. And when the lyrics for the resolved one came to me, I called it 'Bemused: Third Canto.'

That was already more than I'd accomplished all day, and I continued to 'diddle,' until what she said to me about our 'Mystical Encounter' being a matter of record came back to me, and with it, music and lyrics, too, almost faster than I could transcribe them—not something I *heard* on the other side, but something *inspired by a visit* from the other side."

"Tell me you're not messing with me," Rodney muttered.

"You asked. Are you planning to eat that pastry?"

"Yes, and I might even order another one!" Rodney snarled.

"So, *Knight on the Town* was a success, despite all my 'doom and gloom.' You heard her wish me luck?"

"She didn't just wish you luck," Rodney said. "She gave you her blessing! Remind me to send her a dozen roses."

"Send her a dozen roses," Morgen said.

"We're lucky it's a Halloween special," Rodney continued. "I can say it was all hype for the show."

"But it wasn't," Morgen said, turning serious again.

"Please refrain from telling the world that 'Mystical Encounter" was inspired by an imaginary goddess."

"But it was," Morgen said.

"The truth is, she's gone back to the supernatural world from whence she came, and you're still here," Rodney replied.

"Truth serves not," Morgen replied. "It is its own unbending master."

"That sounds like something you read on a fortune cookie."

"Something I just dreamed up," Morgen said.

Morgen excused himself when Rodney's cell phone buzzed. As he left the table, he heard Rodney say; "Good morning to you, too. Did you? Yeah. No, that's all genuine."

On Monday morning, they moved out of their Cotswolds hideaway, and checked into a hotel, far enough from the ruined abbey to avoid attracting attention. Early in the day, some of the band and some of the Trashbabies went sightseeing, but that afternoon, they were all taken to the abbey to assess how the production setup was coming along, and do a walk-through of the show. The location was on the chilly side, but they were glad to work on the large, deep stage, in front of the ruined abbey wall.

High above the stage was a canvas roof, and there were wings erected on both sides of the stage, housing large propane heaters hidden from sight that heated the stage area. They were especially excited to see the camera crane anchored in the center of the audience seating area that would allow for high-angle Busby Berkeley-style shots of their "In This Place" cosmic dance number.

During and after the walk-through, they were invited to partake of the snacks on the craft service table and told that their dressing rooms, makeup trailer and mobile green room would all arrive tomorrow, and be set up in the same area they were for the May Eve concert. That wasn't much help to Trish, who wasn't a Trashbaby then, but her partners all assured her they wouldn't let her get lost.

After the walk-through, they took digital photos of each other in areas where they thought the pictures would help tell their stories, but by 4:15 p.m., it was getting dark and the temperature was dropping, so they went back to their hotel, where, after supper, they looked at each other's pictures. At 10:30, Morgen went to bed, but with all he'd seen that day, and all he was hoping to accomplish on the morrow, he didn't get to sleep until after midnight.

Morgen awoke early, had an entire triangular box of Toblerone chocolate for breakfast, and asked one of the band's drivers to take him out to the ruined abbey. The remote location TV production van was already there, as were some of the crew. He entered what had once been a great hall, but now, without a roof and its walls in ruins, was back stage for the production. A motor home with a green room sandwich board sign in front designating it as the performers' lounge, the makeup trailer, and a honeywagon, were already in place. Morgen crossed the once great hall to see the view from the collapsed hole where once a huge window stood, but noticed a small flowering vine with tiny blue flowers, growing out of the cracks in the wall.

Morgen reached out to touch them, but hearing footsteps at the far side of the hall, turned to see who was there at that hour of the morning.

A woman, wearing a smock over her street clothes was crossing toward the makeup wagon.

"Excuse me!" Morgen called.

"Yes?" answered the woman who stopped and turned to see who challenged her.

"I was wondering . . ." Morgen began, but the woman recognized him and blurted out, "Oh my goodness! It's you!"

Morgen pointing at the scraggly vine, and asked, "Do you know what these flowers are?"

Frowning, the woman approached for a better look.

"I couldn't say, for certain," she said, "but I think my mother called them Periwinkles."

"Periwinkles," Morgen repeated. "I've heard of them, but I don't think I've ever seen them before."

"To be perfectly honest, I'm not sure if she meant the flowers or the color, but they are pretty, aren't they?"

"More than pretty," Morgen said. "We call this a ruin, but what's in ruins is our work, stone and mortar meant to last for ages, but today, in these ruins, seeing Nature reclaim her own. These tiny, pretty flowers, are working their way through and around the stones, are literally re-covering our rubble."

"And to think, that every year, they probably cut them back before the start of the tourist season," the woman said.

"And every year, off-season, they return," Morgen said with great satisfaction.

"It's amazing what you can see, if you just pause to take a closer look at what's all around us."

"It is," Morgen agreed. "Do you know if this abbey was built over an earlier, pre-Christian site?"

"I really wouldn't know. I'm not from around here," she answered, wondering where this conversation was going, and made slightly uncomfortable by his question.

Morgen noticed, smiled, reached out to shake her hand, and said, "I'm Morgen, and I'm not from around here, either."

"Oh, I know who you are," the woman replied as she smiled back and shook his hand. "I'm Irene, the makeup lady, and pleased to meet you."

"You, too," Morgen said. "I guess I'll be seeing you, later."

"You will," Irene said, studying his face. "I'm the one who has to see that you're presentable."

Morgen laughed. "You'll have your work cut out for you."

"I'll do my best," she answered as she turned to walk toward her makeup trailer, but looking back over her shoulder, added, "Luckily, it's Halloween. Worst case, I'll put you in a mask."

"Excellent!" he said. "I like a woman who comes prepared."

Irene, before entering her trailer, paused in the doorway just long enough to favor him with a smile and a wave. "Later," she called, went inside and shut the door.

Morgen glanced back at the scraggly vine, and said, as if saying it made it so, "Periwinkles."

George arrived in the second passenger van, at 10:15 a.m.

"I knew you'd be out here," George said.

"Déjà vu?" Morgen asked.

"You have direct access to the stream of consciousness, don't you?" George asserted.

"So do we all. We decided it's inherent, remember?"

"But you know things you've never studied."

"I sometimes think I do, but that may be more hubris than proven ability," Morgen replied. "Didn't we agree that we all have innate knowledge, that comes to the fore in times of dire necessity, severe emotional distress, or sometimes joy?"

They both fell silent for what seemed like a long time. Finally, Morgen said, "We are both actively involved in the stream of consciousness, especially when we have these discussions, but since you brought it up, I'd like to share what I think may be a useful flow chart."

Seeing Morgen's grin, George remarked, "Pun intended."

"Think of my recent experience and inspiration as carried by the brook that flows from the Tomb of Every Hope, a tributary emptying into a subconscious stream that floats my music, lyrics and hopes into the Sacred Pool, a repository for all human wisdom, inspiration, experience, and conjecture, a pool of knowledge where all subconscious aspirations are mixed before they flow from the subconscious into the Stream of Consciousness, and become randomly available to all.

"You are every bit as much a tributary to the subconscious stream as the brook and I, and we meet in a pool of knowledge, where our skills and talent are mixed and flow into the stream of consciousness. We're not alone in there. All experience, all inspiration, all thoughts, all possibilities, vibrant and latent, flow into that pool and blend into currents that include Rodney, too. Still with me?"

"I think so," George replied. "So far, you've got you, me, and Rodney, all splashing around in the same puddle."

"Splashing around in the same puddle. I love it! You're the one with the gift for words, George. You should be the one laying out our verbal flow chart!"

"Maybe later, after you tell me where it's going," George said with a happy grin.

"Fair enough," Morgen continued. "Now you, with your special skills, insights, and your band of musicians, meet up with me, and we team up with Rodney, with his fortune, artistic enthusiasm, and supporting terpsichore, and together we develop and release our works, our purpose and our hope, to be carried by that stream, and made available to all."

"Terpsichore?" George asked?

"George! You not only know the word, but you pronounce it properly, rhyming it with hickory, so you must know it means 'females delighting in dance and choral song,' but did you hear anything I said after 'terpsichore'?"

"I have a degree in music," George replied. "I know Terpsichore was the ancient Greek Muse of dance, but frankly, the choral song angle is new to me."

"An activity clearly exemplified by the Trashbabies."

"Do you think we'll make a difference?" George asked.

"I do, and that's why I'm compelled to do it."

"You once said the short, thin thread called for skill."

"And we have proven we have the skill," Morgen replied. "It's now a matter of record."

"But the thread is still short and thin," George observed.

"And now, it calls for hope," Morgen concluded.

A brief silence ensued, during which Morgen hoped George was mentally considering their conversation.

Suddenly, George announced, "I haven't had any breakfast."

Morgen sighed, and replied, "It's too early for lunch, but craft services will have coffee and snacks. I'll walk you over."

CHAPTER TWENTY-ONE

It was early afternoon, and Morgen was going over his lyrics when Rodney suddenly appeared at the ruined abbey.

"There you are!" Rodney exclaimed as he rushed to Morgen. "Come on," he continued, taking Morgen's arm and pulling him to his feet. "You've gotta see this!"

"See what?" Morgen asked, surprised to see Rodney at the abbey.

"The Busby Berkeley shot! The director is setting it up and invited Linda, Jasmine, and us to watch."

"I thought you'd be hobnobbing with the powers that be," Morgen said as they hurried toward the production van.

"No way," Rodney answered. "Alan can deal with that crowd. I'm staying right here and keeping an eye on my investment.

"The director has a chair set up for me inside the production van, so I will be seeing the entire show as it's broadcast."

Inside the van, one monitor showed a big white oval painted on the stage floor. Another held on an image of Jasmine's Shiva figurine, setup on a green sheet.

"You're just in time," the director said. "Don't mind the oval. That's the camera angle. It's a circle on stage."

They watched as the camera angle in the van was adjusted to match the camera angle on the crane over the stage, and then enlarged to exactly match the oval. Once aligned, the director faded up the statuette, and faded down the white oval.

"And as you see," he continued, as he demonstrated proudly, "I can bring it up or down at will. I'll probably only do it once, but it should work beautifully."

"It's magnificent," Jasmine said.

"I going to try to get a slightly higher angle, more like a real Busby Berkeley, but as you've seen, we can superimpose it to exactly match the stage. When it's dark enough, I'll want you to do a camera run through. You dancers aren't flat drawings, and I want to be sure you're in focus."

"Thank you," Linda said. "Give us the word and we'll be out there in a flash."

"So, what do you think?" Rodney asked Morgen.

"I think it'll be sensational," Morgen answered.

"We do what we can," the director said modestly, obviously delighted that they were pleased with his demonstration.

Outside, Linda and Jasmine hurried on ahead.

"We've got to tell the girls what we just saw," Linda said.

"Pretty great, huh?" Rodney called after them."

"Brilliant!" Jasmine called back.

"So," Rodney said, "how about you? You all right?"

"I'm fine," Morgen answered.

"Ankle all right?"

"Ankle's good," Morgen assured him.

"You want to get a cup of coffee?" Rodney asked.

"I've had enough coffee for today, tonight, and tomorrow."

"Okay. Catch you later," Rodney said, and set out for the craft services table.

Morgen went back to his hole in the wall, and was staring at the tiny blue flowers, when Alice appeared.

"You all right, Morgen?" Alice called as she approached.

Happy to see her, Morgen answered, "I'm fine."

"Linda and Jasmine just told us all about the Shiva demonstration. I wish I could have seen it."

"You will. We'll all get copies of the entire show."

"Was it as brilliant as they said?"

"Here, in the U.K., it was brilliant," Morgen replied, "but by the time it gets to Boston, it'll be wicked!"

"Wow!" Alice exclaimed.

"Wow is right!" Morgen agreed.

"You're not putting any weight on your ankle," Alice said.

"Really? Well, if I sat with both feet on the floor, I'd get a stiff neck if I tried to look out over the countryside, or, if I sat with both feet dangling outside the wall, I might slip and fall down into the rubble, below, so I decided to sit sidesaddle."

"Okay," Alice said, "Just checking."

"But before you run off," Morgen said, "you wouldn't happen to have an ace bandage in your gear, would you?"

"I'm a dancer. Of course, I have ace bandages in my gear. You want me to wrap it?"

"It's not terribly sore, but it's a bit warm and a little stiff."

Alice shot him a sly look.

"We are still talking about your ankle, aren't we?"

"I am," Morgen insisted. "The left one."

"Right!"

"No, left."

Alice artfully wrapped Morgen's ankle, tight, but not too tight, and supported it with as little bulk as would do the job.

247

"Better?" she asked.

"Brilliant," he answered.

Although it had grown dark, people with tickets were still coming through the gates. The Trashbabies were back from their camera run-through, and inside the green room, Morgen was sharing his interpretation of the significance of the location and date of their Halloween concert.

"Back in the dark ages, Christianity systematically replaced old, heathen religious traditions, cutting down their sacred groves, throwing down their shrines, and erecting, in their long-standing sacred precincts, churches, abbeys and monasteries, symbolizing Christian ascendancy and dominance through the suppression and demonization of the more ancient cults.

"I don't know if this ruin is one of those sites erected atop an old heathen site, but if it is, seeing it in ruins today might suggest that the one God hadn't fared any better than all the old ones. But all gods aside, one thing is certain. Nature is currently reducing these man-made stone walls to rubble, and recovering them with flowering vines and shrubbery.

"The last time we played here was on May Eve, one of the two nights of the year when the liminal barriers between our world and the mythical otherworld are believed to be weak, or possibly nonexistent, allowing gods and monsters, good and evil spirits, alive and dead to pass between the worlds. My adventure, perhaps instigated by some benevolent or hostile force still dwelling beneath our feet and awakened by our May Eve concert, ended on Mayday, and led, however indirectly, to our reappearance here, tonight. Happily, the May Eve spirits we roused proved more playful than threatening, but the spirits prowling abroad on Halloween, are considered more threatening than playful, and more dangerous than benign."

Trish, who only joined the Trashbabies after the May Eve concert, said, "That's kinda spooky."

"What's spooky?" Irene asked, poking her head in the door.

"Halloween," George answered, in his spookiest voice.

"Well, that's as it should be," Irene replied, and added, "You're it, Morgen. Last but not least."

"Promise to be gentle with me?" Morgen teased.

"Only if you behave," Irene said.

"Yes, Ma'am," Morgen replied as he joined Irene outside.

Inside her makeup trailer, Irene was all business. "Sit," she said, indicating a chair that looked like a cross between a barber's and a dentist's chair.

"Yes Ma'am," Morgen answered and sat.

At that moment, Rodney stuck his head in the door of the Green Room just in time to hear Sylvia say, "He certainly knows how to set a mood."

"Okay, people," Rodney shouted, "on stage in five minutes."

Alice quickly poured herself a cup of tea. "No, you don't!" she exclaimed. "Without my tea, I'll never hit the high notes!"

"Tea?" Sophie blurted out, "I'd need a major operation!"

"Come on!" Roger jumped up, yelling, "Let's do it!"

Rodney's eyes searched the Green Room, but Morgen was nowhere to be seem. George said, "He's in makeup."

"Makeup?" Rodney squealed, and pulled his head out of the doorway.

"Almost done," Irene told Morgen, "Now, close your eyes."

Rodney poked his head into her makeup trailer. "What's the holdup?" he demanded to know.

"I'll just be a minute," Irene answered, as she continued working on Morgen's makeup.

"You should be done with all that by now," Rodney whined.

"We want to look our best, don't we?" Irene replied.

Exasperated, Rodney snarled, "Well, hurry it up, will you?"

"It reflects on me, too, you know," Irene said, snarling back.

With less than 15 minutes to go, the crowd screamed and carried on the way crowds do at rock concerts, as cameras and spotlights panned the audience, then the lights came up on stage revealing three tiers of an all-female choir, all wearing coronets of autumn leaves, and some with tambourines, as their choir master signaled the opening of "Sweet Mystery." As soon as the choir began to sing and sway, the crowd noise subsided as they listened to the choir, initially supported by orchestral percussion and harps, and eventually, by the entire 72-piece orchestra, in an enclosure on the ground in front of the stage.

"Life giver! Ageless Miracle! Love!
Freya! (Freya!) Janu! (Janu!)
Ishtar! (Ishtar!) Danu! (Danu!)
"All conceiver! Joyous Harmony!
Freya! Janu! Ishtar! Danu!
Freya! (Freya!) Janu! (Janu!)
Ishtar! (Ishtar!) Danu! (Danu!)
Gentle Deceiver! Eternal Weaver!
Freya! Janu! Ishtar! Danu!"

The rest of the lights came up, illuminating the entire stage area, where Beantown Home Cookin' began playing the heavy rhythms and wailing guitar lines that signaled the Trashbabies' entrance, dancing their way across the front of the stage, bringing the excited crowd to its feet as behind them, the choir continued to sway and sing.

"If a song can touch the true you,
Influence the things that you do,
Let this song flow in and through you,
And feel its power passing to you!"

The Trashbabies each extending an arm, calling attention to Morgen's entry, as he bounded onto the stage and joined the Trashbabies, supported by the choir and orchestra as he sang.

"Come nearer! Let me see you!
Let me feel your loving touch!
Breathe life in me with your kisses!
Only you can do so much!

250

Near you the wildest beast stands tame.
Sweet Mystery!
Sharing the wondrous magic in your name!
Life giver! Ageless Miracle! Love!
(Freya!) In your bower, keep me! Soothe me!
(Janu!) Let me feel your warm caress!
(Ishtar!) Fill my ears with your sweet music!
(Danu!) Grant me peace and tenderness!"

Morgen sang the next verses, carried over into the chorus.

"Your perfect love is your great fame!
Sweet Mystery!
All is made greater when made in your name!
All conceiver! Joyous Harmony! Love!"

Beantown Home Cookin' and the orchestra took over, playing the instrumental release while Rodney watched from inside the production van, thrilled by the record-breaking crowd reaction leading into the vocal release.

"If a song can touch the true you,
Influence the things that you do . . .
Let this song flow in and through you . . .
And feel its power passing to you!"

And the choir came in singing again.

"Freya! Janu! Ishtar! Danu!
(Freya!) Lie with me in sunny meadows!
(Janu!) In darkened groves, be by my side!
(Ishtar!) In swift flowing water, bathe me!
(Danu!) Reveal your nature! Be my guide!
Mistress of Earth, Air, Water, Flame.
Sweet Mystery!
All feel the awesome power of your name!
Gentle Deceiver! Eternal Weaver! Love!

The orchestra and Beantown Home Cookin' took over, building to an instrumental final cadence. The crowd continued to roar as the lights dimmed over the choir, the band, and the

Trashbabies, leaving Morgen alone on the stage, motionless, held in a follow spot, until the crowd quieted, and Beantown Home Cookin' began to play "The Reprise of the Fool," slowly and gently, as Morgen stood quietly and sang the solo.

> "I lived in a cave for a year and a day,
> Fathered by a sun ray.
> Once I was a bull. Now I can't say.
> You'll have to find your own way.
> Chief bard of the Ancients am I.
> Wit is my singular tool.
> Beloved am I, of the Ninefold Muse,
> Or am I simply a *Fool*."

Leading to a segue begun by the orchestra string section, reintroducing the flamboyant, rock version of "The Fool."

> "I've been around the universe several times.
> Wine flows from my grapevines.
> I've taught your musicians. I've taught your mimes.
> Poets learn from my rhymes.
> At home on land, in sea, or sky,
> When I pass the trees sigh.
> You knew me before, but I never did die.
> I merely transmogrified!
> Chief bard to immortals am I.
> O'er fantastic realms do I rule.
> There's none to whom I need bend my knee,
> Honor your mentor, *The Fool*!

Morgen hung his head and stood silently as the band and orchestra segued into the "Morningstone (Fate) Theme," sung solo by Sylvia, and as it rang off, the band played the growling entry to "Flying Snakes" and the crowd went wild as Morgen was "reactivated" and the Trashbabies joined Sylvia on stage.

> "I've seen snakes fly, trees cry, and holy men lie!
> Your life may be a mystery.
> You just appeared miraculously.

Well, if you say so.
You live in your reality, but if it seems unreal to me,
Perhaps I'm just slow,
But I've seen snakes fly, trees cry, and holy men lie!
Your after-life is groovy.
I've seen it in a movie. Yeah!
But it seems while you still live here,
You've something more to give here. Yeah!"
The growling synth, and other instruments played a spaced-
out instrumental that led into spoken lines, that Morgen started.
"You say that you're just passing through."
Followed by two Trashbabies, each taking a line, saying,
"And that may work just fine for you,"
"But should that prove to be untrue,"
And Morgen spoke the last line . . .
"What harm would then come to you,"
That led back into the song.
"If you spent a little time,
Helping us to hold the line,
Before you go."
"I don't just ask for me and mine.
You tell me that you're doing fine, well . . .
If you say so.
But I've seen snakes fly, trees cry and holy men lie!"
"I do believe you're clever,
Bound to live forever. Oh!
But I've got mortal things to do,
And I don't ask so much of you,
But one thing you should know.
I've seen snakes fly, trees cry, and holy men lie!
Lie!
Lie!
Lie!"

253

Morgen and the Trashbabies exited into the right wing, where Morgen collapsed into an overstuffed chair, placed there for that purpose, and the Trashbabies regrouped for the real finale. The stage lights dimmed, except for a spotlight on Beantown Home Cookin', playing the gentle intro to "Dog, Roebuck, and Lapwing," Morgen closed his eyes to better concentrate as the Trashbabies began singing their song and their solemn procession from the right wing, out and around their circular mark and on to exit into the left wing.

"Dog, Roebuck, and Lapwing,
Your nonsense song makes my ears ring.
Between the lines, I hear you sing,
Dog, Roebuck and Lapwing."

As Morgen listened, eyes closed, the pale, white creature appeared to him, perched motionlessly, a miniature ghost, bold in the bright moonlight, black eyes staring, a visitation by an old friend, and Morgen was not at all afraid. They stared at each other, neither one moving. The figure wasn't very large, and there was something peaceful about its stillness, its unblinking stare, its heart-shaped face framing and emphasizing its black, hooked beak, and wearing its radiant golden glow like a gossamer shawl over its head and wings, blowing gently in a mild, night breeze, a thing not quite of this world. The owl blinked, and said his name.

Linda was the last Trashbaby to exit as "Dog, Roebuck, and Lapwing" began to fade, and as the stage went dark and the huge banks of portable Musco lights illuminated the audience area, the roar of the crowd became deafening.

Rodney burst out of the remote production van, and began hotfooting toward the right wing; the Trashbabies, guided by security staff with flashlights, hurried across the backstage area from the left wing back over to the right; and George led Beantown Home Cookin', closest to the right wing, across the dark stage to where Morgen sat in his overstuffed chair, his eyes closed, a faint smile on his lips, silent and motionless.

A BBC camera crew was there to shoot the post-concert celebration, but when Morgen failed to respond to George's attempt to awaken him, the horrified director switched immediately to panning shots of the excited crowd, still roaring enthusiastically.

Tears began to well in George's eyes, but he forced a smile as he softly told Morgen, "Let's stay in touch."

A security guard knelt by Morgen's side, and nudging George aside, tried to find Morgen's pulse. The silence backstage, in contrast to the cheering out front, alerted Rodney, and he pushed his way through the stunned Trashbabies, to see the security guard, his ear to Morgen's chest, listening for a heartbeat. Rodney screamed Morgen's name and rushed to his side, pushing the security guard away.

The security guard said, "He's gone," but Rodney ignored him and shouted, "Get a doctor!" Linda crouched behind Rodney and hugged him close, trying to comfort him. "Somebody get a doctor!" Rodney screamed. "He's gone," the security guard repeated. Wild-eyed, Rodney looked at the silent, stunned group, and shouted, "George!"

He saw George, standing nearby, looking up at the lighting grid above the stage. His eyes followed George's stare, and saw the larger-than-life barn owl looking down from the grid, as did almost everyone backstage at that moment, including the quick-witted BBC camera crew who captured the now famous, but rarely seen footage of the larger-than-life barn owl as it silently took wing, flew out into the night, and disappeared into the darkness.

THE END

APPENDIX: MORNINGSTONE'S TOPOGRAPHY

Morningstone's topography is important to understanding where locations are in relation to each other. The Stream of Consciousness is one of the boundaries of Morningstone, flowing between it and the Liminal Zone, a veiled, no-man's land between the natural (conscious), realm, and the supernatural (unconscious), realm. Western tradition holds that the Liminal Zone's size waxes and wanes with the seasons, and the veil between the two realms is thinnest and most penetrable on May Eve and Halloween, the two ancient heathen holidays midpoint between the equinoxes and solstices.

Morningstone's main attraction is its megalithic shrine, fronted by a stone circle (not shown), with a Stonehenge-like trilithon entrance, located near the top of a hill. In the center of the stone circle, stands a man-size monolith, a solitary upright stone that on special occasions is cloaked and crowned with a masked, antlered headdress for ceremonial observances. Beyond the monolith, built into the hillside to the left of the dark cell shown in the illustration, is the larger, dark entrance to a man-made stone chamber in which is hidden a low narrow shaft, little more than a long, dark, confining crawlspace, leading down into the Tomb of Every Hope, a natural cave within the hill, modified for ceremonial purposes.

A brook flows through the cave, eventually merging with a larger stream, that flows out of the hillside and empties into a Sacred Pool. The overflow of the Sacred Pool forms the Stream of Consciousness that flows past the Guest Cottage, on the sloping back side of the hill, and not far downstream, narrows into a series of rapids and waterfalls, carrying it to the bottom of the hill, where it widens and proceeds peacefully under the Bridge that connects the Liminal Zone with Morningstone. Just over the Bridge, a sign, hidden in the trees, points the way to Morningstone along an overgrown seldom traveled, dirt road that finally arrives on a slight rise, overlooking the tiny village.

Smythe's Forge and Auto Repair is located in the village, as is the Village Bakery, behind which a steep, but well-worn foot path shortcut leads up to the clearing in front of the megalithic shrine. Beyond the village, on the paved rural road that serves the valley and its farming community, is The Owl pub, sharing a wall with the Morningstone Inn. That same paved road, continuing on from the pub, skirts the hill to a more gently rising slope and a pony cart path that winds its way up to the megalithic circle, continues over the crest of the hill and down back, through the woods to the Guest Cottage on the liminal side of the Stream of Consciousness.

T. E. P.

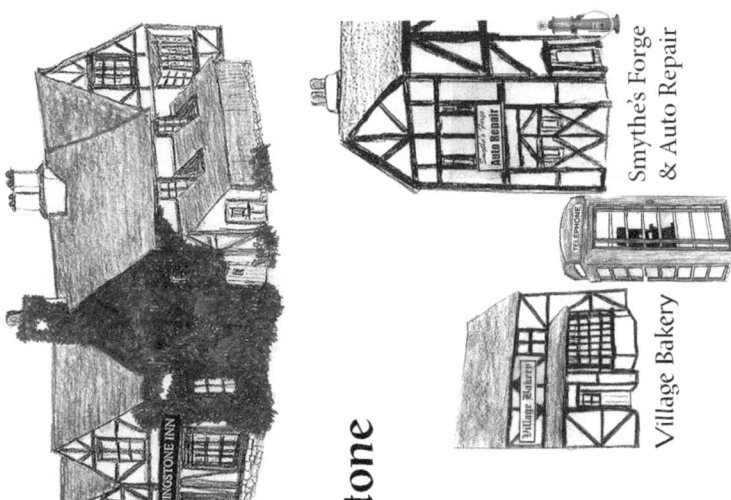

The Owl Pub and Morningstone Inn

Smythe's Forge & Auto Repair

Village Bakery

Morningstone

Monolith Dressed for May Eve Ritual

Entrance to the Tomb of Every Hope

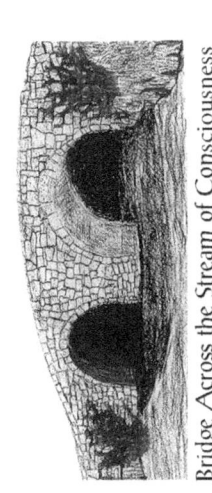

Bridge Across the Stream of Consciousness

Wellspring of the Stream of Consciousness

The Guest Cottage

Liminal Zone

257

www.ingramcontent.com/pod-product-compliance
Lightning Source LLC
Chambersburg PA
CBHW070220030726

47505CB00006B/1748